BULB

NICHOLAS TURNER

Bulb

Nicholastrieste.com

Nicholastrieste.wixsite.com/nicholasturner

Leave feedback at:

Nicholasturnerauthor@gmail.com

Twitter: @nicholastrieste

Instagram: @nicholasturnerauthor

Facebook.com/nicholasturnerauthor

ISBN-13: 978-1-7342915-5-1

First edition

Editor Tell Tell Poetry

Illustration © Tom Edwards

TomEdwardsDesign.com

Printed in the U.S.A.

For my mother
Thank you for understanding that I was sometimes too busy working
on this to spend hours on the phone

1

A man sat in his massive apartment in the city while watching television. He sipped easily on a beautiful glass of scotch from the Aboveground. Outside the light was now artificial, bright in neon. Projections of ads displayed themselves while artificial men and women walked around begging customers to come into their shops and purchase whatever wares or bodily orifices they were pitching. On the television was the man's favorite reality show. It was perfection Below. He smiled to himself.

There was a knock at the door and the electronic voice of an accented woman came over the speakers. "Sir, you have a guest from the local Capitol."

"What can I help them with?"

"They say they would like to discuss immigration."

"To the Aboveground or to the GUC?"

"Both, sir."

The man sat a moment as he calculated the risks of letting

those still Above, living lives separate from those underground. He thought whether it would be beneficial to bring them down Below, and to let the world know of all the secrets they had been keeping. That there was no mass destruction during the second world war. That everyone had been forced to live underground as a science experiment. The world had recently gone to hell, and now he was asked real questions about revealing the truth. He mulled over the idea of mass immigration of a lesser society. The same question had cropped up for decades, and he always gave the same answer.

"Tell him the answer is 'no.' No one comes in, no one goes out." His answer was law. "They stay there. They don't learn about us yet, and we keep control of those who are too ignorant to know there is still life Above. The narrative of nuclear war stays in place for now." *This Utopia must not be tainted until the last stragglers are on the brink, then, and only then can they be allowed here. Maybe I choose to let them die off entirely. Population Control.* He felt elated by the power he commanded.

"He thanks you for your time, and should anything change he would appreciate a conference with you and your superiors."

"It won't happen anytime soon. The Aboveground is closing in on two full years and they're still wild. They haven't developed class or structure since our experiment. We can't afford to let them in."

"He understands and has departed, sir. Please, enjoy your show. Shall I arrange for any entertainment tonight?"

"Just forward any calls to my secretary, except from the bosses. Forward those directly to the living room Holoscreen and blackout the apartment. Overlay business casual attire and"—he thought for a moment— "how about black mahogany for my desk should they call."

"Understood. Have a good night, sir."

* * *

Cars zoomed through the streets, flashing lights and humming as they hovered off of the ground releasing zero emissions into the purified air of the Greater United Capital. Jeremiah sat outside in the piss and shit of the gutters. The Slums was filled with men and women like him. It was home to all of the lower class schlubs who were the descendants of the first brave souls to volunteer or the criminals who were dragged down. It was a life he had come to know very well, sitting in the gutters, yet, most days he wished he could go back to his old way. The small shacks surrounding him were dimly lit, and though the air was purified from pollutants, a smog still crept from the hot blast furnaces with the regular coal that burned to power the area and keep the lights on. It was nothing like the clean energy the UC and the Capitol had. The streets there were clean, they had little crime, and food and water flowed like rivers into bellies already full.

From his gutter, Jeremiah could see the Capitol building of the city looming above the entirety of the GUC. It was triumphant, a symbol of man's power and victory over itself. Glass shimmered with spotlights which ran twenty-four hours a day, and illuminated the center of the GUC as life hustled and bustled in each ring of the city. From the UC, to the Deep, and the Slums, night never came as work was done around the clock. Life never stopped Below. Even when people turned off their lights and tried to sleep, the Capitol building shined bright. At the center of their world was their sun, their god which governed over them. Jeremiah heard that other cities had towers like this, but traveling was too costly—at least for the workers—and he barely had enough credits to get by day-to-day. Rumors circulated that there was even a life of more wealthy people somewhere in the country below. It was a land of ivory and gold. A land he would never see.

A bell sounded louder than the whirring of machines grinding and crunching which kept this section of the city running. Jeremiah stood up and wiped chunks of fecal matter off of his work jeans, then rinsed his boots off in a mixture of the human fluid which gathered near a corner of a bodega with pink and purple neon lights. The characters were in Chinese, a language he had never learned. He made his way along the side alleys as police vehicles blasted by, making no noise, all while their red and blue lights reflected off of the tin shacks and bed rolls which collected near each other on the ground.

There was an emergency door, covered in graffiti and red letters that stated AUTHORIZED PERSONNEL ONLY. He wasn't authorized, but no one working in the Furnaces was. They just shoveled into the red mouths as they scorched away. Sweat mixed with black dust and ran down toned arms. Ten-hour days of nothing but shoveling made their bodies wiry, and strong, but low pay and hunger made them weak. Most of them only just got by, surviving until the next shift so they could continue to eat and work one more day. It was in their programming, to be subservient, good workers. Posters on the black walls which ran down the stairs through the door reminded them every day.

The words GOOD WORKERS ARE HARD WORKERS. HARD WORKERS DON'T SPEAK were plastered on pictures of stoic looking men and women, with arms bigger than body-builders, and chests which wanted to burst through tight army green shirts. Jeremiah looked at the poster and at himself. His shirt was green once, when the credits were good and he could afford simple things, like a roof over his head. But time, greed, and corruption took that away from him. Now his clothes were torn, tattered, and he couldn't even afford to get new work-issued shirts. Not since they started charging half a day's creds for a pair of socks and three full days for a pair of shoes. He didn't even like to think about how much new pants would cost him, as he looked down at the holes starting to get bigger in his current pair. *If only I was back on the force.*

He was bumped in to. It was a friendly gesture from another worker. He was daydreaming, taking up space on the clock rather than shoveling. If he was caught, the floor manager would ruin him. A public beating, a day's creds, loss of job, or even throwing him personally into the furnace. The punishment list was endless. It would be a warning to all of the other shovelers to keep their shit straight as they worked. It was all relative to the floor manager's mood and how his bosses treated him that morning. Some days the floor manager wouldn't even appear to watch them as they heaved black chunks into glowing metal. Other days he would pace and stand over them like a hawk waiting for its prey to make a wrong move. Today the floor manager was looking for anyone to take his frustration out on.

"Jeremiah, you need to fuckin' move before that sack of flesh gets ya."

Jeremiah, finally shuffled over to the huge piles of coal which were getting picked up by cranes and swung over to the massive furnaces. His shovel, though small, quickly made the pile of coal next to him dwindle away until he turned back and saw the pile had been replenished. Infinitely it came back no matter how hard he tried to make it go away forever.

Time flew by as his arms and back seared from the weight, and before he knew it his shift was over. He trundled up the steel grates of the stairs back to the streets above, returning to the neon glow and flashing lights of the city. It had begun to rain, though not naturally. The city set off massive sprinklers far overhead where they couldn't be seen. They were used to give the feeling of outside life. It helped the rich feel at home, like they were actually in a world outside as they looked out of their windows, but for the working class it made sleeping more of a chore than a relief. Jeremiah didn't always mind it. Some days it was nice to clean off the grime and sweat from the furnaces. Today was not one of those days.

Turning down alleys, and passing mongers on the side of the streets, Jeremiah waved his hand over a small electronic pad which scanned his fingerprints, almost regretting how many creds it had cost him to make a small steaming bowl of noodles in the goopiest brown-black broth he had ever seen to pop out of a darkened window. As he pulled a makeshift spoon from his pocket and dug in, the broth sucked back at the noodles, like feet and air getting trapped in knee-deep wet mud. It wasn't the best tasting meal, but it was loaded with the calories and nutrients he needed. *Better than those nasty calorie-cubes.* He shuddered at the thought of them. Some scientist long before he was born made them in a lab to help fight the food crisis. Now it was easy to feed people on as little as possible. That's the story Jeremiah heard anyway. His stomach still felt empty as he slurped the gelatinous broth. He wanted more noodles but could not afford spending more creds to satisfy his stomach.

Jeremiah turned and wound his way through the maze of thin metal frames and poles holding up the small buildings. He soon found himself back at the row of cots and floor mats which lined the alley just off of the main street leading to the Furnaces. Nearby, there were men and women selling themselves to whoever wanted a piece. Ass, mouth, whatever someone wanted was for sale only for a few more creds and the dream of escaping this hell where it artificially rained whenever someone with an agenda wanted it to.

Jeremiah found an open cot, which did not belong to him and lay down on it. He slept and did not dream. Jeremiah somnambulated through his days, never really relaxing, simply going through the motions.

Jeremiah watched as water dripped from the rooftops of the metal shack onto his face. The air was warm, warmer than usual. He sat up and noticed the sound, or rather, the lack thereof. All around, men and women in tatters stood near the emergency door Jeremiah had become so accustomed to. He stood and made his way through the crowd and towards the door. Rain fell and resounded on the smooth black concrete and metal all around. The neons caught the droplets as they bounced off the street.

"What's going on?" he asked to no one in particular.

"Explosion. Someone brought a pipe bomb down there and tossed it into one of the furnaces."

"There was a small cave in on the stairs. They're trying to get out," someone else said to the crowd which had begun to get larger.

"How many are down there?"

"No idea. Cameras cut out a few hours back. Knocked the power out for half the Slums."

Jeremiah looked around and noticed that it was way darker than it normally was. Neon lights had gone gray, while streetlights didn't illuminate any of Sleeper's Row. The Row was almost peaceful and kempt looking. Bloodstains were only dark circles which could be mistaken for any shadow cast.

He backed away from the crowd surrounding the door and walked a few blocks until no one was within sight. He picked up his pace to a swift walk, then a full-on sprint. A labyrinth of streets and alleys serpentine in their making. Jeremiah drifted through the lanes until a familiar yet small alcove came into view. Quickly, he input a procession of numbers on a small keypad which blended in perfectly with the surroundings. A low churn of a machine slaving tediously away could be heard louder than Jeremiah would have liked.

A door opened a block or so away, and Jeremiah made his way casually over to an alley which he had to squeeze into, then tucked himself into the back of an old closed down shop. Inside he found his old, worn police issued weapon, some coins, and his Holobadge. It was green-bronze, caked with dust, and filled with memories of when Jeremiah ran the streets as a cop in the UC. Before distrust and corruption dug its claws into his friends and colleagues.

Jeremiah left the small opening and made his way back to the street. On the side of a large garbage can was a black jacket. He lifted it and pulled his arms through. His pistol rested on his right hip, partially charged, and he looked in the distance at the Capitol building. Pure white reached up until it faded into the ether.

The streets were still dark, but lights had begun to flicker on here and there—either coming back to life or clinging to it. Jeremiah watched movement come back as he escaped the Slums and made his way to the lower-class sector of the city. Blue and pink neon began to switch over to reds. Symbols from all languages hung outside buildings with glass windows. Inside men and women gyrated with music, some playing on poles, and some putting them inside themselves. This land was foreign, but familiar at the same time. Glass was rarely used in the Slums, mostly metal. The glass here in the Deep was dirty—coated in film from years of use and abuse—coated in human fluid dried from time.

A woman wore full black latex as she slid up and down a

metal pole in the middle of the room behind the glass. Her ass fitting the warm rod between her cheeks and slowly began to raise her ass up as she brought her face and tits toward the ground, never breaking contact with Jeremiah. Her eyes were deep blue, like sapphires freshly cut. Jeremiah felt desire for the first time since he left the UC to hide out in the Slums. He walked up to the glass, flashed his Holobadge over a black box, and a door to his left opened. Inside the walls were burgundy and the leather couch a deep stained black. He sat down waiting to ask questions. This brothel had been known to be a meeting place for some, and always heard the rumors going on in the lowly sectors of the GUC. Jeremiah learned that while on the force, and that creds could get him almost any information he wanted.

The woman from the window appeared. Her latex tight, and clearly dirty from other people. She reached under her chin, and unzipped the suit from the mask, then ran her arm down her back so she could slip out of the suit. Her breasts were firm and large which made Jeremiah ache. She walked over, keeping the mask on, and didn't struggle with pulling him out of his disgusting jeans. Within three minutes she had finished him off with her warm hands. She pushed herself off of her knees, giggled, and walked to a corner. Jeremiah heard water running and quickly put himself away.

"Come back anytime, dear. You'll be my best client if that's all it takes."

Jeremiah flushed, stood up. He felt for his gun which was still attached, though his coins were a bit lighter.

"I have a few questions for you."

"What makes you think I'd answer?" she asked coming back into the main room.

"The coins you're hiding from me are a good place to start." He flashed his Holobadge to assert authority he no longer had.

"Nothing gets by you, honey." She returned the coins from her cleaner hand.

Jeremiah made his way toward the exit to make sure no one was waiting in line. The windows burst and glass came flying toward him. He raised his hands to cover his face and felt hot shrapnel tear into his body as he fell backward. A woman screamed. The world slowed down from a punch of adrenaline.

2

Crow and the group were panting as they ran. The Traders were behind them. Wood splintered as they kept up the best pace they could with the recent snow. Crow felt the wet cold seeping through his jeans and wondered how Bernice was fairing. He stopped a moment to look over his shoulder and saw Jamal doing his best to drag her along. *She's holding us back,* he thought.

"She's going to be the death of us."

"I'm gonna help them, man," Fox said.

Crow conceded the fight before it even started. He watched Fox jog over and throw one of Bernice's arms around his neck. Him and Jamal lifted her off the ground. Crow waited for the Traders to appear through the trees. They moved further on once everyone had caught up.

Crow kneeled behind a massive rock which was able to hide all of them. He rested his rifle on it for balance. Fox did the same. Everyone waited for the men to come roaring through the trees like the savages they were. Taking people and turning them into their own personal objects for any use they wanted. They all hated the Traders, and knew none of them deserved to live. Morality had gone out the window without electricity, and the devolving of humanity was rapid. But there was still a code to live by. Never become a Trader.

They waited, passing glances back and forth. Crow watched Bernice take off her shoes and start to rub her pale feet.

"Where the fuck did they go?" Jamal asked.

"I dunno, man," Fox replied. "I'm going to take a look."

Crow watched him scurry off before he could tell him to hold his position. Almost like he was psychic, Crow could see the situation play out in his head immediately before it happened. The trees around them splintered and bullets bounced off the boulder they hid behind.

"Shit, shit, shit!" He pulled his rifle close to his chest, as he turned away from the oncoming men. Everyone looked to him for guidance and right now he knew the only thing they had in their favor was Fox. Crow shook his head, took a breath, and peered over the rock to see if the Traders were rushing them.

In the winter light, he could see the flashes of earth tones as the Traders ran tree to tree. Their feet were heavy as they bashed through the snow. He fired a round and watched it completely miss his target. Crow tried to steady his breathing. *Relax. Deep breath. Hold. Squeeze.* Another bullet left his rifle, and he saw it hit the side of the tree one of the men stood behind. More bullets started to whiz by from his left, and he ducked behind the rock after he saw the man he shot at run for better cover.

"Did you get one?" Jamal asked.

"No, but I scared him off pretty good."

"We're dead," Bernice said, a blank look in her eyes.

The whoosh of a bullet glancing off of the rock checked Crow back to the fight. The tearing of the wind reminded him of early childhood arguments where he and his friends would throw any object they could find back and forth until they doubled over from laughter. Only this time the stakes were higher and no one was laughing.

"I need you to lay down a few shots so I can sight one of them," Crow said to Jamal.

He watched him gulp nervously.

"I don't know how I feel about this."

"It's our only chance, then we go back to camp and continue on." Crow gave Jamal a reassuring look. "Now go to the right side, and just shoot. Don't aim down the sights, but send bullets their way. Got it?"

"Yeah, I got it," Jamal said. Crow watched as Jamal's body shook harder than the rustling leaves of autumn. *God,* he thought, *if only we could go back to those days.*

Crow waited as Jamal fired off a few shots, then spaced out a few more. Less than five altogether.

"Good?"

"Yes. Just like that."

As Jamal leaned against the rock again, the snow near him began to kick up. *Perfect.*

Crow lay down, opposite Jamal, and sighted the first Trader who had leaned back behind his tree. He squeezed the trigger as the man peaked out again to get a look at the situation. The .223 hit him just above the collarbone in the soft space of his trachea. *Good enough*, Crow thought, though he had been aiming for center mass. The man crumpled to the ground grabbing at his neck, trying to put pressure on it. He was dead, no amount of help now would save him.

The other Trader looked over to his dying friend. Crow saw him drop his magazine and reload his rifle.

"Fucker," Crow said as he watched Fox creep up on the man. *He's good.*

The Trader crumbled as his friend had. Fox's knife caught him in the neck. It was a quick kill. He'd bleed out in less than a minute from his severed carotid.

"Just two?" Crow asked as he jogged through the snow.

"The third was back there." Fox pointed with his knife.

"Taken care of, I assume?"

"Yeah, man," he said, his eyes downcast.

"You think it's the last of them?"

"Absolutely not." Fox looked up as the rest of the group joined them in looting the bodies. They'd get left there for the animals. No need to bury Traders. *They don't deserve the respect.*

"Where's the rest of them?" Janet asked.

"They'll be through soon. It was just a scouting party," Crow replied.

"We should get as far from here as possible then."

"Of course we should, we just need to see what else these guys have." He handed Janet a rifle. "Hold on to this. I don't see any extra ammo on any of them."

"They're traveling light, man," Fox said. "Just a little food." He pulled a can of corned beef and hash from the man's pack, and put it in his own.

"Then let's get going." Crow stood up and started leading the way through the woods.

The sun drifted lazily as they walked, eventually cresting the distant New York mountain line. Crow knew they were somewhere North of Orange County, but without the river or the main roads, he couldn't say for sure. *Fox will probably have a better idea.*

They set up camp as the last of the light began to dim, then turn into shadow and darkness. It was a quick set up. Crow's shelter was a small tarp hung off a downed tree with rocks to keep it on the ground. It was modest and able to stop the wind. He had set himself as far from everyone else as he could, but stayed close enough to see them without any obstructions.

He lay down then dug in his pocket and pulled a few photographs. He pulled them close to his chest and did not dream.

3

C row stood in the open air overlooking a valley from the hill. The crisp air brushed trees as the wind struggled to blow the leaves at his feet. Slick mud mixed with blood on his calloused hands. The color of shit and crimson ran down his fingertips and back to the earth where it belonged. *This doesn't feel like New York anymore. I can't believe it's been over a year since the bulbs burned out.* He had tried to keep track of the exact day of the week, but after the months went by, Crow decided it was no longer necessary. Whenever the power came back, if at all, then he'd figure out what day it was.

A deer wandered through the woods unimpressed by its familiar surroundings. Leaves, trees, snow, and feces littered the path it trundled down. He saw it from afar and let the animal pass. It was not meant to die today—only a passerby in the crumbled world. Crow wondered what it had seen in its life. *Was it alive when the bulbs burned out? Was it there when the clouds blocked out the sun and the cold stayed through the summer and never left? Was it there when everyone knew what a normal life was?*

He moved away from camp making sure to cover his tracks as he walked through the snow which could cause even the most careful of feet to slip. The canteen on his bony hip was full as he walked, his belly only slightly empty.

Miles passed until the bridge appeared. Halfway through the tunnel, he stopped to take off his backpack and leaned the old rifle against the gray bricks. Crow rustled with some of the old stones, feeling for the loose ones he had dug out days prior and pulled them from the wall. Inside the food was still there: jerky, old cans of apricots and mandarin oranges, which would not go bad for a few more years. *I need to scavenge and smoke more meat before the deep winter comes again,* he thought. Winter brought out the worst in people, but Crow always enjoyed it the most. The quiet that engulfed the world as the snow fell from the sky was something to be desired when the lights were still on. Now, everyone in the world longed for that noise and movement again. Everything was too quiet, and winter never left. It only brought deeper snow, colder days, death, and starvation. Crow left his small hiding place and found Janet waiting at the edge of the camp they had made.

"What'd you do today?"

Crow reflected on his morning. "The usual. Nothing special. Only watched the doom and gloom."

"Yeah, I guess that summarizes it well. But I don't see the point in the way you described the world around you."

"It's just how it is. We live in an apocalypse. There's no control anyway. How else am I supposed to describe what I did today besides watch the world around us be dead?"

"That's bleak at best."

It isn't bleak if it's true. What don't you get? You can't look at a pile of shit and call it gold. He held his breath and saved the thought of arguing with her for a better day. He looked at Janet covered in dirt and dried blood standing atop the hill overlooking the valley and noticed the still green needles struggling to keep to the trees. Sometimes he hated Janet as he stared through her to the pines.

She was no different now than when the world ended, he imagined. She was this spiritual, connected to mother-Gaia kind of woman. She believed that spirituality could change the world, make it better, and that the greater being who governed it would be appeased by her goodwill. *How self-gratifying. Who wants to change the world for a greater being rather than change the world simply because it sucked?* It was a messed-up way to change the world, or at least he thought so.

"You know I hate it when you look off while I'm talking."

He snapped back to reality as her voice broke through his thoughts. He realized he hadn't heard a word she had said. Maybe it was better that way, to simply stew in his own thoughts while she mumbled on about whatever it was that was on her mind.

"Sorry, I was just thinking about the past and if there was any way it related to the now," he said trying to change the subject and keep the tension down. There was no reason to bring the drama back into the camp. Keep it to himself.

"How could it relate to the now?"

"It's not really that important. Let's just get going. The sun will set soon and we don't want to get stuck out in the dark trying to find our way back home."

"Yeah, I guess you're right. We aren't really that far from camp though. It's just a small patrol I was doing, looking for any food or people who might be a problem. Tell me about your thoughts while we walk back." She smiled.

He looked away. "I think I just want to walk back in silence. I prefer it when people talk less most times."

"Why's that?"

"Because I find most people who speak have nothing really worth listening to." He looked back at Janet and didn't smile.

"Okay, I guess we don't have to talk while we walk back home. It would be nice though." Crow breathed a sigh to himself. *Finally, just some peace and quiet.*

They walked and walked and walked some more before making it back to their little piece of civilization with the other three members of their clan, or whatever people referred to it as. Crow went to his makeshift tent made out of camouflaged blue tarp, and watched Janet go to hers. His was strung from a tree to block the wind in case he felt like making a small fire. He never did though, at least, not without everyone there to keep watch while one of them cooked and the others wandered the perimeter in case of an attack from the Traders.

They were bad news. He thought about how Bernice had been able to escape from them, but she never spoke about it. She carried something the rest of them didn't.

Crow sat under his camouflaged tarp, waiting for something to happen. He felt it in the air, unsure of what it could be. The air was cold, enough to give goosebumps when it blew, but not cold enough to shiver when the wind was still. The leaves rustled behind Crow, dressed in his all black attire, stained with browns and hues of red. Fox came through the woods, scrawny from being overworked and underfed. Behind him he dragged a small doe carcass. Its eyes were pallid and glazed over, yet the dilated pupils stuck out as if they had come to peace with existence and how their life had ended. Crow knew Fox had made it a quick death but still wondered how long the agonizing pain lasted before the deer's consciousness winked out.

"Where'd you find this one?" Crow asked in his hoarse and aged voice.

"I found her while walking down stream, maybe a mile or so from where you keep your small stash."

"She's small," he retorted, not making the comment that he thought no one knew about his stash. He knew this is how things were, strangers coming together, yet still not trusting each other. That's why he had a stash, and that's why Fox must have tracked him one day to see where he was going. Unless, of course, Janet told Fox about it, which was entirely possible. She was the only one Crow had told. His weakness for intimacy led to pillow talk between them one lonely night.

They had lain under the stars, not anywhere near camp, fucking until the sun had come up. The most primal of urges had stirred inside, and they had succumbed to them, knowing the possible consequences.

"Tell me a secret," Janet had said as they lain on a sleeping bag in the snow.

"I don't really keep secrets."

"Well there has to be something about you I don't know."

Crow had mulled it over before thinking, *Fuck it.* "I had a family once, a wife and a daughter, they're dead now. I buried them myself a week after the lights went out." He had hoped being depressingly forward would steer her from furthering the conversation because silence sounded the best right now. He always seemed to prefer it.

"Can I ask what happened?"

"I'd rather you didn't."

"Tell me something else then."

"I keep a picture of her and my daughter in a small stash nearby every time we make a new camp. This time I tucked them under a bridge behind some bricks." He had doubled down on the sob story.

"Is that why you disappear so often?"

"Perhaps."

"I'd like to see the photo of her one day."

"I don't think that'll happen."

"Okay, well if you want to talk about them, I'm here to listen."

"I just want to go to sleep right now. Get your clothes together and let's go back to the camp."

"That sounds like a good idea. We should check the snares on the way to see if we caught anything. It's the least we can do for everyone since we were out having fun." She had smiled as she had bent over to gather her clothes and tried to make light of everything, but clearly had understood that Crow had shut himself off from all of them.

Crow watched from his small tent as Fox set to skinning the doe, being as careful and precise as possible as his hands shook. *Probably from hunger, or exhaustion.* He wanted to help but knew Fox would not allow it. He sat and watched, taking note of his deft hands, and how they did not appear as skillful as they once had. They shook and trembled even when he did not make any movements with them. Crow hoped he was not getting sick. Fox was the best they had.

The meat sat over the fire as Janet, Fox, Crow, Jamal, and Bernice, came around to watch as it cooked. Half a doe was laid over the fire on a small chain-link fence. It used to be part of a whole which was covered in the typical green plastic-paint. They had melted that off of it when they came across it.

They all watched the fire, captivated by the whips of flame and smoke. It was the awkward time before nightfall where the sun was still out, almost sunset, still bright, but just dark enough that a fire could be seen further off than in the daylight. The smoke, formless, drifted into the gray sky, snake-like and fluid. It was filled with prayers and hopes that no one had seen the fire and were making their way to check it out.

The wood crackled and a piece of it shattered, bringing Crow and everyone else back from their hypnosis. It was sharp and loud, but it did its job, because no one else could escape their own thoughts in the quiet solitude. The days had become physically draining and long as food became harder to find through hunting and scavenging.

Crow watched the smoke drift lazily to the sky, getting lost in the darkness. Gray on black, until it no longer existed. He sighed and looked back into the warmth. He enjoyed nights like these.

"Don't turn. There's someone behind you, Bernice," Fox said.

"I'll take care of it," Crow said as he stood up, and walked away to fake a piss. He caught a glimpse of the man who had lain down. He acted like he didn't see him and kept walking to his left. Crow felt the man's eyes on his as he turned his back, and pretended to urinate.

"Don't move." Janet stood over him with a rifle aimed at the base of his skull.

"Fucking bitch," the man replied.

"What the fuck did you just call me?" She slammed the barrel into the back of his head and pushed. His face hit the cold snow and broke through to the ground below.

"I'll take this." Jamal reached down and grabbed the rifle as Crow made his way over. Fox and Bernice stayed near camp keeping an eye out for any more people who might be watching the scene unfold.

They let the man up and forced him to move closer to camp, all of them walking behind him as the snow melted against his clothes. The man shivered as they walked.

"Look guys, I'm just hungry. I've been living off of berries, and nuts, and roots, and whatever small animal I can get my hands on. It's been a long winter," he tried pleading with them as they got closer to the fire and felt its warmth. The smell of cooked meat hung in the air.

"Who are you?" Crow asked him, allowing Jamal and Janet to keep the rifles aimed at his back while Fox and Bernice sat on the opposite end of the fire.

He didn't answer. Crow watched as he continued to stare at Bernice.

"Hey, asshole. Who the fuck are you?" Crow called out again.

The man took a deep breath. "Name's Logan. I've been running ever since my house got burned down with all of my supplies."

"He's lying," Bernice said, as she rubbed her feet. "He looks familiar, but I can't place it." She looked up at Crow.

"I know he is," Crow said. He crossed over, grabbed the man by the back and pushed him to the ground. His head dangerously close to the fire.

"Crow, we need to decide now what we're doing with him. This isn't a matter of morality anymore, man. It's dark now. We have to put out the fire soon, and he might not be alone. There's a lot going on here. A lot of factors we have to take into account. We're going to have to pack up and move, tonight, man," Fox said.

Crow looked up and swiveled his head to look at everyone. "What do we do with him?"

"We can let him stay the night and keep guard until tomorrow. We can take his stuff and send him on his way while we disappear into the woods. Or, we can kill him, man." Fox stated the only options as he emphasized the latter.

Crow felt Logan twist and spin beneath him just as he shifted his body weight. Logan spun out from under Crow and threw him to the ground, fist flying as the other hand gripped Crow's throat. Crow slammed his forearm into the ditch of Logan's elbow.

"I know who he is!" Bernice shouted.

"What?"

"He's not who he says he is. I know him."

"Well, who the fuck is he?" Crow asked as he stood up, wiping blood from his nose.

"He's a Trader from the camp!"

They all turned to look at him. His face had mutated, contorted into a ball of twisted rage. The light from the fire exacerbated his emotions and features as the smell from the fire tried wafting in between everyone. The deer meat was clearly overcooked and burnt at this point. The smell was no longer delicious but acrid and unpalatable.

"Fuck you. I loved every moment."

Bernice picked up the rifle near her as Jamal and Janet backed away. She lined up the shot, even though she was the worst one and pulled the trigger. The rifle slammed into her shoulder as the bullet exited the barrel and ripped into the man's neck. Blood spurt out onto the white snow. Logan's eyes never broke contact with Bernice and his face never changed from the twisted smile he gave her. Crow could see the hate that flowed through him until the last moment before his eyes washed over and dilated. And right before the life left Logan's eyes, Crow could have sworn he saw relief.

4

Crow slept next to Janet and dreamt of another woman, completely self-aware of his dreams.

They were standing in the trees, a day of hiking when they were still young and didn't have a child or a care in the world. She was beautiful, her brown eyes caught the sun and the rays shown in her hair. I don't want to be here, he thought. I don't want to be seeing this memory again. I want to wake up, but I only see her. She is shorter than him, at most five foot five. Her frame is small, peaking maybe around a hundred twenty pounds. She smiles at him as they walk through the crunchy dead orange leaves. He's in black and khaki. He has terrible taste in clothing. She's in leggings and a T-shirt. She looks immaculate in it. Showing him up in every way possible.

She took her time walking behind him so she could take pictures of him that day. He was so infatuated with the scenery. She only had eyes for him. Every picture was of him with some trees, but he was always the focus. She lay next to him and stared while he looked at the sky and closed his eyes to hear the birds. I don't want to be here, he thought again. I don't want to relive these moments with her. I miss her. I feel that cold depression in my sleep. Please, let me wake up.

They walked back toward the car after their hike. She clung to him. When they got back to her place they sat in a bath for over an hour. The water was scorching in the jacuzzi tub. They got dehydrated without even knowing it. They figured that out when they stood up, pouring sweat, and discovered their legs didn't want to work. She dressed in lace that night, red with black trim. They didn't sleep. They were so in love that any time apart was an atrocity to their feelings. I don't want to relive this, he thought. Please, God, just let me wake up. I don't want to face such a beautiful memory that I can't go back to. I'd give it all back to go back to those days where we were together and happy. Please, let me wake up.

Fox watched as Crow stirred at last to the smell of rabbit over the fire. There were bags under his eyes and a look of despair. No one asked him what was wrong when he didn't take food. Fox knew he was in a mood, but not sure from what. *Best to leave him alone,* Fox thought as he watched Crow venture off into the woods without saying a word while everyone sat around the fire eating.

"I wish he would talk to us," Janet said.

"Me too. I feel for him. You can't make someone open up," Jamal retorted.

"I think he'll talk about whatever it is in time, man. He's got an air about him, but he ain't so bad, just a little aloof, man." Fox spoke quickly as he always did. "Anyway, we should probably figure where to go today to get some more deer. We're running low on our jerky and that doe isn't going to last long. It's going to get rough soon. I wish we lived in elk country. You guys would love elk, man."

Fox waited for Crow to be completely out of sight, then he put his finger up to his lips for everyone else to see. He grabbed his rifle and tailed him. Fox watched as he sat on a damp rock under the bridge where he hid them. *Probably going through his memories. He definitely feels like shit, man. One day he'll be okay, but he's gotta let it all go. They're gone and they ain't coming back. They all need to accept that. Their old lives are gone.* Fox walked away and left Crow to his own photographs, memories and emotions.

Time to explore, he thought to himself.

The road was clear except for one scraggly man walking down it. If anyone had seen him, they made sure not to give away their position in the wooden cottages which adorned either side of the road. It was an old place with old, white money. Mostly the cottages were once owned by old people who needed a second home to talk about with their friends over dinner in rich suburbia. Fox noticed that it was a different kind of tacky in this town. People had decorated their mailboxes to look like different animals, ducks and birds mostly, but some had painted wolves, or hung signs of dogs from the old-world tools. Now they collected dirt, dust and snow, and had their paint get bleached away by the sun.

It was still a nice place, Fox noticed. It was small, and no house was too close to the next. People here must have spoken to their neighbors as they passed by, but were not forced to interact with them if they didn't want to. The idea was nice, quiet, alone, but close enough to not feel isolated.

He wandered into one of the small single floor houses through the back-sliding glass door which led into a kitchen that was openly connected to the dining room. The table and chairs were covered in a thick dust. It had settled across everything, even the floorboards, from years of not being used. If anyone had been in the area, they had definitely not come through this house even to scavenge for some canned foods. Fox made his way into the living room.

Above the mantle of the fireplace was a bear pelt. It was real, that's for sure, but he highly doubted the owners had been the ones who had killed the bear. The area was too rich, too secluded, too neighborhood friendly for someone to be a real hunter here. Fox had been wrong before, but his gut said this was purchased for a lot of money just for the sake of spending it.

In the back corner of the house was a small bedroom with bunk beds. Attached was another small room with a tiny bed, made only for preteens. Fox took off his pack, made sure the door to both rooms was closed, and he lay on the bed. It was hard, but anything was softer than sleeping on the ground under the trees. He loved exploring old ruins for this reason. They were quiet and it was peaceful. The alone time on the bed reminded him of the time when the lights were still on and he wouldn't have had to made sure the wooden window curtains were latched shut to keep any peering eyes from looking in.

Fox slept until it was dark, then slept until it was light again. The house was barren, but there were supplies which still resided in the cottage. Fox had found a can of beans, and a can of sausages along with a small bottle of rubbing alcohol, gauze, and some medical tape bought from a dollar store if only for the sake of having supplies in the vacation house when the family returned to get away from their real life. He also found a small stash of potato chips in the closet of the room with the bunkbeds, but they had already gone stale and lost the crispiness he longed for. He had returned back to camp before Crow had.

"Where'd you go, man?" Fox asked when Crow returned, though he knew the answer already.

"I just needed some alone time."

"So, the bridge." It was a statement to try and draw Crow into opening up to everyone. A sharing of burdens.

"I just needed to spend time with my wife and kid."

"They're gone, man. You know that."

"Of course I know they're gone. I live with it every day, and I see it every night."

"I wasn't trying to offend you. I have no clue what you're going through, or what you went through, but we're all here for you, man. I just wish you'd let us in sometime. Maybe one day that'll happen, but it's obviously not going to be today."

* * *

Crow was still annoyed, but he wasn't sure why he was annoyed. Fox had made complete sense, but he wanted to hold onto his anger and depression as long as he could. He wasn't sure he had the right to. Did he have the right to not focus on surviving and being part of the group he had put together?

Crow opened up the gates and let the deluge flow. "I don't understand why the world is the way it is. I don't understand why people can't look at the world objectively, at themselves objectively, at their friends objectively. Maybe it's because no one wants to take responsibility for themselves, and they don't want to criticize their own friends and loved ones. Avoiding conflict, I guess. I never did that with Maria and Lucy. I just wanted Lucy to be the best she could be, and to do that I wanted her to recognize that she was flawed at a young age—that we're all flawed. Maria always said that's the perfectionist in me, and she wasn't wrong. At the same time though, everyone is so bad, and no one wants to do anything that doesn't inflate their own ego. Maria said she understood when I said this, but I don't think she actually did—

maybe no one actually grasps that. Maybe I'm just hoping that people will be better than they actually are."

Crow was stuck in his thoughts, speaking openly to the wind. "I'm not better than anyone though. They sat home, with the curtains drawn, just trying to make it through the first night of the bulbs burning out, and he had come in trying to steal everything we had. I heard a gunshot as I came back, and I ran upstairs knowing what I'd find. I'd do it all again though, I know I would. I'd watch him beg for mercy as I stabbed him over and over, and watch him choke on his blood. I would do it all again, and I know it's wrong, because he had a family too. I knew him and his family. They lived in the building next door. I took him from them, and I knocked on their door and told them I came across his body and did all I could, but I was too late. His wife screamed and cried, and I was cold and uncomforting. I just wanted to see someone else sharing the same pain I was going through. What I did was cruel. She was dead shortly after. I came across her and her kids about a week later when I came back to the building to grab some photos of my family. I decided I needed to leave the city, and get as far away from that life as I could. It's all fucked. And now I'm here, just with some old photos and people I hardly trust."

Crow felt like the world was dismissing him even though he felt Fox staring at him while he spoke. *He's probably faking it, just playing the part of a listener instead of actually being one.* Ever since he lost his family, everything felt cold, and too often did he feel nothing—not apathy or depressed, but emptiness. As if the void of the world resided within him.

Crow looked up. "Sorry, didn't mean to share my life story with you."

"Nah, man, it's cool. Get it off your chest."

"I probably offended you by saying I don't trust you guys."

Fox laughed. "You think I trust your asses? You gave me some cans, but I know any day there can be an argument or a hungry day and the weakest of us will get killed. It's all a matter of patience and feeding another mouth. I get it, man."

Crow smirked. "Well I hope I'm not the weakest who gets killed off when someone here gets hungry and wants to control what everyone else does as a group."

"I doubt you will be."

5

NEW YORK CITY, 2012

J ames stood in Grand Central on his birthday waiting to meet a woman who he had been talking to for months for the very first time. The station was cold. It was the end of December and the Christmas decorations were still up.

She appeared near the escalators, saw James and quickly crossed over through the sea of tourists. She was bumped and bashed into by everyone who was too fixated on their phone. She had dark brown hair which came down just below her shoulders and deep brown eyes that looked bland from far away, but up close were deep and defined. James was immediately in love the moment he met her.

"It's so great to finally meet you," Maria said as she threw her arms around him and squeezed him tightly.

"Yeah, you're so much more beautiful in person." James smiled back. Nerves rattled him and his personality took a hit for it.

"I wish you would've worn something other than all black to

meet me though. You look like a crow with your beard, the pointy nose, and the small, dark eyes." She laughed and put her arm around his waist as they walked toward the subway.

"I only wear black, you know this."

"Yeah, but still, put some effort into meeting a beautiful woman for the first time why don't ya?" Mischief danced in her eyes.

"Since this is your first time in New York City, I have a treat for you." He changed the subject, not able to keep the secret which had been welling up in his chest ready to spill onto the floor.

"What's that?" Maria questioned him as they were going through the turnstile below the main floor.

"They're running the old New York street cars today. People are wearing clothes from the 1940s."

"No way! Like the green ones with the old ads?" She had seen the photos in an article and sent them over to James saying how cool she thought it was that the city still even had the old train cars around—gathering dust like a second skin.

"Yes, and they still have the ads from that time period. Nothing is current. We'll see a lot of their history."

Maria started running to the closest staircase. "Well, hurry up," she yelled back to James.

He laughed. "You're going to the wrong one. You're going downtown. We need an uptown train. This way." He led her to another set of stairs and they went down to wait for an eternity. It was the usual subway lines in New York City, never on time, even when the small ETA signs said the train was arriving. The new construction, which had been going on for at least ten years, had seen to delays every day. James was used to it by now.

"Are the wait times always this long to get on the subway here?" Maria asked, echoing his thoughts.

"If you only knew. They never get their shit straight. Even

when they have no construction or changes in trains, they still manage to fuck things up for everyone."

"That's harsh, don't you think?"

"Nah lady, your man is right. They can't tell their ass from their elbow," someone chimed in from the platform.

James saw the puzzled look on her face. "Don't worry. Everyone talks like that here. It's a New York thing."

The train barreled through. Maria stepped back from the rush and noise of it all. It flashed emerald green among the white tile walls. In the train cars stood men and women in old over-coats, fancy hats, and dark heels.

"Oh, James, they're so beautiful. It's like a time warp. This is the best." She hugged him and dug her face into James's chest. He felt some tears through his shirt. "They're happy tears, don't worry," she said. *Already knows what's on my mind before I even say anything.*

They hurriedly got on the train before the doors closed and it disappeared into the dark tunnel.

James and Maria went to dinner at a restaurant with a name punning on dogs. Inside were multiple pictures of dogs on the walls, and in the booths.

"Oh, the Dog Bowl is literally just a bunch of shit in a bowl," James said looking at the menu.

"I was thinking of the Wire Haired Jack Russell with Meatballs."

"Why not just go after the Fried Golden Retriever Snot."

"I do love mozzarella sticks."

"Then it's settled."

"What's your favorite dog? Or did we just end up here by chance?" Maria folded her menu and placed it on the table.

"I actually wanted to take you to the place across the street, but you know, the lights are out, and I didn't want to say I didn't do my research. So I just made it seem like I wanted to be here. Also, it's a pug."

"I knew it. You looked totally lost. Before that you knew exactly what was going on, but the second we got on this street, you looked dumbfounded."

"Was it that obvious?"

"Do I look that dumb to you?"

Their waiter brought over their food and placed it on the table in front of them.

"No, no, no, that's not what I was trying to say."

"Oh, relax, you're so wound up." She chuckled. "It's kinda cute." There was a pause. "We should go to Long Island tonight."

"I'm down," James said as he tried to stop his mozzarella stick from stretching for what felt like an eternity. "What do you wanna do there?"

"I know someone's house we can squat in. Apparently, he's got a jacuzzi tub."

James tried not to choke on the cheese which would not break down no matter how long he chewed on it. "Okay, where's the guy though?"

"My mom said he went to Florida. Snow bird or some shit. Y'know, the kind of rich person who has two houses just to have two houses—like every politician ever." Maria laughed.

"I see what you did there."

"Good. At least you're not completely inept." Maria winked.

"What's that supposed to mean?"

"Oh, you know, just figuring out where we gotta go and eat and such."

James blushed.

"It's fine, I don't care where we eat. I'd like your company even if we ate fast food."

"Well, now I know I can take you on a cheap date next time."

"I'm just so easy to please."

"I knew it from the second I met you."

"Hey now."

"What? You don't like when your date gets sassy with you, Maria?" James smirked, knowing he finally could get back at her.

"Oh, boy, are you in for it."

"I'll wait."

"Hey, waiter, can you bring me the check? It seems my fun date here, James, would like to leave your establishment for some dollar burgers."

"I-I-I I never said that!"

"Oh, I'm sorry. I thought you just wanted to please your cheap date as easily as you could?"

"I'm sorry. She just wants to embarrass me because the restaurant I picked was closed, and I tried to go with the flow."

The waiter stood there looking between the two to try and figure out what was happening. He disappeared to go get them their check. *He probably thinks we're weirdos. Tourists even!* James guessed as he caught their waiter looking over while conversing with another employee.

"You are so going to get it later."

"I dare ya." She leaned over the table and kissed him on the mouth. "Make a move."

They left the restaurant. James leaving a fifty percent tip on top of the bill.

"Excuse me, walk closer to the road like a gentleman. Didn't your mother teach you anything?"

"Hardly."

"That's okay, I'll teach ya."

James and Maria made their way to the empty house. The car ride was long. Even though it was late, there was traffic and traffic cones for no reason—there was no one actually working on anything, and everyone slammed on their brakes the entire way to the bridge and off of it for no other reason than to slam on their brakes. Once they arrived and got settled, all of the frustration of late-night traffic was forgotten as they enveloped each other in the folds of the other's body.

* * *

Crow woke from his love dream, wishing that he would be in that bedroom again with the mirrors on the walls and ceiling, the jacuzzi tub, and a glass shower. He wished he was waking up to Maria wearing her red lingerie with black trim. He wished he saw her smile, but all he saw was a dark sky. A depressing nostalgia lingered on his chest and pressed down. He sighed, and a little of the sadness melted away, leaving only a cold ache deep in his ribcage.

"You were talking a lot in your sleep." Janet's voice broke through the darkness, a faint crackle in the night, something too afraid to speak.

If only Maria was telling me that.

"Just some bad dreams," he replied.

"What were they of?"

He lied and told her an old nightmare he had after the bulbs burned out to keep her from asking more questions and saying he never spoke. "I saw a dark sky, and a red ringed sun with a black spot over it. The world was lit up in a red-orange glow, and all the buildings were crumbled in the distant horizon. They looked like metal spikes covered in blood. I guess that's symbolism for the way the world is now—just an empty husk full of death and disease."

"Don't you think that's kind of meta? You know, to explain

what you think a metal and the color red means when we already live in the apocalypse?"

"Why are you questioning it?"

"I was only making an observation."

"Please, keep the observations to yourself the moment I wake up. I have a myriad of thoughts going on when I open my eyes. First one is probably why I'm still alive in this shithole."

"What's that even mean?"

"What?"

"That word."

"Myriad?"

"Yeah, that one."

"It's a 'great number.'"

"Thinking of dying doesn't seem to be more than a single thought."

He glared at her, annoyed with the back and forth which was becoming common.

"I don't want to hear stupid English terms for playwrights and other nonsense to make me feel dumb when I'm only trying to have a conversation with you," she said.

"I'm going back to sleep."

"Enjoy the red sun."

"Fuck off, Janet."

* * *

Janet sat on her rock, looking over everyone as they slept, wishing Crow would open up a bit for her. She cared for him, but he was dense, cold, and cryptic. She wished the lights were still on and she was back with Rob in their cute apartment with pink curtains and cream-colored walls. Janet wished her dog, Taco the Pomeranian, was still greeting her every morning and that his little feet pitter-pattered to her every day for breakfast. Most importantly, Janet wished still felt that warmth of being loved and cared for.

* * *

New York City, 2018

It was Christmas, and Janet was standing over the stove making omelets and corned beef hash for Rob, her, and Taco. The smell of peppermint hung off the tree where the pine aroma resonated. It was gloomy outside, and the sun fell lightly. There was just enough snow to coat the ground and make it impossible to see what was beneath. She heard the door shut which was connected to their bedroom. *Rob must be awake, finally,* she thought. The toilet bowl flushed, and the sound of running water reverberated off the walls of the kitchen.

"It smells delicious, babe," Rob said as he strutted into the kitchen, putting his hands around her waist, and giving her a squeeze.

"I'm glad it smells good. Now tell me it tastes all right."

"Yeah, I guess it's edible," he said after Janet fed him a small piece off of a fork. They watched Taco demolish the small plate of eggs and hash then beg for more.

"Well, he'll eat anything. You on the other hand choose when you want to eat." She smirked. "Now eat the omelet and let's open some presents."

"As you say, master." Rob's voice was soaked in sarcasm. He ate some eggs and walked shirtless in his red pajama bottoms over to the living room and plopped down on the recliner. Taco ran alongside, and sat adoringly at his feet, never taking his eyes off of the fork which kept going back to the ever-dwindling omelet and hash on Rob's plate.

"Here, open this one first," Janet said as she threw a big box at Rob. He caught it almost crushing it. She knew it was light and he wasn't prepared for the catch.

The lights flickered. "Hmm? I guess it must be windy outside for the lights to do that. There's no way an inch of snow made that happen."

"Yeah, or some asshole driving on Christmas morning struck a pole. Who cares? Open the box."

"Jeez, relax for once." He put the remaining eggs and hash on the floor where Taco was waiting patiently and saw his chance to get a second helping of breakfast. Rob opened the box and inside was another, smaller, yet not so delicate one.

"Oh, I see. Ha ha, a box within a box," he said unwrapping the slender wooden casket. "No fucking way, you got me Superbowl tickets?" He exclaimed. "But, how?"

"I know a guy. A friend of a friend."

"What'd you pay for these," he almost yelled.

"Hey, we don't do that for Christmas. Remember? No money talk."

"Holy fuck, babe." Rob stood up and grabbed Janet while just missing Taco with his right foot who was still licking the plate clean. Rob kissed her forcefully on the mouth and hugged her tight.

* * *

"I wish he could still hug me like that," Janet said to herself sitting around all of her friends sleeping on the ground.

6

NEW YORK CITY, 2019

James heaved a backpack around his shoulders filled with small cans of tuna, some canned green beans, and mandarin oranges—his favorite. He hooked a carabiner to a loop of rope, and tied it to two gallons of water. It was time to get out of the city, and head north. He grabbed his bat, put a small hatchet in his jacket pocket which he had stolen from a neighbor who never came back after going to the supermarket one night.

The lights had been out and they were not coming back on. He trundled down the stairs away from his loft apartment and went to the park where he had buried his wife and daughter.

It was about to become daylight outside, and there was little commotion on the street for the first time in all of the aftermath, but James knew it would not last long. Soon everyone would be running on the streets, using up gas, shooting the shit out of each other, and looting whatever was left.

James made his way quickly down the street, sticking to little openings and alleyways as he went. The buildings of gray and red held a little cover, but not too much. Just enough to stay a moment and move onto the next spot. Grand Central wasn't far, and he knew the tunnels were dangerous, but not nearly as dangerous as trying to hit the George Washington Bridge, and head to Jersey. It was open season on the bridges and the highways. James felt he would be decently safe, at least, until he hit Harlem-125th Street. Then the tracks opened up until he got into Westchester.

What am I doing, he asked himself as he saw Grand Central a few blocks down the road. *I have no idea how to navigate those tunnels. I'll get myself lost. Fuck. Maria. Lucy. I'm sorry.*

James pulled himself down an alley. It was now mid-day, and James hopped in a dumpster and pulled the lid closed. *I have to head up to Harlem. From there I can take the tracks north.* He knew them well. It would be long and arduous, but he made the trip north to Croton-Harmon many times. After that, who the hell knew, but it wasn't Manhattan, and it wasn't nearly as densely populated. *I shouldn't have left.* Tears rolled down his face.

James camped out, grabbed a tiny nap, and waited for nightfall. The walk to Harlem-125th Street was long, taking most of the day. James stopped multiple times when he heard gunshots close by and tried to stick to the shadows whenever cars started to speed through. Recklessly they would drive through the streets, trying to drift around tight corners with no one to stop them. Those people would slam into cars still parked or already wrecked, and keep going until their vehicle finally gave up—the life sputtering out of them. Sometimes he was glad when he saw headlights hoping they would be upon him soon and he'd be joining Maria and Lucy—he was too scared to do it himself and he knew that. Other times he was not as fortunate. When a car had flashed by and he didn't know it until the sound was on top of him, they simply drove by or swerved to avoid him as if they had a sense of morality. No lights, just the engine chugging away. It felt like some were getting their adrenaline fill and expected the lights to come back. James didn't think so. Better to leave and come back, than to stay in the city of old ghosts and dead family.

James slept in another dumpster close by as the sun rose and a light snow drifted to the ground. It was the kind of snow that started early in the morning which would have made the street lights cast an orange glow if they were still on. Now, the snow only dampened all of the noise around him, like the world itself had gone to sleep. He could see the platform of Harlem-125th from where he was. He had always seen homeless people sitting on this corner in front of the red brick building just under the platform and now he was stealing from them. Living a life they lived which he had never had to. He was a stranger to this. A stranger to being cold and alone.

James decided to make his way up the staircase and heaved himself over the turnstile. He jumped down on the tracks, and started walking. From above he could see all the garbage in the streets, only now noticing the bodies he had been avoiding the entire trek.

"Wow." It fell from his mouth as a gasp. He had been so focused on getting there that he had not stopped to take a look at the world around him. He knew what was going on and what had happened, but for the first time since he left his apartment, the fog in his head rolled back the curtains and he was fully aware in that moment—struck with a thick dose of reality. He smelled death, shit, and heard all that raucous noise which still permeated the streets of the city he once fell in love in. The serene white snow reflected on blackened footprints from dirt, and red which ran down the curbs into the sewers, unless it had already frozen. He closed his eyes, took a breath as he let the scene wash over him. He started walking before someone saw him up on the tracks and decided he had something valuable, or, at least, something they wanted. He heard the little of a small handgun in the distance, almost like popped balloons echoing through the corridors. *Maria. Lucy. I'll come back one day.*

* * *

A distant gunshot pulled Crow from his dream of memories. The bright sun reflected off of the snow, blinding him while he tried to shake the remaining traces of sleep.

"We need to get moving," Fox said while the others had already begun to pack up their camp.

"Any clue what's goin' on?" Jamal asked his words drawn out with his city accent.

"Not a clue," Janet added to the mix.

"Who cares? It isn't us, but the shooting's close, so we need to move," Crow stated matter-of-factly while trying to shake the past from his head. The switch in Crow's head set itself to survival, and all of his dreams were quickly forgotten. They all heard it grow louder as they shuffled around, the pops and bangs echoed through the woods.

"He's right, man. Whoever it is could be here shortly, and we don't need any of that shit," Fox said. Crow stared at Jamal who was looking at his watch. Crow wondered what was going on in that man's mind at a time like this.

* * *

New York City, 2018

Jamal stood in the foyer of the rundown theater looking at his watch. He and his friends were squatting there making a home out of a bad situation. The torn red fabric seats made for poor sleeping arrangements. The weather was cold, and the snow kept coming down as Christmas loomed just one day away. They had cleared out a few of the seats with some bolt cutters and a lot of muscle so they could bring in a few barrels to start fires in. Brandon, Jonathan, and Mikal were all he had. His family wasn't around much, but he didn't mind. The streets were more comfortable to him now than being stacked into a small apartment with too many people. The black watch around his wrist ticked away slowly counting the seconds until the sun set and Jamal would have to start a fire with some torn scraps of clothing he found in a dumpster outside the nearby mall.

Jamal looked over at Brandon. "Yo, is your new girl coming through tonight?"

"Yeah, my dude. She prolly showin' up."

"Where's she at anyway?"

"I dunno, man. Prolly tryna get food or some shit."

"Go find her and bring her here. Get her ass outta the weather for tonight."

"Yeah, I guess you're right." Brandon walked over to one of seats and pulled a torn coat patched together with duct tape over his body and made his way to a side entrance. The main doors had been boarded, taped, and had paper glued over them long ago.

"I'll be back," Jamal said to the air around him as he as he made his way over to the door following shortly behind Brandon.

"Where ya goin'?" Mikal asked

"I dunno, just wanna get some air before I gotta spend another night in this drafty ass theater." Jamal moved a piece of plywood and let himself out. He made sure to pull the tagged piece of thin wood back over the door to keep as much of the cold draft out as possible. *He probably doesn't want to be left alone in a drafty theater.*

The snow was blowing hard on the road in the city. It made seeing more than ten feet a chore. Jamal pulled the hood of his sweatshirt over his head and began to truck through the snow which had garnered more than eight inches on the sidewalks. Wind bit through the layers of clothing and still brought a chill even to those who were well clothed. Jamal kept his hands in his pockets but snow still managed to gather on his watch face despite being buried there.

As he walked, Jamal realized he was hungrier than he thought. Not far away was a fast food joint which never closed—even in the worst weather. Jamal was grateful. It was cheap, but more importantly, reliable, unlike most things in the world. He made his way slowly but eventually arrived to find the doors still unlocked as the weather worsened and it grew dark. The doors opened as another customer made their way inside and Jamal followed behind making sure to kick off as much snow as possible. He ordered a few burgers for just over three dollars. He pulled out two crumpled bills and a wad of change.

"Have a good day, Jamal," Joce said with a smile.

"You too, Joce," he said. It was always good to see her again. They had been old friends who grew apart after trying to date once. They didn't hate each other. They knew that together they would never work out. Jocelyn's parents gave her an earful for dating a guy who ran away from home and never graduated high school. He didn't have the patience to deal with her family—having to jump through hoops to spend time with her.

"You stayin' warm?" she asked.

"Of course," he replied.

"If you ever need anything, just let me know, and I'll find a place for you to get some good shut eye."

"It's all good. I'm at the theater still with Brandon and Mikal and Jonathan."

"I'm glad you got them."

"Me too. Me too." He grabbed his white bag with burgers wrapped in yellow paper and made his way to the door.

"See you around," Joce yelled to him as he threw up a peace sign with his right hand.

The walk back was harsh. The wind had picked up and whipped the bag of food around. The snow had become so dense that it almost fell like snowballs. Seeing anything was impossible in the blinding white. The street lights flickered and shut off for a few drawn out seconds. Jamal felt the dark might stay and envelope him, but the lights came back on and stayed the entire way back to the theater. He remembered years ago when the power went out all across the city at the end of the summer. People freaked out all over. He heard it went out all the way up to Canada. He was scared when it happened back then, not being able to see at night, and hearing all the people around the city going crazy. It was wild, not having stores with power. Everyone relied on it so much. Sweat poured from their bodies and food went bad. The city was miserable on a good day, without power, it was an atrocity.

The theater was close, almost close enough to see. The snow had already begun to cover the makeshift side door down the alley even though he was gone for less than an hour. He pushed the board to the left. It left a track in the snow. Inside the fire was still going. Brandon was back with his girl, and they were curled up close to the barrel with their shoes off trying to dry their wet feet. Jamal went and sat next to them, pulled off his shoes, and stretched his long legs close to the fire after he had taken off his socks and laid them next to the barrel. He took a look at his watch. It was just after six, and it was dark as all hell outside. The fire shimmered and cast shadows on the wall and on the faces of his friends which made them all look like skulls and dead men.

7

B oots crunched through snow, like biting through potatoes which hadn't been fully cooked. It made a bitter noise which wasn't unpleasant, but definitely drew looks from people who were curious as to the origin. The sound was quick, thorough, and Crow was not pleased as they trucked through the woods to put distance between the camp as everyone followed behind trying to keep their feet in the tracks he had already made. Fox brought up the rear, doing what he could to make the tracks look less human and more of a mess.

The gunshots had died down from a frantic battle between surprised foes, to the occasional popping off of people behind cover. Ultimately it ended with one side having a victor, or maybe both sides died out from wounds. Whatever the case, Crow needed to make sure they were away from it, and moved uphill where they could get a better view of the land.

They reached an overlook with a small valley to one side, and a massive cliff to the other. From there, Crow could see where they had come from, and further, a small area of red marked the snow in a clearing among the trees. Not far from the clearing was what looked like a small cabin they must have missed. *How did we go completely around that?*

"Whoever stayed there either fucked someone up, or got fucked, man." Fox looked down into the valley, noticing the red and the cabin.

"Maybe both sides got screwed," Crow retorted hopefully.

"I'm gonna go over there and take a look at what might be leftover," Fox said looking down at Crow who was crouched and taking inventory of what was in his bag.

"Do what you gotta do. We'll wait here until the next morning, then we continue east."

"What the fuck's east of Nowhere, New York?" Jamal wasn't used to all of the trees and nature, Crow guessed. The steel was his home.

"A small city, a few miles from the college. There are some caves nearby that would be good shelter for a bit, and plenty of old orchards which attract all the deer," Crow said.

"You sure seem to know a lot about the area up here," Janet stated.

"Used to come up here with my family in the spring and the fall. My parents were a couple of Leafers growing up, at least, that's what the locals called them." *And Maria and Lucy loved to come here and go apple picking.*

"What are 'Leafer's?'" Bernice asked.

"People from the city who would travel to the small upstate towns to hike during leaf changing season every year."

Jamal laughed with Bernice. "Leafers," he said mockingly.

"Yeah, can't give them any credit for originality, but hey, most of the locals were nice enough when we came through, and some of them gave pretty good directions to local swimming holes. People rarely want to explore caves when there's food and beer nearby, but if you ask the right people, you'd be surprised what's around for a day you just want to explore."

"Yeah. Well, if these caves are all fine and dandy, then maybe we have a place to get out of the weather for a bit. I say we wait for Fox, and if that dude doesn't come back, then we head for them." Jamal was probing the thought process for the group.

Crow nodded and pulled some cans of tuna from his bag, a pack of jerky, and one can of peaches. Everyone else pulled something from their bag as well, and they all split what they had evenly. No one cooked that night so as not to raise any suspicion from any possible onlookers. The night was calm, clear and warmer than normal. Warmer didn't necessarily mean warm though. The wind had died off entirely, and everyone felt it was below thirty. Definitely cold, but warm considering their standards. *Why trust one man for all of our survival? If those caves are so safe, maybe someone's there already,* Crow thought about the possible consequences.

The dark had started to creep in as Fox continue to make his way back down the way they came. This time he did not worry as much about covering his tracks. He took a mental note of them and where they were as he continued on.

He intertwined himself through the brush, weaving in and out, disappearing from lines of sight in mere seconds. He was a shadow in the dawn, something you could have sworn to have seen out of the corner of your eye, yet left no trace of where he went or where he came from. Fox was an apparition creeping closer and closer to where the gunfight had occurred. Overhead a bird circled way higher than was normal. He watched it closely and it rarely seemed to beat its wings. It glided along, as if it were following and watching him. Its movements were static and odd. Fox heard the crunching of icy snow and got his head out of the clouds. *Someone? Maybe only an animal.*

He approached the small cottage, run down, worn by the weather. The wooden structure desperately needed to be redone. The sun had lightened the color and the constant weather had worn down the roof and overall stability of the house. Windows were glazed over in a thick white film while the door looked like it was about to fall off its hinges at any moment. Fox crept around the back, and popped his head up to the sill. He gazed inside taking note of any danger which might have lurked. There were two bodies near a gray stone fireplace. They looked bloodied enough and stiff. *Probably dead.* Fox backed up and dug around his backpack.

He pulled a large rock from it and launched it from a tree which he had quickly clambered up. The rock struck the window and shattered it. Fox waited and waited. No one came running from or towards the cottage. Two hours must have passed by his judgment of the sun. He finally decided to come out of the tree and creep again towards the window he had broken. He lifted his head and the two bodies laid next to the fireplace, clearly dead. *That's good*, he thought. The back door was unlocked. Fox quickly swept the one room cottage with his rifle and made his way over to the bodies so he could begin to pilfer for any useful supplies. On one of the men he found old gum, a few bullets, a small flask of whiskey, and some coins which he thought could be one of the more useful supplies should the thaw ever come. Coins made for great distractions when they resounded off of concrete. He left the bodies and started back towards the mountain, hoping to catch the crew before they left.

"What'd you find?" Crow asked.

"Just some supplies. No survivors in the cabin. Didn't want to get too far away and see who they were fighting, man. I'm guessing they assumed the two inside were pretty shacked up and decided to not shoot it out with them anymore, or they're dead as well."

"All right, now what?" Jamal asked knowing they were going to start moving again.

"Let's get to the city east of here, and put as much distance between us and them as possible," Crow stated.

"Should we hang out for the night?" Jamal asked.

"I think that's a good idea," Janet interjected.

"Let's take a vote on it," Jamal said.

Crow voted to leave along with Fox, but Bernice, Janet, and Jamal voted to stay the night and actually relax, though they would not be able to light a fire.

"So we stay. I'm not happy about it," Crow proclaimed.

8

J eremiah opened his eyes as he rolled over onto his stomach. His head ringing so much that he could hardly see. Gray static flowed through his vision, making the reception to his brain hurt. His hands were coated in blood that had begun to dry. He wondered how long he had been out for his hands to start to clot and scab, unless—he looked around and saw body parts strewn around him. The blood wasn't all his. *Fuck, fuck, fuck. Head down. Keep your fucking head down.*

Jeremiah struggled to stand and hobbled toward the exit. He walked into the street where it was even more chaotic than the torn couch and dead sex worker. The police hovercars were already parked and the area quarantined off with their Projection Staffs. They were long and black, with a metal base, which allowed them to stand about three feet off of the ground. The black metal was thin. On each side was a slit which sent out a yellow light to the next. White words ran through the beams, POLICE INVESTIGATION KEEP OUT. *Simple technology,* Jeremiah thought.

Officers started to rush toward him and he reached in his jacket pocket for his ID. His thumb flicked a button on the back as he opened it. PRIVATE INVESTIGATOR. SECURITY LEVEL CLASSIFIED flashed in small red letters underneath his photo.

"Yes, sir. Sorry, sir. Do you need medical attention, sir?" one of them asked frantically as he stepped out of Jeremiah's way as fast as he could. *He knows not to piss me off or the Precinct will string him up. How did I survive that blast?*

"I need a Sep-9 shot, a pack of Medi-Flesh, and I need to acquisition the closest civilian hover vehicle." Jeremiah walked to the other side of the road and sat on the curb, waiting for his Sep-9 shot. He kept his head low. *Best not let any more people get a look at me.*

The officer returned and Jeremiah placed the Medi-Flesh over his face and hands. The soft nano-skin formed to his facial structure and tightened over the cuts which began to sear with pain. He was now only slightly bleeding. The officer handed over the Sep-9 shot, and Jeremiah wondered why his hands were shaking. *Maybe this is his first dead body.* He glanced over to the human remains strewn about as he took the needle out of its holster and jammed it into his thigh. His adrenaline kicked in from the shot, and the nano-skin activated with the increased rush of hormones as Jeremiah grimaced in pain. The chemicals reacting with the nano-skin forced his body to heal faster than it should have been able to.

"Where's my vehicle?" Jeremiah asked.

"I got a man two minutes out. First thing he could find was an enclosed scooter."

"Damn." They were notoriously slow. Reliable, but slow. He would have to hijack and reprogram the computer inside so he could rest while it took him away from the scene.

The egg-shaped scooter arrived after taking its sweet ass time. Jeremiah hated the look of them. Two suspensors, one on each end, kept the thing floating off the ground. It was always cramped inside, and simply puttered along the streets while every other vehicle flew by. Jeremiah said nothing as he flung the door up, stepped inside, reached, and pulled the door back down. He put his badge up to the steering wheel and waited for his override to take control. A keyboard projected in front of him and he typed away quickly on the projected keys. The windows of the scooter immediately darkened so no one could see in, but Jeremiah could still see out as if nothing had changed. The code was easy to break, and he quickly installed his AI into the system.

"Where would you like to go today, sir?" The voice was pleasant and he was glad to hear it for the first time. *I always hated these things. Don't trust 'em one bit.*

"Just drive around the police perimeter, taking random turns so as not to be tracked. Make the drive as inconspicuous as possible. If we get tailed, wake me up, otherwise stay within twenty blocks of this scene. I need a few hours' sleep. Wake me when my vitals stabilize from the Sep-9."

"Understood, sir. Would you like anything played while you sleep?"

"Can you play something relaxing?"

"As you wish."

Jeremiah reclined the seat and closed his eyes as the scooter puttered along, putting distance between them and the explosion. Inside the sound of water on metal surrounded him. *Goddamnit. Rain on Slum shacks? Really?*

People ran back and forth, frantically trying to discover where the explosion had originated, all while figuring out why it had occurred in the first place.

Jeremiah swayed from one side of the scooter to the other,

never fully sleeping, but never being fully awake. It was a nap which only made him more tired. He heard all sounds in his half-sleep.

"Sir, I've intercepted a radio message from the local police which may be of interest to you."

His eyes snapped open. "What is it?"

"They seem to be on the lookout for someone of your stature, wearing an overcoat passing himself off as a high-level Private Investigator. They have a photo of you up on their monitors, and they have a photo of this scooter." *Shit.* Jeremiah knew they were onto him. The old, hacked Holobadge could only keep them away for so long. Soon, the whole police force would come knocking.

"Pull over immediately and let me out. Does this scooter have a wireless earbud connector?"

"Yes, on your right side next to the brake."

"Download yourself into it." Jeremiah put the device in his ear. It was small and black and did not emit any light. He hopped out of the vehicle and went into a dark alley.

"I need to know how far I am from safe house number four."

"About three miles. Sir, there's an access tunnel a few blocks from here which leads to the sewers. It will take you within eight blocks of the safe house."

"Overlay a blue marker to my optical inlay. Take me to the tunnel."

"As you wish, but, sir, there are police barricades on the way there. They're saying you caused the explosion and audio has been released on a threat to local politicians. That you threatened some who frequented the glass brothel."

"Trace the signal back to its source, eliminate any background noise from any other radio signals. Search for keywords: 'over-coat', 'explosion', 'brothel', and 'Deep'. Then cross check these with any photos of me. See if that gets me any results about which Precinct is putting out the dispatch."

"Three sources discovered. One in the Central Precinct you used to work at, one from the UC financial district, and one of the signals is coming from the Capitol building itself."

"Let's start with Central, since it's the closest to us. How far are we from the Capitol?"

"Not close, sir."

"Any chance of me grabbing a FastTrack there after the safe house?" A FastTrack would get him out of the GUC and to another city, he knew, but it was a huge risk. He'd never been to another city Below, and if they caught him boarding, he'd be no better off when he arrived somewhere else.

"Soonest is thirty minutes, next one after that is two days away."

"Okay, so I need to lay low. No chance of me making that first run and running through security checkpoints isn't gonna work." Jeremiah tucked his face into his overcoat as he popped the collar. A small implant in his eye created a blue line for him to follow as it twisted and looped in on itself to the sewer.

"Would you mind sending out jamming signals at three-minute intervals, unless you notice a camera, then jam it immediately. Respond when you do it so I can change my course to make tracking me more difficult."

Police sirens loomed in and out ricocheting off of the walls as Jeremiah made his way to the access tunnel.

"Cameras are becoming more consistent. They're catching on to us."

"Run voice verification over the radio. Redirect police units behind us. Flip the video and project it to their cruisers."

The cruisers flew by Jeremiah as he continued toward the

police barricade. He saw everyone gathered in front of the access tunnel.

"Any chance you can redirect power a block away and cause some of the transformers to blow?"

"Already done. I don't think they'll be gone long. I'm not hyper-connected to the grids here. They'll catch on soon."

The barricade quickly dispersed as officers responded to the explosion. Jeremiah ducked towards them, and snuck quickly through the massive metal door. He climbed down the ladder on the side of the wall, and splashed to the floor.

"They're on their way back. One of their AI discovered me already. I'd hurry if I were you, sir."

"AI, activate night vision." The tunnel turned a pale green as the optical implant churned over to old settings. Jeremiah made his way quickly through the tunnel. Minutes passed and Jeremiah felt exhaustion again for the first time since the Sep-9. He came across an alcove, and sat down. He leaned against the wall and closed his eyes.

"Sir, we do not have movement in the tunnel. Please, continue on."

"How long have I been out?"

"Two minutes at most. They got a tip saying they saw a shady figure going through an access tunnel. My signals are weak down here. Getting them to believe a redirect will be nearly impossible, but I shall try." The small, metallic voice rung in his ear.

"No, it's okay. I'll take care of this if I have to." Jeremiah stood up and scooted across the left wall, pulling his gun from its holster, and set it to stun.

"You have enough charge for five shots, and fourteen lethal rounds left."

"Thank you. How far until I can reach the exit?"

"Just over two miles. At current pace, you'll be there in forty minutes. At a decent run, around twenty minutes."

Jeremiah turned and jogged briskly, trying to keep his feet away from puddles so as not to make any more sound than he already was. He turned left down an offset tunnel, looped right twice, then made a left. It added a few minutes to his escape, but it was worth throwing some distance between him and the police.

"Sir, they're coming down the other access tunnel. They have anti-material rifles. You will be disintegrated and your body turned back to dust and atoms."

"Shit." *Fucking AI always knows how to put things in the worst way possible.* Jeremiah stopped in his tracks, found a gap between the walls, pulled his pistol, flicked a few settings, and waited until the last of the armored men had passed by him. He leaned out and fired a non-lethal round into water below them. The corridors turned to static as their systems overloaded from the charge.

There was a groan and the man taking up the rear was unconscious. Jeremiah stripped him of his rifle and set it to stun. He fired and the team fell quickly.

"What's that noise? Has he been subdued?" A voice cracked through the helmets of the four men at Jeremiah's feet.

Jeremiah reached down to one of the matte black helmets, and pulled it from the man's head. His eyes were still open and flicked back and forth, trying to figure out what had happened. The stun setting of the rifle was reliable in rendering people useless. Sometimes it would knock them out, other times it wouldn't. The man on the ground was fully conscious, but had lost all movement in his body. His synapses were firing randomly from the electrical impulses. Jeremiah noticed his mouth was tightening in the corners like he had something to say and his fingers were contracting into a fist and smoothing out randomly. He put the helmet's microphone to his head.

"I'm still here, and I'm coming your way." Jeremiah dropped the helmet to the ground, and jogged toward the oncoming squad.

The tunnel was narrow and dark, and the sensors in their helmets were beeping frequently of an incoming target. He moved quickly, turned the corner, and stopped directly in front of them.

"Sir, I don't see anything," said one of swat members as his voice echoed down the access tunnel to Jeremiah.

"Hold your fire," one of them told the group of men with him. "I'm going to have to ask you to lay down your weapons, and approach with your hands raised," the man shouted down the tunnel.

Jeremiah didn't answer. The tunnel began to fill with smoke.

"Sir? There's nothing on my thermal imaging. Not a single heat signature that isn't our own."

Electrical bursts began to hit the walls surrounding them. They returned fire while trying to dodge any incoming blue bursts. The electric-blue continued and was sporadic, hitting walls and clipping their arms and legs. None of them took any direct hits. The firing stopped.

"I think we got him, sir."

"Laurence, go down the hallway and find the body."

Jeremiah watched a short and stocky man slowly walk down the hallway and begin searching for him.

"Sir, I didn't find a body, but I did find one of our rifles. It looks like the trigger was taped, and left on the ground."

Jeremiah slammed the hatch behind them with a loud metal clang.

"Thanks for hacking their sensors, AI. Really helped me out back there. Give me a minute while I weld this hatch shut." He pulled his pistol and flipped through the settings until a high-powered ray erupted from it. He ran it over the hatch until the metal melted and cooled itself to create a seal he was proud of. The charge in his pistol had completely run out.

"Anytime, sir. I recommend making your way to the safehouse before they get the hatch open."

"Exactly what I was thinking."

A door creaked open and Jeremiah stumbled through it, worn out and tired from his trek. The drugs were wearing off and he needed to sleep desperately. Long sleep, no dreams or nightmares, just the empty void which none could remember. Disappear into the ether, and return to reality whenever his body was ready to do so. *Lie down and fuck off.*

The safehouse was sparse, mostly made of wood with aluminum accents which caused the single yellow light in the middle of the room to reflect throughout. Though the light reflected everywhere, the room was still dim, casting shadows into corners and amongst the reticent furniture. He was a stranger here, and everything felt as if it were telling him to hurry up and leave.

Jeremiah strode across the room, found his way to the small desk, and smacked it open. He fumbled around and found the syringe he was looking for, pressed it to his wrist and depressed the button on the side. It activated, and Jeremiah felt his body rush with the concoction. He grew tired. He pulled his overcoat off, laid it on the ground, and snapped his fingers. Machines whirred and chunked their way to life. The ground shifted, twisted, and rolled. The jacket disappeared into the floorboards where it would be cleaned and pressed.

Jeremiah made his way sloppily to the couch, his boots slipped off as he went. He pulled his gun from his waist as he did so. He laid it on a small piece of hard black plastic. The gun lit up and began to charge its cells. He collapsed on the couch and slammed into the world between worlds, but it was not empty.

Jeremiah dreamed. He saw body parts, he saw explosions, he saw himself taking lives of people around him. Jeremiah saw men and women choking on blood, he saw glass tearing through bodies, and he saw fire. He became aware of his dreaming.

Around him the aluminum walls were a hot, red-orange. Smoke swirled and encased the room. He tried to cover his nose and mouth with his torn shirt, but the thick black smog pushed into his watering eyes. He choked on the air as a banging grew louder.

Jeremiah woke to his door being bashed in. He ducked behind the couch, input a code, and disappeared under the floor into a small room.

Jeremiah grabbed a small bracelet from his cubby hole, and shoved his hand through it. The bracelet rotated and cinched around his forearm, creating a black sheath up to his elbow. He tapped keys of blue light on the keyboard which projected onto his arm. The holopad turned into a screen, and Jeremiah saw a swarm of armed men corner checking his small safehouse. They did their sweep and put their guns to their sides. None of them moved much and only turned to see if any of the others had missed any open spots for hiding.

One of the men began to bang on the floorboards with the butt of his rifle, while another carefully tapped away on the ceiling of Jeremiah's small sanctuary. They found a hollow spot where his jacket had gone under and unloaded an entire magazine along the frame. The floorboards splintered away, and beneath they found his jacket. The machines under—and the clothes he would have put on if there were no bullet holes in them—were utterly destroyed.

Another person walked in, clearly outranking all of them.

Everyone stood at attention and saluted. *Military?* He couldn't hear anything they were saying, because he never got around to wiring the place up with mics. Jeremiah cursed himself under his breath for it now. *Who are these people and why are they trying so desperately to get me? No ordinary cops would try so hard to do this.*

He racked his brain over and over, trying to come to some conclusion as to why he was being hunted after the explosions, why he was being hunted for impersonating an officer. Why he was being hunted...

Jeremiah's brain thought about it but no recent events had led anyone to him. No recent events, he thought, and then his eyes widened, and Jeremiah finally came to a conclusion that might have made sense. *Someone found me. Someone knows. After all the time I put in, someone knows.* He crouched down in his one room box, and fumbled as quietly as he could through some piles in the corner. From the piles he pulled another gun, though this one was much older, and the ammunition was finite and could not be recharged. He flipped open the revolving chamber and loaded six large bullets into it, then tucked the handgun into the back of a pair of black jeans he had managed to find and squeeze his way into. It was an old gift brought down before his time.

Jeremiah slid a small panel open, tapped on a keypad quietly, and caused the entire safehouse to rumble, lurch, and sway. A piece of the ceiling collapsed, he could see on camera, and pinned one of the officers underneath a solid beam. They all rushed over, attempting to free the man whose leg had clearly been crushed and shattered.

A small crevice appeared and Jeremiah began crawling through, stomach to the floor. He had done this many times before. Above, the safehouse was collapsing. In his mind, everything was collapsing. He heard screams and light lit up the darkness. Men and women were wandering aimlessly, trying to make sense of what had happened. *An explosion? From inside the Precinct?* He shook that memory from his head and tried to focus on the now. Jeremiah crawled through the long chute he had created.

He couldn't let that memory creep back in, not yet, not now. He had to get out of here before the safehouse went completely up in a roar. The blast seat was directly behind him, in that small room. By his estimate, he had less than two minutes. Possible, but he needed to focus. He reached and pulled, reached and pulled, turning corners and squeezing through any obstructions and debris. He thought he had cleared the chute of all the dust and bricks long ago, but heavy traffic and construction must have caused small cave ins. The end was in sight, but the light at the end of the tunnel was small and dim. Rebar and massive slabs were in his way. He rushed ahead on his stomach, and began to push and pull on anything that would move. The ground shook, and Jeremiah knew the small homemade bomb had gone off. If anyone still stood in that room, they were dead and gone, either impaled or blown apart. He struggled faster to clear his way out. The heat from the explosion would hit him from behind any minute, he'd live but it would not be pleasant.

A chunk of reinforced concrete moved, and he pressed his arm through, then pulled his head and second arm against the outer edge of concrete, and grabbed for leverage. He felt his feet grow warm, then hot, then scorching. He smelled his flesh sear. He hadn't had time to get any boots on his feet. They would have found him. The hole gave way, and his body fell through into an open area, full of water and human waste. Directly inside the wastewater treatment facility. *Disgusting. Why did I ever put this place here?*

He tucked and landed on his back in a pool of water. It felt good on his now burned and blistered feet. Ice on a heat-burned face, like when he worked in the Furnaces. It was cool and temporary, but still Jeremiah felt the warmth between his toes, uncomfortable and uninvited.

Jeremiah pulled himself from the clean pool and lay on the concrete to dry off. His feet rested in the water and drifted he off to sleep.

9

GUC, 2015

Jeremiah sat at his desk. He had a pile of paperwork as high as the Capitol building. The light from the lumines-cent ceiling cast an eerie, foreboding shadow that high-lighted all the beams and pointy bits. It blacked out most areas where the windows and doors would be. Jeremiah reached for the top folder. It was thick, made from some form of repur-posed vegetable or grain, maybe a supremely heavy hemp, either way, it was heavy, and exacerbated by how much bullshit holopaper was in the folder. He laid it on his desk and began to thumb through it.

A black and white photo displayed itself on the first page. A man stood at attention, blinking every so often and fidgeting about. He was bald and tall, but not lanky or skinny from what Jeremiah could see. Rather, he was burly—as "large" would be a poor adjective—and even then, burly seemed to fall short, in Jeremiah's opinion. The man had no visible neck, not from an excess of fat, but from very large shoulders, which in turn, had a layer of muscle on top of them. Jeremiah had wondered if the man worked for the Irons close to the Furnaces. He had clearly been able to eat better than the shovelers. He looked sleep deprived, his eye bags sagged lower than Jeremiah's when he was on rotation for OT.

Mason Davis, age: 43, height: 6'6", weight: 279.3 pounds. Iron Worker.

I was right.

Big fucking boy, Jeremiah thought to himself as he continued to thumb through a series of charges ranging from petty theft, assault, attempted murder, until a final declaration of excessive force during an altercation, assault with a deadly weapon, assault on an officer, and murder. Glossing over the reports, the arresting officers had declared Mason's elbows and knees deadly weapons on multiple occasions. Reading further, the report quoted Mason as preferring to use them rather than anything around him. While being interrogated, he said he liked the feeling of bones crunching and breaking against his body. He laughed as he said this and asked for the officers to release his handcuffs so he could show them how much he liked it.

Jeremiah shuddered. Mason would seriously hurt him at any given moment, and Jeremiah was the lucky one to have been handed the case of, *Why the hell is Mason Davis being released within a couple hours?*

Jeremiah closed the folder, pulled his jacket off of his lousy chair, and made for the exit of the Precinct. Mason would be smelting iron, or so his public work schedule said. Outside it was dark and humid, the only real light radiated from the Capitol which was maybe a couple of miles away. Jeremiah found his police cruiser, opened the door, and sat inside. He fingered a few buttons and thumbed some switches, pulled up a map in his optical relay, and set the cruiser to a brisk speed, only going slightly faster than what was recommended. He needed to get to

Mason, but he wasn't in any rush to go faster than he was asked to go.

When the car jolted to a stop, Jeremiah begrudgingly opened the door to the cruiser and stepped out. *Why do these things always brake so hard?* He waved his Identification Badge over the door. The car lowered and put itself into lockdown. The windows dimmed to a void-black, the exhaust ports slammed shut underneath the vehicle so it would be a dragging brick rather than a floating one, and the handles started running an electric current through them. If anyone tried to open the doors, they'd be shocked, their fingerprints analyzed and placed into the system for attempted theft of a police vehicle. If they were dumb enough to try again, they'd be stunned with a slightly less than lethal blow which would paralyze them for up to ten minutes as a chip was inserted into their hand, producing electric charges until someone arrived. Jeremiah had to test it in the Academy once, and pissed himself the first time. The second time, he remembered, wasn't nearly as funny as he lay on the ground convulsing with his fellow cadets.

Jeremiah strode through the winding alleys and found himself at a massive entranceway, big enough for the largest of machinery and vehicles to get through side by side by side. He took a small walkway on the right, and made his way down the long tunnel, following the dimly lit orange lights which were slammed into the concrete walls. They were obviously rushed during their installation by the telltale cracks and fissures which spread from them. *How long had this place existed?* Longer than Jeremiah definitely. *Maybe longer than Mom and Dad? What about their parents?* His grandparents had been the first to be born down here. Their parents had been selected to be a part of this new life, he recalled.

He remembered the stories he was told growing up which

were passed down one generation after another. His grandparents told him what they heard about the sunlight. Shortly after his great-grandparents moved here, everyone heard stories that there was a war Above, a war which killed everyone instantly. They were told nuclear weapons incinerated everyone and everything, so not even dust remained. His great-grandparents told their children they had seen movies from Above of what those bombs could do. Entire cities were leveled. He tried to imagine it but couldn't. The stories described it as giant mushroom clouds which relieved skin from bone. Jeremiah had never seen a mushroom before, so he did not know what to imagine, but he had seen people burned, and he had seen muscle and bone before. When he asked what a mushroom was, he was told it had a shaft with a dome on top. His only frame of reference was rather phallic. *If only those movies were still around,* he thought once. But the Capitol had stopped distribution of them.

He wondered what people in the Above had seen in their last moments and how lucky he was to be descendants of people who were randomly selected by lottery to come down and be a part of a new life.

The long tunnel to the Irons began to open up. It had clearly become hotter by how much Jeremiah was sweating. His mind wandering as he meandered to his target. He needed to find Mason and confront him without incident. *Please, for fucks sake, let there not be an incident.* Jeremiah sighed. *Why did I get assigned to this bullshit?*

"Mason Davis?" Jeremiah walked to the largest man he saw. He wasn't exactly hard to miss.

"Who the fuck is asking?"

"I'm Detective Jeremiah."

"What the fuck you want, pig?" Mason kept on working,

walking around Jeremiah as he lifted machinery and lugged wheelbarrows full of iron ore to dump in a pile.

"I just had a few questions—mostly on your last case."

"What you wanna know? I was acquitted of that bullshit charge." He stopped and looked at Jeremiah. Mason tensed his muscles and Jeremiah could see Mason was itching for a fight.

"Did you know the victim?"

"Man, cut the shit and get to the fuckin' point. Know you read my file—all of 'em. I damn knew that lyin' cunt, and you know damn well it was declared self-defense after I snapped 'er neck for comin' at me witta knife." The Slums dialect was coming through strong. *Never mentioned he was from the Slums. Makes sense. Probably abandoned or sold off by his family.*

"Okay, sorry, Mason." He was trying to cut the tension which was clearly escalating. "No bullshit. Why did you really kill her? We both know you planted that knife and stabbed yourself with it. What did she have that you needed so bad?"

Mason stepped closer and crouched down next to Jeremiah, his mouth next to his ear. "You step back right now, and avoid the road yer 'bout to go down. If I don't kill ya, someone else will."

Mason went to pull away. Jeremiah grabbed his shirt and stared the hulking mass right in the face. "And that is exactly what I want to know. Who the hell is getting you off on all of these charges and what you're doing for them?"

Mason laughed, smashed down on Jeremiah's wrists like a steel beam, and brushed him off with the outside of his forearm. Jeremiah landed on his ass and felt embarrassed by the man in the torn and dirty clothes. He needed to set an example in front of everyone or else he could never show his face. Mason turned around and started to walk away.

Jeremiah grabbed a shovel that the men down here used to shovel from the piles of iron ore into their wheelbarrows. He closed the gap and slashed Mason in the back of his thigh. He created a huge gash and forced Mason to take a knee as he held onto the muscle which was thicker around than Jeremiah's entire body. *Write it up as self-defense. He moved first. No one at the Precinct will dispute that.*

"You fucked up, boy. You fucked up real bad!" Mason screamed at him.

"I'm going to need an ambulance down in the Irons. Mason Davis. Gash on back of right thigh." He radioed to the familiar voice through his holobadge. *AI or person? Does it matter in the end?* Jeremiah quickly handcuffed him and wondered why Mason didn't put up a fight.

When the ambulance arrived, Jeremiah rode with Mason. White lights lit up the entire spacious cabin. It hummed and beeped with little voices talking to each other and to the EMTs who could decipher their alien language.

"When I get to the hospital, I'm gonna kill ya." Mason stared directly at Jeremiah. "And I'll be done 'fore anyone can blink."

"Just tell me who it is, what they want, and where I can find them. I can offer protection through the Precinct for your word." Jeremiah tried to reason with Mason and be blunt enough for his soft brain to comprehend.

Mason laughed. "That Precinct is bugged and so is the hospital you're takin' me to. Every single Precinct is. There ain't a single place that isn't corrupt. So, I'm gonna kill ya, like I said. Then, I'm goin' to continue workin' for 'em. Livin' my life, wastin' any motherfucker they want me to." He spit directly into Jeremiah's face.

The ambulance pulled into the Emergency entrance. The driver put the ambulance in park. Jeremiah watched the driver through the hatch separating the compartments. He slipped his knuckle against a sensor and unlocked it from the inside, allowing him to turn and push the door open with his right hand. As the driver opened it to exit, a bullet tore through the front of his skull. No bang, no clap, just a sickened thud and squirt as blood and brain matter exited his head and he slumped to the ground beneath the no longer floating ambulance.

Jeremiah sprung from the back, through the small doorway separating the two areas. He pulled the door shut and slammed his badge over the sensor. The ambulance immediately lifted off of the ground and started screaming with blue and green sirens. It had gone into lockdown mode and autopilot. It sped towards the Precinct attached to Jeremiah's badge. Bullets dinged off of the hyper-enforced windshield and could be heard thudding against the metal carapace.

That's not good.

He shouldn't have been able to hear bullets hitting the husk of the ambulance. The electro-barrier should have been slowing down any metallic objects that came close to it, as was standard with all emergency vehicles. Preventing any damage to the people inside was of the utmost importance, even those accused and convicted of the worst crimes of humanity. Jeremiah's mouth dropped at the sound of bullets ricocheting of the vehicle. *No way that should be happening. The nanites and electro-barrier should be stopping anything from coming into contact with this thing.* If Jeremiah was hearing the bullets hitting, that meant that military weaponry was being used. Maybe black market and Jeremiah knew he was in serious trouble. His mind was spinning as Mason cackled behind him.

Despite his hands being shackled to the bars of his ambulance bed—his feet as well—Mason's smile told Jeremiah that knew he would be freed. It was only a matter of time.

"Tell me who they are," Jeremiah demanded as he returned to the back where Mason still laughing. The two EMTs that remained were nervous and huddled in the emergency lockdown section of the ambulance. In front of them was thick glass, bullet-proof and reinforced with small nanites ready to matterweave themselves against any projectiles. Once they did, nothing would be able to get through. The armor they would create would be too strong to penetrate without destroying them entirely. The glass shimmered and flowed as the nanites spun and swam through their home, active and alert to the emergency sirens which rang all around them.

"Fuck. Off," Mason grunted.

Jeremiah turned away and sighed. There was no getting through to him, not here at least. But, once he got to the Precinct, maybe, just maybe he'd be able to get through to him. Jeremiah ran his hands through his hair and rubbed his eyes. He looked down at the strands which kept falling out and could see the follicles at the ends. They had been falling out for a while now, but the stress of the job only furthered the hair loss by his temples. His fists closed out of anger and he grabbed the police issue baton from his pant leg.

Mason was still laughing with joy. Jeremiah returned and smashed Mason's fingers against the handrail of the bed with his issued baton. The knuckles popped and phalanges broke. *Tired of hearing this sicko's laugh.*

"You fuckin' pig! I'll kill ya!" Mason screamed and strained at the handrails. Beneath, the bolts pulled against the point at which they connected. Jeremiah could hear it, a few more tries and he would be free from the handrails of the bed. Then he would have full reign over the vehicle until the ambulance arrived at the Precinct. They were maybe ten minutes away by his judgment, but that was a long time to be stuck in a cramped space with a monster.

Jeremiah slammed Mason's other hand, breaking more bones,

and then for good measure, he laid into his shin. It didn't break like he had hoped. He hit him again hoping that the pain Mason felt would distract him from the weakness in the handrail. Mason jerked and each time the nuts and bolts strained under the stress of Mason's body. Jeremiah stopped from exhaustion, returned to the driver seat, and closed the hatch between the front cabin and Mason. He sealed it and put the driver's cabin into lockdown separate from the rest of the vehicle. He relaxed momentarily and let the adrenaline in his body take its course.

The ambulance wailed and whined through the city, twisting, bending, and shrieking through the corridors of slow passing time. Jeremiah heard a heavy shudder door crank and groan open, allowing the ambulance to pass through.

Finally.

The ambulance slowed and sifted the dust of the mostly empty Precinct garage around a bit, then shut itself off. The green and blue strobes still flashed and whirred, illuminating any pillar or cruiser in a ghastly undertone of sickness. No sound resonated off of the concrete walls. Everything was quiet, except for Mason who no longer laughed, only let his breath fume from the back of the vehicle, waiting for someone to open up and let him out.

Jeremiah stepped from the ambulance, opened the back doors after releasing the lockdown with his badge and let the two EMTs free from their nanite prison.

Jeremiah grabbed a receiver from the wall of the garage and radioed to anyone upstairs who may have been in the Security room. "I need backup in the garage." Three officers arrived briskly, asking Jeremiah what had happened. Quickly he explained and told them they needed to move Mason Davis to a holding cell.

Two of the officers moved to the back of the ambulance and pulled the bed out with Mason still attached to it. It began to hover off of the ground and waited for the officers to direct it to their next destination. One began to make his way around to the head of the bed. He was short and stocky. Jeremiah didn't know his name, but he had been there longer than him and looked familiar enough with his dark hair shaved tightly to his head, conforming to its shape. Jeremiah watched as Mason pulled one more time as hard as he could. He freed a bar from the bed and in one motion swung the entirety of the handrail around with tremendous force, using the handcuffs as an extension of his arm. The handrail swung and connected with the man's skull below the left of his jawbone with a sickening crunch. His neck gave way and snapped as his body slumped to the floor. His head cracking against the pavement. Dead before his skull gave way on second impact. Teeth separated from their sockets and clattered on the ground, like a necklace of pearls being ripped from a woman during an armed robbery. They cobbled at the feet of the second officer. Polished white with a red sheen.

The second officer released his weapon from its holster and set the gun to stun.

"Don't move, Davis," he shouted as Jeremiah looked on still in awe at what had occurred so suddenly.

"Pigs." Mason spit on the bed between his legs, still attempting to gain any feeling other than pain in his fingertips. "I'll kill you all, right here, right now. And I'll take my time with that prick Detective!"

"Put your right hand up, now, Davis." The officer aimed directly at his chest.

Mason kicked and the cuffs attached to his legs and the bed could no longer hold the weight, strength, and the inertia he was able to put forth. The officer shot.

Mason was hit in the chest with a small concentrated burst of electricity. Jeremiah saw as Mason lost his breath as he fell back into the bed he was trying to lift himself from. Like waking from the dead, standing up from his coffin, and falling back to sleep among the soft velvet. Jeremiah blinked.

"You're gonna die," Mason grunted. His eyes half open, pupils tight. He took a breath and stood up again.

The convict lurched up before the officer could get off a second shot. Mason flung out his left arm still attached to the bed. The remaining handrail broke free, and the hoverbed detached itself, flying towards the officer. It impaled him before he could get his hands fully up to protect his face. It smashed into him, and Jeremiah could practically *feel* the officer's bones breaking in his body. Falling backwards the officer hit his head on the way down. The white lights above shimmered between blue and green as Jeremiah watched on, stunned by what had just happened. *I came here for help, not to bring death in my wake.*

A slew of officers rushed in behind Jeremiah dressed in their riot gear. Batons, stun rifles, and pulse shields illuminated the one entrance and exit which wasn't locked down. In front of the men and women in their armored black suits and helmets, they could see two of their dead compatriots. Two lives gone out amongst the world that they had been trying to make better. And all they had was a man they all knew was guilty. But they had a job to do and a duty to bring him in alive. Let their justice system, the one which they had sworn to defend, decide the harshness of his crimes and which punishment to receive.

Mason was struck and he lost control of his limbs as the stun rifles hit him. He collapsed. Jeremiah watched as Mason struggled to keep conscious and force his body to work the way he had intended. Breaking every bone in the bodies of the men and women around him. When Mason had finally lost consciousness from another volley of stun rifles, the officers all rushed over to drag the hulking mass inside. Jeremiah watched as Mason was taken by, his legs dragging on the ground. He looked back to the entrance and saw his colleagues dead on the ground. *I should have killed him.*

Jeremiah opened the door to the interrogation room in which Mason was once again handcuffed. The walls were deep blue. One wall was replaced with glass neither of them could see through. He knew people were behind it. Rage was filling Mason's face as he kept squeezing his hands. *Broken hands.* Jeremiah could see each time Mason squeezed, the pain just made him angrier. Mason pulled frantically against the static-cuffs linked to the table. They cut into his wrists and warm blood ran down his fingers, onto his nails, and dripped to the table in front of them. The blood pooled quietly, like a secret festering among friends, quiet and brooding. Something which should not be seen, but both parties longed to share it with the world.

A squeak broke the silence and frustration. Mason looked up to Jeremiah as he laid his holopad on the desk, and stepped back. Behind the glass, everyone from the garage looked at their stand-off. The air was still and most were holding their breaths, except for Mason who was breathing heavily, reliving his broken bones.

"Mason, let me explain something to you." Jeremiah looked intently at him. "Everyone here wants you dead. I want you dead. We have a few options and I'm going to tell you them before we even bother getting you an attorney or recording anything. You can either one, be the piece of shit you are and act up, where we will—most definitely—retaliate and kill you this time. Two, you can hide behind a lawyer and live your life in a small white electro-cell as you're transported from prison to prison in the GUC while we drag our feet and prolong your trial for as long as possible. Or—my preferred—three, you help us and we work together on who keeps getting you off the hook and why you're working for them. Which, in turn, will unfortunately allow us to release you back to the shithole job you have."

Mason stared at Jeremiah, mulling over the words he was being told. He spit in Jeremiah's face. "Listen, pig. I want to make one thing very clear. I hate every. God. Damn. One. Of. You. I'd rather die here fightin' this entire Precinct before I help it. I'd watch the entire damned human race choke on its own blood. I'll be out by tomorrow to do it all. You all deserve to die and your families too. You're nothin' but a cog in a system of oppression and abuse. Going around, struttin' like you own the world."

Jeremiah squeezed the small flap of skin at the top of his nose between his eyes. Mason was not going to make this easy, and something said, he was telling the truth. Someone would pull the strings so he would be out by tomorrow. Jeremiah left the room and went upstairs to his holoscreen without saying a word to anyone along the way as he trudged through the dense, open space. His feet like cement on the light gray stairs. He tapped away on the augmented reality keyboard in front of him, dragging pictures and files to corners and flipping through whatever information he had on Mason. Past murders, accomplices, and attorneys who worked with him.

"AI, compile recurring names along with Precinct numbers and judges for Mason Davis. Background check them with known family members, coworkers, bosses."

A blue bar appeared on the screen as it pulled from Mason's past trying to find any names which appeared more than once. Minutes passed as Jeremiah stewed, rocking back and forth on his feet, waiting for any clue which would help him get Mason into the system as fast as possible. The holoscreen dinged and Jeremiah looked over the results. Nothing. Not a single name appeared more than once or linked to any known family member or gang in the prison system.

Jeremiah sighed through his nose. "AI, background check all attorneys with local politicians. See if any two attorneys work for the same politician who also worked on any of his cases."

Jeremiah left his holoscreen running and went back down to Mason. He walked in to find an attorney sitting with the man.

"Excuse me, you need to leave. My client and I are speaking and no one is allowed in here or the room behind us."

Jeremiah stepped out quickly knowing his time was running out. He ran back upstairs to find out who let the attorney in already. *How had he been able to call an attorney already? Was he chipped?* The Captain wasn't present and neither was his Lieutenant. In fact, it seemed all of upper management had been called away from the Precinct. All who remained were some detectives and rookie cops running back and forth for their high-ranking partners. The Precinct shook and a siren went off.

"Emergency. Explosion in basement Interrogation area. Emergency. Explosion in basement Interrogation area."

The Precinct was evacuated. Jeremiah ran around trying to find anyone familiar. All officers were unharmed after a quick headcount, along with everyone in the holding cells, that is, everyone except Mason Davis and one attorney who had checked in. They remained missing. Jeremiah started to panic.

Through the chaos and smoke rising from the Precinct, officers from Central began to show up, asking questions. It all droned on, and on, a buzzing of questions over the low clicking of footsteps, breathing and the normal goings on of life down near the Capitol. Jeremiah was dejected. Officers had died today. Mason was missing. He took a breath. The Captain showed up.

"You know, we have your back in this." His blond mustache bushed from his face, so much so you could only see his teeth when he forced them to be shown. His whiskers wiggled and noise in the form of words escaped in return.

"But, sir, there's nothing to have my back on here. All of the tapes will show that. I was upstairs and was not informed of an attorney being presented. All of the film and audio is there."

"You're right, Detective. All of the film and audio is there, including the film of you breaking that man's hands and threatening to kill him and stating the entire Precinct wants him dead. Now, we didn't have time to erase all of that audio with how fast Central showed up, you know, having a bombing and all in a State building. Unfortunate as it is, they're on my ass because of what was said. And, while I feel that the world down here is better off without him, the law states he is allowed a fair trial. So, like I said, we have your back on this one."

Jeremiah mulled over everything that was being thrown at him. *Are they going to throw the book? Even though Mason deserved the death he got?* Everything suddenly felt claustrophobic and Jeremiah needed to sit down.

"Why don't you go home and take a breather? I can answer the questions that need answering and I'll postpone a formal interview for forty-eight hours. That should give you enough time to tell them your side of the story and let them know how emotional of a day it was. That the things you said to Mason were out of anger, along with the things you did. After all, you did watch him kill your brothers in blue and almost lost your life yourself. You will have to explain why you mashed his hands up so good in the ambulance, though."

Jeremiah looked up, realizing what the Captain was saying. He was directing his thoughts to a defense. *A formal interview. He's coaching me on the right words to say so none of this can be blamed on me. No case against me or him. Protecting his job.*

"You're a good one. Now get home and take an X-Relaxer to get you through the night."

Jeremiah nodded and slipped out before the paperwork

started to pile up along with the questions. There would be no need for him to be at the Precinct now. His case, he assumed, was dead and he needed to prep for any aftermath which was on its way.

* * *

His apartment was empty, and for the first time in years, felt cold and did not welcome him. He left shortly after arriving, coasting between the Deep and the Slums. Between the twisting sheets of metal and cloth, he found a small building, long abandoned. Inside he put down his gun, jacket, and holobadge. If they were going to bring a case against him, he would need these one day, hidden, where they couldn't be taken away. *Someone way too high up was pulling strings too fast and hard for Mason to have gone missing so shortly after being booked. Maybe the entire Precinct is bugged.* Jeremiah pulled out an inhalant, cracked it, and stumbled through the metal slums, groggy from fatigue and drugs. Maybe they were going to put all of it on him so he stopped looking. Maybe he was going to pass out on the side of the road in a ditch of water and piss.

Jeremiah kept his high going for days, longer than he was supposed to have taken off. He let his last high wear off, then decided to return home.

Outside of his apartment, lights flashed and there was a police line set up. He approached.

"Hey, man, what's going on here?" Jeremiah asked as he approached an officer from Central in all black standing next to the hololine.

The officer with his black helmet and dark visor quickly pulled his gun. "Detective Jeremiah, you are ordered to lie on the ground and put your hands behind your back. Any sign of non-compliance will be met with force."

"Wh-what is going on?" He raised his hands.

"You're under arrest for the murder of Mason Davis, treason, and conspiracy. Get on the ground. Now. You will not be told again."

Jeremiah started to bend over and place himself on the ground. He rolled quickly to his left behind one of the cruisers, and pulled his spare pistol from his inner jacket. He set it to stun and fired at the Central's legs, causing his body to convulse until he lay on the ground with Jeremiah. Jeremiah got up and ran. Gunfire rang out behind him. *The Slums.* That would be where he could get away and make any sense of this. *Blend in, disappear, re-assimilate when possible. Set up a few safehouses, come back for anything I need. The Furnaces take anyone on without background checks.* The small kernels of information clicked in Jeremiah's brain while he tried to formulate a good plan of action. For now, run like hell and never look back.

10

NEW YORK CITY, WHEN THERE WAS STILL POWER, 2018

The world around them slowly went dark. It started as flickers and eventually winked out with one surge. Jamal knew it was bad when everything got bright near them and the sky turned blue, only for it to go back to the same dark gray and black he was used to for this time of year. His gut churned. It was wrong. Very wrong.

"We need to leave," Jamal said to everyone in the theater, hoping they'd listen to his innate feeling.

"What? You scared of the dark?" Mikal was being sarcastic.

"Nah, man, this is bad. This ain't normal."

"The city lost power. It's happened before."

"Yeah, but never turned bright blue before. This is gonna be bad."

"Man, just fucking relax."

Jamal stood there, feeling uneasy surrounded by empty chairs and vacant bodies. He started to get his things together and heaved his backpack onto his shoulders.

"Where are you going? It's a fucking blizzard out there."

"I'm going to head for the tunnels, wait for the snow to stop, and get the fuck out of here. I have an uncle up north."

Mikal laughed. "You're really being a pussy right now. Freaking out over no power."

"Dude, it's not gonna be good if the power doesn't come back on in the dead of winter in New York City. At least up north I know my uncle has more shit."

"Whatever man. You're gonna freeze to death walking that far."

"You guys are gonna get killed here," Jamal retorted, regretting what he had just put out into the universe, but knew it was true.

"Have fun." Mikal was short and direct, clearly miffed by Jamal.

Jamal left the theater. It was dark—real dark. The kind of dark that nightmares hid in waiting for someone to make the wrong move so they could reach out and cut their life short. He started to run and made his way to a small entrance to the tunnels of Grand Central. He knew what it'd be like down there. He had a flashlight and knew exactly what track he needed to get on from all the time he spent down there with the homeless as a teenager.

One of the first times he was down on the tracks, he got lost and almost got killed by one of the trains coming through to birth its passengers into the living city. Now, he was sure he could get through the tunnels and on the right track out of the city in almost complete darkness. He knew the problem awaiting him. *How many people were trapped in the train cars? How many people were hiding in Grand Central? It'd get worse the longer the power was out.* He kept thinking it over to himself. He needed to get down there and out of the city before security took over and started to shut everything down and block access. He ran faster.

He knocked on the door to a house after being on the tracks for five days. His uncle opened the door and hugged him. The last time Jamal had seen him was at least two years ago. He was the only family member who had his life together and didn't ask for a handout. They had spoken about getting Jamal out of the city and onto his feet where he had a chance to make something of himself, all he needed to do was "commit and put in the time," his uncle had told him.

"You can stay here indefinitely," he said after they embraced.

"It's only until the power comes on, then I'm going back to the city," Jamal said hoping he wasn't a burden.

"I don't think that's going to be anytime soon."

Jamal looked at him. "Yeah, me either."

The power hadn't come back on anywhere. Jamal noticed during his trek up. Every town he went by was dark. The world was on its way south.

* * *

Jamal waited and waited. His uncle was still out there, and though it was light out, he felt that it was odd for him to be gone all night and into the day. He'd never been gone that long. He let time pass and sat on the couch. *Been here this long and it's the first time he's been gone longer than half the day.* The couch he sat on was drab, torn on the sides from cats scratching at the brown fabric. It sat in a living room with piss stains and spilled beer on the carpet from the last tenants. His uncle lived alone. His kids gone to make their own families. His ex-girlfriend left him for someone else. Jamal was the best company he could have asked for. The lights had been out for a few months, and they had started to take turns scavenging anywhere for leftovers.

"Man, fuck," he whispered to himself. "I gotta find him, no way it takes that long to check the gas station for shit."

Jamal stood up and went to the kitchen with the stained fake tiles, and the steel sink filled with old dishes. He grabbed his backpack off of the dining room table covered with a plastic tablecloth which had flowers printed on it. It was tacky, but his uncle always said it reminded him of his childhood—growing up in a house of fourteen kids, it was easier to clean up a shitty table-cloth than a shitty table. He hooked his arm through the strap of his pack, grabbed a gallon of water, and tied it to the other. Then left the house only after making sure to hide the spare key to the back door under a jar of old cigarette butts his uncle had welded a false bottom to.

Outside it was clear, the sun shining brightly off of the snow —definitely midday at least, Jamal reckoned by the position of the sun. It didn't help that he had slept a lot longer than he had thought he would. But it was nice sleeping inside a place which wasn't a rundown theater in the city. *I wonder if they're still alive down there? That's a lifetime ago now.*

He saw the gas station off Broadway and slinked closer, sticking to the side of the street and hugging the walls of the building. He wondered if they had had seen his uncle the day before. If the walls had secrets, whisperings among them his uncle carrying his rifle. If they knew, they chose to keep quiet as Jamal passed by.

He entered the gas station and found it empty. All of the shelves ransacked, and only some open, crumpled bag of chips were left behind, along with the occasional beer can or smashed glass on the floor. Jamal left and walked around the back, just to get outside and think everything through.

Where had he gone? There's no way he came here and just decided to not come home. What's that old man doing right now? Jamal leaned up against the dumpster and looked towards the sky trying to figure out where his uncle had gone and what his next step was. He looked to the right and saw a ladder. *Go up and take a look at your surroundings. At least get a feel for the area.*

It was a short climb, his hands slick and cold against the metal. On the roof he saw a body of a man lying in a pool of blood. He noticed the backpack and the clothes, everything familiar as the last time he saw his uncle walk out. A black bag, blue jeans, and a thick, heavy brown jacket. Jamal stumbled over, taken aback by what he was seeing.

His uncle's head was busted open, clearly shot and his brains baking in the cold sun. The smells emanated off of him churned Jamal's stomach and he threw up what little food he had eaten. Jamal started to cry. He felt rage, felt grief, and the need to do something with his uncle's body. He ran back to his uncle's house, letting the buildings on the side whisper and gossip about what he was about to do and how he wasn't taking any precautions to not be seen. His emotions were getting the best of him.

Outside was a red can Jamal had grabbed after taking off his pack. Inside he grabbed a rag, and ran back to the gas station.

Jamal got on the roof and started pouring gasoline on his uncle's body. It was way too cold to dig him a grave and if anyone was going to try and come back here, he wanted to make sure they'd find nothing left. *Hopefully there is still gasoline in the tanks, enough to blow this entire fucking block off the map.* Jamal thought terrible things to himself and cried as he soaked his uncle's dead body and then the rag. He was a child new to death—unsure how to cope with trauma and grief. Out of his right pocket came a lighter, and he lit his uncle's pants on fire, then quickly got off of the roof, and started pouring what little gasoline was left inside the building and on the floor. He lit the rag and threw it in. He watched everything start to light up. Warmth radiated off of the flames as it grew larger and larger. *Better to burn, than let his body be picked at by animals or people.*

Jamal contemplated joining his uncle. He had nowhere else to go. No one else to see. He could go back to the city, but it would be a mess, and he'd probably die there with everyone else. *They're all gone anyway. Everyone you ever cared about is gone. Your parents didn't give a shit. Your friends are dead. Joce was the only one and you left her in the city. Now your uncle is dead too.* Tears ran down his face.

Jamal backed away. He watched the old buildings as the gas station went further and further into an inferno and was swallowed up by orange flames and black smoke in broad daylight. It was immense and beautiful against the gray sky. Jamal felt his old life drifting away in heat and haze. He wondered if anyone was watching as the streets around him remained quiet.

11

UPSTATE NEW YORK, 2018

Jeremy made his way through the woods, his beard getting longer as the days turned to nights and back into days. He had been wandering for months after having his mental breakdown. Work was monotonous, boring, but proved to be fruitful for him, yet, he hated every moment of working for big business. Sitting in a windowless office typing away was a form of insanity. It was solitary confinement. Cruel and unusual punishment. He remembered the night he changed his life.

He was a clean, freshly pressed man who walked down Main street, and found a couple of homeless men and women sitting on the corner of the sidewalk. They were a common sight. The town was a hub for traveling homeless youth—a resurgence in the hobo culture.

"You good for tonight, man?" Jeremy asked one of them sitting with his one-eyed dog wearing a red bandana around its neck. Supposedly a protector at night. The dog walked right up to him and brushed its head against his leg. Jeremy assumed it wanted to be pet. Generations of domestication running through its DNA, the dog must have forgotten that maybe there was hostility in a stranger.

"We could use some food, if you got anything to spare. Or cash." The homeless man tried to emphasize the money issue. Jeremy knew it wasn't so he could eat. He needed a score and swindling people out of their money was what they always tried to do. He had seen the same people on the corner every weekend trying to get tourists to feel bad for them. Jeremy was better at getting people to give him their money. Five dollars was nothing compared to what he got from people with the promise of bigger profits.

"I have something for you, man." Jeremy dug into his pockets and pulled out his keys and wallet. "Walk down the road that way for three blocks," he said pointing with his left hand, "and you'll find a long driveway on the right-hand side. That's my house. Inside you'll have food and running water."

"Woah, what? That sounds fishy as fuck."

"Nah, man. It's fine. I work in finance and I'm done working for this scheme we've been led to believe in. I just wanna disappear into the woods and live off the land." Jeremy left his keys and wallet at their feet, not waiting for a reply. Maybe they could understand what it was like wanting to be free from "the man". Free from the bounds of society living under the ageless stars and timeless sky. "If you don't want to take the keys, you can take the money and credit cards in there. I'm not calling the banks for fraud. Just spend a little at a time and they'll let everything go through."

"You sure about this?" The man asked, reaching down to get the keys and wallet. He handed half the cash to the white woman with dreads sitting next to him, and the other half to the man sitting in torn camo to his other side who must have been pretending to be asleep the entire time. Miraculously, the man was awake and alert once they had been given money. *They need to work on their skills a bit more.*

"Yeah, just do it, man. I got all I need not far from here."

Jeremy started to walk on and make his way down towards the small river at the base of the mountain which overlooked the small town he lived. He overheard them say just before he was out of earshot, "Crazy motherfucker that guy was. I guess we're having fun tonight!"

In a small dugout near a drainpipe laid his bugout bag. Next to it was his rifle with a large carving knife and a few boxes of ammunition, warm clothes for when summer ended and winter brought the cold snow.

Jeremy stumbled into an open yard while reminiscing about that night he turned his back on the world and walked up to knock on the backdoor of a house which was lit up in the darkness.

"Who the fuck is there?" A gruff voice ruffled the air and came to the door. "Who the hell are you?" The man was burly. Stomach huge from drinking, most likely.

"I'm Jeremy, man. I've been out here for a few months and I just need some water. I haven't been able to find any for two days," he said as a woman appeared behind the man in the doorway.

"Why have you been out there for months?" The man pestered him.

"I used to work in finance and I just couldn't do it anymore. I left my keys and wallet with some traveling hobos and left it all behind, man."

"Just let him in, Dad."

He looked over his shoulder at his middle-aged daughter. He let Jeremy in.

"Yeah, all right. I got some water for you to drink. The gun stays outside and so do your shoes. And you get in the shower immediately cause you smell worse than shit, ya hear?"

"I understand. Thank you, man." Jeremy took off his shoes, unslung his rifle, and stepped in the warm house where the fire was going. His stench wafted from his feet to his nose, and he understood what the man had meant.

As if reading his mind, the woman said, "There's a candle in the bathroom. It'll make everything smell better. If you go down the hall, second door on the left." She pointed with her left hand in the direction she wanted him to go. "Lights have been flickering a lot these last two days. We're running half the house on and off, just in case. Here's a glass of water. Now go shower."

Jeremy's bony hands reached out and grasped the glass. He had been losing strength. "I appreciate this so much." His hands shook and fingers let the glass slip under the weight of the precious elixir. He put one hand under the glass, preventing it from crashing to the floor.

"Yeah, go shower, boy," the gruff man said.

Jeremy made his way down the hallway and took the first hot shower he had in months. He thought about going back to his old home and shuddered at the thought. *No reason to go back there. Don't want to become a cog in the system again.* As he took off his clothes, Jeremy overheard the woman talking to her father. "He looks terrible. Like an underfed fox with that facial hair."

Her father agreed and then was out of earshot. Jeremy imagined the man probably mentioned how he couldn't be trusted and decided Jeremy should get out of the house as soon as he was done showering.

Jeremy wrapped himself in a towel, then stepped into the hallway. His shoulders and collarbone protruded through his skin, like a body trying to rip its way out of tight latex.

"There's a set of clothes in the bedroom," the daughter said to him. "I'm Denise by the way."

"Thank you, Denise. I'm Jeremy. I appreciate everything you're doing for me. I'll be on my way come morning."

"No need, there's a shed out back you can stay in. It's our guest apartment. My father agreed you can stay there until it really starts to warm up if you'd like. You'll have to do your own hunting throughout the winter."

"I appreciate it, but I'd rather not stay indoors. I'll stay the night and get on my way."

"Okay. Would you like some dinner?" She motioned towards the kitchen.

"I'll have a tiny bit of food. I probably should get the calories with the cold and snow."

"I'll be in the kitchen when you're all dressed."

Jeremy made his way into the bedroom, found an old classic rock T-shirt on the bed next to a pair of green boxers and gray sweatpants. He quickly threw them on, then ran the towel over his wet hair. It had matted itself while he was in the woods and didn't feel soft like it used to when he would condition it every day meticulously. He missed the feeling of showering twice a day. Hot water running over him, soaking his hair and running over his sore neck. It was his stress relief to sit in the shower longer than he needed. The heat pressing against his neck and upper back.

His first shower was a godsend, warm steamy water fixing his chilled bones. He felt good, almost guilty that he had taken one after committing to such an arduous life out in the mountains where the only place to go was the next spot to camp. His home was among the trees, with the animals trying to scavenge and survive. Jeremy's eyes were wide every time he saw one scurry by. His mind in awe at every twist and bend of the tree limbs and his

94

soul full of color just as the leaves that had fallen were. Now he was indoors and he felt terrible about it as he went to the kitchen to have a home cooked meal. *This isn't real life—only a minor escape from reality to keep society and civilization in check or the idea of civilized.*

A dish was slammed down in front of him by Denise's father. "It's venison stew," she said as she pulled up a chair across the table from Jeremy. "With some rosemary, potatoes, and carrots. I even threw in mushrooms I foraged and dehydrated a while ago."

"It smells delicious," Jeremy said as he spooned some hunks of meat towards his nose, sniffing it, then shoveled the bowl down his throat. He was hungrier than he realized or the food was so delicious that he needed as much of it as he could possibly get.

"Slow down," her father said gruffly. "You'll make yourself sick on all the richness of it if you've really been out there that long."

"You're right," Jeremy replied as he realized his stomach felt full and bloated, as if he was about to regurgitate everything or shit himself. His diet had not had much fiber in it and the vegetables, he reckoned, were about to push everything out of his colon.

Jeremy finished quickly and excused himself to the bathroom. In there he could still hear Denise and her father speaking through the walls.

"I bet you he made himself sick. Stupid fuck. Why am I letting him in my house again?"

"Because, Dad, it's the right thing to do. He's been out there away from everyone for whatever reason he needed to come up with to leave. The first time back he deserves people who will take him in without too many questions."

"And what if he's a bad person? And we're housing him?"

"Does he really give off that vibe to you, Dad?"

"No. But, that's the thing about those psychopaths, they're

manipulative and people persons. We should have left him outside or I should have run him off with the Winchester."

"What good would that have done?"

"I wouldn't be sitting at the dinner arguing with my daughter about who I let in my house. In fact, I should go get the rifle and order him out now." Jeremy heard the scrape of a chair.

"Sit down, Dad," ordered Denise. "If he's such a bad person I'll make sure to handle him myself. I don't need you getting worked up over this."

"Oh, stop it, Denise. Don't make this about my health like you always do. I'm fine. I'm healthier than ever before."

"Your doctor says you really need to relax and destress. I know you're eating better, but your blood pressure still isn't good —and you can't have another heart attack. I need my Dad. I need you."

Jeremy finished up in the bathroom and came back into the kitchen, breaking the silence and snapping Denise and her father out of their debate. He hoped they didn't know he could hear their entire conversation.

"You're going to be staying on the couch down here tonight. There are flashlights should we lose power again," Denise told Jeremy.

Denise's father shot her a look. "I didn't agree—"

"It doesn't matter. You're going upstairs to sleep. You'll take any guns with you and you'll be quiet. I'll be up there too."

"And what if this Neanderthal steals what we have left?"

"Man, I really don't plan on taking anything. I think dinner was even too much from you guys. I just wanted to take a small break. I appreciate it all, and if you want, I'll leave tonight."

Her father went to open his mouth, but Denise cut him off, "It's totally okay, Jeremy. Relax for the night. If you need anything, help yourself. We will talk in the morning and set you off with some water." Denise began shuffling her father out of the kitchen and towards the rickety wooden staircase.

"Thank you. I appreciate it, greatly."

Jeremy walked over to the couch as Denise disappeared. Everything flickered. He sat down listening to the silence of the house which was different than the silence of the outdoors. This silence was muffled, almost perfect, except for the creaks and groans of the wind and wood. It was a pervasive grating on his brain, as if the nearly perfect silence was fake. There should have been the sound of leaves blowing, the movement of branches, anything other than the stillness of the indoors. Outside the silence was pertinent and soothing rather than this abrasiveness which Jeremy had distanced himself from. He'd rather hear the animals and wind close up, as the branches swayed and slashed through the night. Inside was sickening. A domestication of silence, unreal and distorted.

Jeremey was awake before the sun started rising. He expected to be out of the house and dressed before anyone was awake. He heard Denise's light footsteps striding through the wood cabin like an apparition. Jeremy disappeared into the bathroom before showing up behind Denise in the kitchen.

"Hey, uh..." he started.

Her shoulders popped up slightly, and she grabbed her chest before turning her head. "Holy shit you startled me."

"Sorry about that. I just, uh, wanted to know if it was okay to flush the toilet if the power is off." The lights had gone out in the night. A silent death.

"Yeah, we can fill the back of the tank from the stream nearby if we have to."

"Okay, excuse me a moment."

"You know, if you keep sneaking up on me like that, I'm just going to call you 'Fox.'"

Jeremy laughed. "You can call me whatever you like." He smiled at her before he disappeared down the hallway. The walls were littered with family photos of Denise and her father. Some had them holding fish together near some body of water. Another had Denise with a buck's head between her hands. She was extremely young in that photo, but her face still had the same exuberance. Her father, behind her, was young, and his face full of hair. He looked like Jeremy had when he arrived last night, skinny and worn. Jeremy wondered why there were no photos of her mother in any of the photos in the hallway. He flushed the toilet.

He returned to the kitchen. "Do you mind if I ask you a question?"

"Sure, of course." Denise turned to give him her full attention, her back now to all of the vegetables she had been cutting.

"Why are there no photos of your mother in the hallway?"

Denise seemed almost taken aback by the question. The look on her face went from confusion, to pain, then to a still calm.

"To be honest, it's my father. My mother died. Cancer got to her by the time I was three and within two years she was gone. He doesn't like to be reminded that the love of his life couldn't be saved. He's a very controlling man, with a good heart, but when he couldn't save her, it really affected him," she admitted.

"Do you remember her?"

"Partly. Most of my memories are towards the end when she was bald and frail. I don't remember her healthy if that's what you mean, or what her personality was like. She's just a, uh, how do I put this? She's a flash of existence in my memory, someone I knew and loved, but was too young to understand the loss of."

"That must have been hard to figure out growing up."

"Yeah. The girl with no mom in school is always the odd one out. The tomboy who goes hunting with dad on the weekends."

Denise laughed. "Dad says I look like her, back when she was young and in love. I have her eyes. But we don't talk much about her, rarely, if at all now. Growing up I would ask questions. I think those questions kept him alive and helped him cope for a while, getting to relive memories and share them with me, giving me memories I could never have with her. An ancestral bond."

"What's his name anyway? I never asked."

"It's Dean," a gruff voice answered from behind Jeremy.

Jeremy turned around and saw him in the doorway to the living room. "Good morning, man."

"Morning, Dad."

"Her mother was a phenomenal woman. The best I could ever wish to know. Without Denise, I would've lost it. I needed to live and be the best dad I could—for her. A promise I had made to her mother before she passed. Maybe I didn't give her the best life, and I made her into a bit of a tomboy. But I tried to find things she liked and enjoyed, even if they were my own hobbies. I tried sharing those things with her as I could."

"They were perfect days, Dad. All of them," said Denise.

Jeremy saw her father's eyes get glossy. He blinked a few times trying to fight back the waves of emotion. Jeremy wondered if the dam holding back the flood was about to crumble and break through years of strain.

* * *

Jeremy woke up next to Denise. Her body small and warm next to his. He was elated, but knew it wouldn't last. Denise was perfect, but she had the baggage of her father and he didn't blame her for it. He needed to be free, not tied down by anyone or anything for the first time in his life.

Denise stirred, rolled and put her arm over Fox's stomach.

Her nails grazed his skin as she lightly scratched his body. Shivers went to his hair and down his legs. Fox rested his arm on hers and, for the second time in his life, wished that he would do the thing he needed to do. But that meant breaking the first right decision he had ever made. *How is it a paradox to break happiness to be happy?* Jeremy thought all the ways he could be wrong while Denise drifted in the space between reality and the fog of sleep.

Her room was barren, mostly a few tattered well-known books, a small brown desk, and a bed in the middle of the room. There was a wardrobe in the corner. It was small, too small to hold more than a few shirts, some socks, underwear, and a few pairs of pants. There were no mirrors in the room, and on a shelf laid two small skulls, one of a coyote, and the other of what looked like a raccoon, but Fox was too far away to really identify what it was.

"I know you're not going to stick around." Denise broke the silence and pulled closer to Jeremy, his focus shifting to her rather than his indecision. He felt the warmth radiating off of her.

"I figured you'd catch on quickly," he said unsure of what else to say.

"It's okay if you need to leave. I know your place is out there and not here with me and my dad. We'll be fine without power. We've been living as close to off the grid as possible. It's been a wonderful few months, but I know you're getting restless."

"I know you'll be okay without me here. I love you and you know that. I never believed in a soulmate until you dragged me out of the woods." He turned and looked her in the eyes, trying to get lost in the space of her dark pupils, trying to find a home in the void where her consciousness resided. The time he had now spent with her and Dean were truly home, and he still could not stay.

"Fox, if you leave, you can come back any day you want. We'll be here until the power comes back on."

"It's weird to me that it has been off for this long now and we've seen no real military or police presence."

"We're in the middle of nowhere. We have our neighbors and that's about it up here. Trust me, we have a generator for a reason. The power goes out often." She laughed.

"I guess you're right, but it just feels off. The world I mean. It feels like the entire world just turned off and now we're left to our own devices."

"Are you scared of that?"

He laughed knowing she was ribbing him. "Never. I've spent a long time out there and I'm sure I'll be just fine."

"I know you will be."

12

The trees felt oppressive as Crow and the group continued east, hoping to find some sort of life in this mess. They remained mostly quiet, except for a few whispers between Bernice and Jamal, Crow noticed. He almost felt like asking them what they were talking about, if only to create an interaction in the group, but decided to let them have their moment. He wished he was able to have his own moment. *Maria, I miss you.*

Janet interrupted his internal dialogue.

"What do you think is going to be over there?"

He sighed. "Nothing. People, maybe. But I wouldn't count on it. The cities are always quiet now. Good for shelter and that's about it."

They stepped over a log into a clearing. It looked like an old sit-down area for locals. Old park benches covered in snow littered the small area without trees. *How long until nature completely retakes this?*

Crow watched Fox take his sleeve and clear the planks of

wood so they could sit together. He left the snow on the table.

"Why not clear this too?"

"Dunno, just feels wrong. Like this isn't our place anymore and we shouldn't make it more comfortable than we need it to be."

Crow tried to understand the logic, but couldn't as he opened his mouth to reply, then closed it again. They all reached in their bag.

"Eyes up," Janet said, laughing.

I hate this way.

"Peaches. Again." Crow sighed.

"Green beans," Fox added.

"Tuna," Jamal and Bernice said in unison as they each pulled out a can.

"Crackers!" Janet laughed. "We're gonna make our own tuna casserole tonight."

Everyone smiled, Crow noticed. He almost felt guilty for not enjoying the game Janet made up. Sometimes it worked out in their favor, but he hated canned peaches. *Worst. Dessert. Ever.*

They all packed together like sardines under Crow's tarp after dinner. It was stretched out to its furthest capabilities with a fire on one side to keep them warm. The wind had grown strong, and the winter that never ended grew cold that night. They all shivered despite the closeness of the fire.

"Hey," Jamal said, "you think this is like a nuclear winter kinda thing?"

They were all awake, Crow knew, even though none of them tried to move.

"I dunno, man," Fox said. "It feels like it. It doesn't make sense for all this time to go by and it hasn't warmed up."

"I always thought it was an EMP, with the power going out," Crow interjected.

"I guess that makes sense too," Jamal said as he sat up, trying to scratch the middle of his back. "I just don't get why. I never saw nothing in the news about it while living in the city. Nothing in the papers about war. Everything was calm, and then Christmas came, and poof. No more joy." He gestured dramatically.

The wind rippled the tarp as they all remained quiet. Crow wanted to see if anyone else would say anything, but Bernice was her usual quiet self, while Janet lay there absorbing everything. *Surprised she's not talking right now.*

"What if it's both?" Fox asked.

"What do you mean?" Jamal replied.

"Man, if they blew up a nuke above us that would cause an EMP and nuclear winter, wouldn't it?"

"How the fuck am I supposed to know? And how do you know that?"

"Finance, man. I used to work in the city making loads of money for people. I remember someone once saying the entire stock market could crash if they took out the power grid. I don't know when or how that conversation came up. That memory is like an echo, man. I can hear it, almost distinctly, but I don't know who said it."

Crow lay back down, waiting to see how the conversation would go. He found everything to be speculative. They seemed to volley ideas back and forth from aliens, to government conspiracies. It was a ping pong ball bouncing back and forth, erratic at times, and calculated at others. He listened to Jamal and Fox laugh as he drifted off to sleep next to Janet, who he was sure still lay awake.

The tarp shook with the wind throughout the night, yet everyone had grown used to the sound and it no longer woke them up. Crow felt the hot sun on his eyelids before he saw it, then heard a cracking noise. He bolted up, shouldering his rifle from a sit position, ready to shoot anyone who made the wrong move.

"It's just me, man," Fox said.

"Why did you go around breaking fucking twigs while we were all sleeping?"

Fox laughed. "That wasn't twigs. It was my goddamn knees." He bent slightly and they cracked again, this time a little quieter. "The cold is really starting to mess with them."

Crow shook his head and lowered his rifle. He noticed everyone else was awake, eyes wide from his shouting. "We should probably get moving now since I've made noise too," he conceded.

The walk was arduous, all uphill through the snow which had become deeper the further they walked. At times it crested the middle of their shins, a clear uptake from the ankle-deep snow to the west. Everyone's breathing had become labored, and Crow felt like his heart might explode at any moment. They took more breaks than they wanted to, to try and get their breath again. It never seemed to come.

"Moving on an empty stomach isn't going to help us any," Jamal said.

"You're right. Let's get to the top of this hill, then we can take a bit to refuel," Crow said.

Janet nodded with Fox, but still never spoke.

The elevation gain on the final hill felt insane to Crow, who was leading the way to make the path for everyone else easier.

"You got any secrets for getting through this faster, Fox?"

"Yeah, man. Put your head down and keep going."

Okay, prick. He breathed deep and kept pushing.

The top of the hill felt more like a mountain. The view was worth it, and so was the food they were about to consume. Each way they turned, the ground rolled like waves. They stood at the highest peak. A notable achievement and advantage they all agreed on. To the east they could see the Hudson river.

Janet reached in her bag first, and pulled out a can of Spam. She didn't wait for anyone as she opened it and started to feast on the salted meat. They remained quiet, choosing to not make a fire. Crow sipped on water, then added snow to another plastic bottle he would keep close to his body to help it melt faster when they started to walk again.

"What's going on with you?" Crow asked Janet as he let Fox take the lead down the hill. In the distance he could see a bridge to the south. *Probably a day or two until we get there.*

"I just want to relax. Find a spot to just rest. I'm tired of all this back and forth."

"You know that's not going to happen, right?"

"You don't think I know that?" Her eyebrows furrowed.

"I'm just saying."

"I'm just saying you're being a real dickhead. You're hot or cold. That's it. And you always have this holier-than-thou attitude." The words hung in the air.

Crow sped up his pace and caught up with Fox. *Not going to start this argument.*

"You think she's right?" he asked as they continued down, closing in on flat ground.

"Man, this ain't my place, and I'm not picking sides when we're all we have."

Crow kept quiet, walking faster to put as much distance between himself and everyone else. His jacket hooked on a tree branch and tore open on the upper right sleeve. *Of course,* he thought. He heard Janet laugh in the background.

"Petty," he mumbled just loud enough.

"What'd you say up there?" she called to him.

"I said you're fucking petty."

"Feels terrible, doesn't it?"

Crow stopped and turned to Janet who was still walking toward him.

"You can say it to my face, if you'd like." She was within a few feet of him now. Her hair matted from sleeping on the cold ground.

"Remember why you're still alive."

"Like I owe you a thing." She stepped up to him.

"Man, can we cut it with the nonsense?" Fox said. He was standing by both of them now. His twig arms were both free. His rifle slung across his shoulder.

"I don't think this is your problem right now, friend," Crow said.

"It is my problem if we're going to still continue on together, man. You're both irritated and too head-strong to admit you're both wrong."

Here we go.

"Guys." Bernice's voice cut in. She pointed to the north. There was smoke from a fire, a lot of it. It crept upward over the hill they were just on. Winding like a snake into the sky.

"That's not good," Crow said. He saw Jamal and Bernice standing next to each other. "I'm going to get a look at that." He cut in front of them.

"That's not a good idea," Janet replied.

"Yes, it is," Fox interrupted. "We need to know how many people are over there. If they can come for us. One of us needs to go check it out, and if they don't come back tomorrow, we leave."

"I'm going." Crow pressed on without waiting for someone else to put their two-cents in.

The walk sucked a bit less as he followed his tracks and everyone else's back the way they had come. It was more like walking on sand now than pressing through deep snow. The hill was the least of his concerns.

Maria, Lucy, is this the moment I see you again? Crow wondered if he volunteered because he had a death wish or because he was genuinely curious about what was over that hill. The sun was starting to finish its cycle as Crow got to the top. He walked toward the other side and heard a branch break to his right. Spinning with his rifle, he aimed, waiting to see who he had sighted. Nothing appeared.

Creeping forward, he craned his neck, and tried to gather as much information as possible with bated breath. He could see trucks, and a large mass of people around multiple fires. On one of them lay a deer. There were women sitting outside of the tents.

"I told you not to make any noise," someone said below him. Crow kneeled down.

"I didn't see that thing in all this fucking snow."

"Whatever. Once we get up top, we can get a better view of everything."

Shit. He tried to slide backwards slowly. *Traders are gonna see me in a minute. All the tracks up here.* Crow slid behind a tree, stabilized his rifle and waited.

The top of a man's head peaked over the ridge and then another's.

"Someone's been here."

"Yeah, we'll have to call back down. Look pretty fresh too."

Crow fired and the mist sprayed from inside one of their heads. He fired again, missing wildly. Then shot off a third round, hitting the man in the arm before he could understand what was happening. Crow ran back the way he came.

Guys, run. He looked up to the horizon before going down the hill. The sun was close to setting. *That'll work in my favor, at least.*

He slung his rifle over his shoulder as he hurried down the

hill. He could see them all further on. They weren't moving. *Don't wait for me, idiots. Go.* He waved his arm in the air in a semi-circle to get their attention, then waved to tell them to go the other way.

The snow was loose as he followed the tracks, almost slipping on his way down. He leaned back as his legs gave out and continued to slide down. *Please, don't roll. Don't roll.* Crow threw one arm to his side as he tried to slow his descent, while the other instinctively grabbed the rifle and tried to keep it close to his body. When he came to a stop, he popped back up and continued running, not looking over his shoulder. There was shouting coming from up top. Crow knew they'd be in trouble soon.

"Stop waiting for me!" he yelled as he reached the bottom of the hill and saw them all further through the snow. "Go around the next hill!" The sun was setting faster.

Crow started trudging through the snow, the path they had made without him wasn't the best, but it was still helpful. There was a pop, and a piece of snow shot up into the air to his left. He flinched, then moved to his right. *There's no fucking cover here.* He cursed as he looked for a tree to hide behind.

"I got it, man," Fox yelled. Crow looked up and corrected his line of movement to meet up with them. Fox had shouldered his rifle, and fired off less than five rounds. *Unless that's more Traders firing back.*

"We need to go. Traders!" Crow was huffing now. A bullet whipped by his right ear and he could feel the air sizzle. He put his hand up out of instinct. He pulled it away thinking there would be blood, but his hand was clean.

He was panting by the time he reached the group. "Why didn't you leave like I said?"

"What would that have done? Besides gotten you killed?" Janet asked.

"It's for your safety and everyone else's!"

"You were running to meet up with us! How is that for our safety?"

"Can you both stop bickering, man? I count two up there." Fox was still shooting off a round every few seconds, but the noise had faded into the background.

I never saw the third, Crow thought to himself.

"Let's get going," he said, finally looking over his shoulder. The sun was almost completely gone, but the night was clear for once. The hill was foreboding, and on the other side lay certain death. They heard the rumble of a truck's engine. *How do they still have gasoline?*

They started to press through the snow as fast as they could, going around one of the rolling hills they had seen earlier, putting distance and objects between them and the Traders.

"We need to get to the trees, and away from the river," Crow said. They all agreed.

To the south was the bridge and shelter. The city seemed like their best bet now. *It's gotta be totally looted by now. And we'll have the buildings to our advantage. As long as no one's already there.*

They continued through the night, and when they finally felt they had no chance of running into the Traders, they sat down. No one unpacked their tents or tarps.

"Just in case we hear them," they all said to each other. Crow lay far from Janet, though they all huddled together for warmth.

Crow felt everyone roll back and forth, knowing none of them were asleep.

Janet stood up and walked over to him. She lay down beside him.

Crow wished she would have stayed on the other side of the pile, but said nothing. The wind stopped and they all lay awake, pretending to get a restful sleep. No one heard the truck's engine again.

13

Morning came and everyone struggled to rub the chill from their bones. A few rumbles could be felt below their feet, but they were distant. Crow rubbed his shoulders. *It's getting too cold out here for us. We need to find some sort of shelter.*

"Earthquakes?" Janet inquired to no one in particular.

"It happens here in New York, not often though," Crow said.

"Never felt one in my life," Jamal replied.

"It's usually tremors from quakes in further states, man."

The group trucked along east until they reached the Hudson. The river was ice on either side, run through by a murky blue-gray which reminded them all of mud. Two bridges still stood between the gap the river created. One had been for walking once and the other for driving. Now, they both stood against time, monuments to days not far behind, yet long gone.

"Should we head north from here? Or cross and see what's left in the city?" Janet asked them.

"Just some shit over there. Might be good for supplies, but

might run into some trouble on those streets. They're tight, not like New York City tight, but tight enough," Crow stated firmly. The skin on his face was tightening. They were all losing sleep and calories. Their bodies creaked and groaned from each day they didn't rest. *Maybe going over there is a mistake,* he thought quietly to himself.

"I could go for some supplies, man."

"Me too." Jamal replied. Crow had wondered why he had been unusually quiet most of the morning. Was it a dream, thoughts, or just wanting to escape from the life he was stuck in?

"Ladies?" Crow looked over waiting for them to give their input.

"I don't really want any trouble, but I think it's for the best if we go over there and try to find something," said Janet. She had her hands stuck in her jacket trying to keep the cold off of her cuticles. Crow noticed they were peeling and bleeding from the raw exposure to wind, cold, and the sun whenever it came out.

"Same," Bernice said.

"Then I guess we walk across." Crow shouldered his rifle and led the way.

Please, don't let this be a bad idea.

The wind blew fiercely, whipping their jackets and loose clothing. It cut through their jeans and made everyone's hair stand up beneath the multiple layers each one of them had donned that night and kept on when morning came. The bridge had deteriorated quickly. From the ridge, it looked normal. Holes showed through the snow-covered road and ran straight down into the frigid river. It was like a broken body begging for someone to reset its bones and stitch its skin back together. The columns had lost their paint and the color of rust had begun to show underneath. The golden days were just a layer of gray, a facade for all to see.

A car was parked closer to the other end of the bridge, black and worn, its tires flat from neglect. Inside sat a skeleton with a hole in the top of its head. Fox and Crow looked in through the broken windows. In the lap of the body lay a small pistol with the bones still touching the grip. The inside was covered with murky brown blood and black which could only have been decayed brain matter. Everyone left the gun alone, but knew they could have found a better use for it. Someone else had probably thought the same thing. They had also decided that if a man couldn't find peace in his life, he should be left alone in his death and not be disturbed. Almost a sense of reverence for the dead. An old law or rule which governed society for decades.

The road began to narrow as buildings piled up on either side, old and gaunt, windows broken and doors left open. Outside, the streets were littered with furniture and clothing. Torn couches, broken chairs, clothes, and bodies started to line the sidewalks. The city had looked decent once, but now it looked like the world around it, barren and immoral.

"Let's head into some of these buildings. Then we can go to the train station. Maybe get a little rest and break from the wind and cold." Crow broke the long silence which had been piling up to an insufferable weight as they walked by the suicide.

Crow walked the familiar streets, and passed by old bars and restaurants he had frequented with Maria six years ago. Inside broken glass, memories played before his eyes. Nights they had laughed at the wooden bar with mugs in hand surrounded by friends, celebrating their engagement. One door down he could see the backroom of the small taco joint, which wasn't particularly good, but had made the best queso dip he could remember.

In the back was a large table. The first time they had been there they sat there. A cake was brought out for Crow which said, HAPPY BIRTHDAY. Maria handed him a card in a pink envelope.

JAMES, I LOVE YOU TO THE END OF THE UNIVERSE AND THE NEXT. YOU MAKE ME FEEL LIKE MAYBE THERE IS SOME SORT OF GREATER BEING GOVERNING THIS WORLD. OTHERWISE, HOW WOULD I HAVE MET YOU? THE LOVE OF MY LIFE. I JUST WANT YOU TO KNOW, WE'RE EXPECTING. HAPPY BIRTHDAY. *Maria, Lucy. I miss you so much.*

A tear ran down Crow's face, as it had the night of his birthday. He turned away from the restaurant and rubbed his face into the crook of the arm which shouldered his rifle. He hoped no one noticed his motion as they followed him.

They reached the brick train station, which still stood formidably among the trash of the city. The red brick was dirty, and aged, but stood out among the browns and whites and tans of the surrounding houses and apartment buildings. Cars sat in the parking lot, destroyed and worn with age while skeletons littered the ground around them. They had died with law and order. Ghosts had littered every crevice of the world now.

Crow looked down as they walked past two bodies. One lay in the middle of the road, and one closer to the long entrance to the train station. He wondered what they had seen in the last moments before death. *What happened that they lay here of all places? What had they seen before they turned to decay and fed the birds? What horrors happened at the end of days?* It was never peaceful to die in the open, Crow knew that. *It was always terrific —in the archaic sense.* He repeated to himself as if having a conversation with someone else.

Crow followed by everyone marched over the two bodies and entered the parking garage where cars had busted out windows and some had been torched. All had been looted already. It was disappointing for them. Some cars held more skeletons, while others held clothes covered in age since the bulbs burned out. They found little, except a decent enough duffle bag which had a hole in the bottom of it along a seam. It could be easily fixed with some duct tape and a sturdy over-the-shoulder sling. Jamal cut two holes in it then tied some rope through the holes. It was easier to shoot a rifle with a backpack than a lopsided duffle bag. A pair of rubber rain-boots was found in the backseat of a rundown sedan. They were dark blue, almost gray, more like slate than anything else. They fit Bernice, though they were still a little too big. She desperately needed a new pair of shoes. Hers were held together with plenty of duct tape, so much so, they were better considered to be fabric with duct tape soles rather than actual shoes. They couldn't afford to waste any more precious silver for the sake of her feet which had been in question for a while now. The air around them was still, and they made their way up the stairs, over the small enclosed bridge, and into the greater hall of the train station.

A news stand stood in one corner inside the main hall. It was raided long ago of any leftover food and snacks it once held. The newspapers were left behind. Titles about corruption in politics and the old nuclear tensions with North Korea. The hall was massive, empty, and grotesque. A beautiful scene for a horror film.

"Man, it's funny how even without electricity or a government controlling this mess, no nuclear warfare has happened, at least, not near New York City. Any of you hear anything?" Fox asked as he put down a paper he had picked up.

"Nah. I'm from the city and nothing hit us. Never heard of any nukes going off when shit went down either," Jamal said.

They looked at each other and no one said a word about it, simply nodded in assent.

"All media scares. That's all it ever was," Crow added.

They scoured the area and found some window cleaner in a janitor's closet, along with one roll of toilet paper, some rubbing alcohol, a small plastic spray bottle which was empty. Though

Fox had thought it might come in handy which was why he carried it.

They piled in the men's bathroom because it had the least number of stalls. It allowed for them to spread out on the floor as they settled in for the night.

"Where are we going from here?" Jamal asked.

"I wanna get into the basement, see if there's anything going on. Then if we take the tracks north a bit, there's an old water treatment facility. Might have some chlorine which could be useful," Crow stated as he set up his pack as a pillow and laid out what sheets or tarps they had between them.

"What are we gonna do with chlorine?" Janet asked while digging through what food they had so it could be split between them. All they had was some tuna and mixed fruit.

"If we can get some lye from the hardware store beyond that, we can make bleach. And then from there we can make some mustard gas if we have to." *Traders are hunkered down in this weather.* Crow thought back to seeing all the men guarding apartment complexes shortly after the power went out. *Hopefully they're all fighting with themselves for food and too many mouths to feed.* He thought back to the army base the night he had first met Fox.

"So, you wanna go up to a water treatment plant to possibly make something? Not even for sure?" Jamal criticized.

"Yeah. Pretty much. They also might have, you know, clean water up there too."

"Man, fuck that shit. I'll sit my ass right here while you go and do whatever you want."

"Anyone else wanna stay back here with Jamal?" Almost all of them agreed, except Fox, who always wanted to wander. He didn't mind doing something risky or foolish, as long as he was outside and not sitting in one place for too long.

"All right, well let's get some rest, then we can take a look downstairs and you guys can hang here for a day while we get up there. If we don't come back in two, just keep moving," Crow was growing more agitated to find too few of them agreed with his plans.

"Where would we go from here?" Bernice finally spoke up.

"Well, if we're dead, or captured, or whatever. I'd probably head north anyway. Unless you want to go east, and eventually hit Connecticut. South on this track takes you passed the nuclear power plant, and eventually New York City. But that's a dead zone. It's been looted and ate through by now. I'd be surprised if anyone were still down there and living better off than any of us have been."

"You think we're doing good?"

"Not particularly. But we haven't starved to death or died of thirst. We stay relatively warm with all the clothes we have, and still have ammo for our guns. So, yeah, maybe we're doing pretty all right for ourselves right now. I'm not saying some days aren't tough, but down in the city, those souls are gone now," Crow stated.

Crow slept fitfully on the ceramic tile with the crusted over mirrors hanging above the dirty white sinks. He noticed he wasn't alone. The others seemed to be struggling as well, though he suspected some caught a little sleep during the night.

Morning came, and they all crankily packed their gear. They had to shoulder all their supplies once more, then made their way toward the stairs leading to the substructure of the train station. No one spoke. The air was hostile and quiet. Fox pulled out a flashlight after they opened a thick framed metal door.

The stairs were metal, and they could see nothing in the darkness. The backup generators had obviously burned out long ago. The emergency lights weren't even on, and everyone was unsure if they ever came on. The group shuffled through, and shut the door behind themselves. Pipes littered the walls, some broken, and some still clinging to the concrete. It smelled of old matter, long decayed. It was almost murky or musty. Somewhere in between the two like a dried-up swamp or a mildew basement with mothballs.

14

Jeremiah woke from terrible nostalgia and found that his feet still burned and his body ached like he hadn't slept except in spurts for periods of abject time. Time had consistently been against him, objectively moving forward when all he had wanted was for it to slow down or stop for him so he could catch his breath. But time kept running its marathon, striving to finish first at the end of all things, where it would not continue on, but stop and greet death. The two lovers always flirted with each other, but time was something death could never have when he wanted it. Their love story was dramatic, coming to an end together when nothing else remained. Soulmates throughout life, yet only meeting and having a single moment together, until they both winked out into nothing. Jeremiah wished time would turn around and come back for him before his life took a turn with Mason Davis. If he could convince time to go back, he would have passed that case onto someone else, even his best friend. Let someone else deal with that shit. He didn't care.

Jeremiah stood up and hobbled on his burnt, sore feet. He felt blisters pop. Liquid oozed to the ground—his flesh raw. Once he returned back to the Slums, he could find something for them, wrap them in rags. Anything at this point would be better than pink flesh smacking the ground.

"Damn, I'm really turning into one of them," he mumbled to himself while thinking about people who were born in the Slums. Those forced to live poorly, with little to no chance of escaping their poverty. Rags wrapped their bodies, trying to keep them warm, or trying to keep out infections. They were all stuck there, working and living and sleeping just so they could work, live, and sleep again. No joy. Only the next day's hard work while someone benefitted from their moroseness.

Jeremiah found a ladder, and the metal dug into the arches of his feet as he climbed. He pressed on, knowing there would be a light at the end of this tunnel. All he had to do was move the manhole cover.

He threw himself onto the street above. He wasn't far from safehouse 2, nor was he close. It was a gray area of being close or far depending on who you spoke to. Maybe it was a couple of blocks easily reached within the hour, maybe it was far, taking almost an hour to get to where he lay. Everyone would say different, but, either way, Jeremiah was within an hour's walk of his safe house, and he knew there was a black-market pharmacy nearby. He'd go there and get some Second-Skin and cloth to wrap his feet. First, he needed to get up and quit wallowing in his own self-pity. Jeremiah knew the Second-Skin wasn't as good as the Medi-Flesh, but it did the same thing and would protect his feet. *Cheap Slum knock-offs.*

The block was empty. Completely empty. No lights from any of the buildings, and hardly any of the street lights worked as it was. No luminous pinks and blues to give ghastly shadows to pedestrians. It was shades of gray on the road, buildings and Jeremiah. If anyone took a photo, he'd be a dark mass at the bottom. It might have looked like a crime scene where a photo had to be taken, and the lumps at the bottom of the picture were a body which had intentionally not been lit up. Whoever took that picture was trying to be decent to the corpse, but they still had a job to do. The background would be a light gray window and behind, pitch black, an empty storefront where anything could be going on. Rape, murder, the drowning of a political enemy as he was extorted for information, money, or a simple vote and signature on a new law. That's how Jeremiah felt about this kind of dark gray area.

He pushed himself off of the ground and slipped the manhole cover back into place with extreme strain from his aching muscles. He could feel the infection growing in his feet, his body getting warm and cold as he began to shiver and sweat. *Not far now.* Only a few blocks to the black market and any injections and highs he could find. Bring back the good old days when he was using chems for recreation on the job rather than trying to stay alive with their help.

Down an alley and around the back, between some plastic sheets and a small tin door, Jeremiah was able to find a man covered in dark—husky with his muscles ripping through his already torn shirt.

"I need chems. Infection. Quick-heal. Second-skin. Anti-inflammatory. Then I need something to make me airy. A few uppers and a few downers."

"'m gon need yih to opn tat jacket of yirs and turn owt yir pockets." The accent of the Slums squeezed through gaps of missing teeth.

"You know who I am."

"Yeah, I seen yih here 'fore. But tat don't mean I know who

yih-are. So do as yir told 'nd get some creds ready." His voice hung in the air on the last modulation of the word.

Jeremiah opened his jacket and turned his pockets out as he was told. Nothing suspicious. He had ditched it outside. He waved his Holocard from the Furnaces over a terminal and transferred all the credits he needed to.

"Tak 'im. Get owt. 'nd dun't tell no-'un where yih got tees."

Jeremiah nodded and dipped through the door he had come through as he shot a concoction of drugs to make himself feel better, followed by an upper so he could find some place to sleep and let everything do its job. He saved the downer. His eyes wide, finally energized, he pulled off his shirt and cut it into strips. He wrapped his feet, trying with all his might to make some kind of cloth shoe out of what he had left for clothing, only after putting the Second-Skin on. It wasn't pretty, but it would suffice until he could get more clothes or new shoes. Now was the time for exploring and finding a good spot to lay low, then pound some downers and sleep for a long time.

Through the darkness, Jeremiah plodded along, trying to find anywhere to duck into. In buildings and behind glass, there were old jackets torn, weathered and passed down the chain of wealth to the poor working class so they could be purchased again, deepening the wallets of those with tendrils throughout the GUC. They were mixtures of black and brown—full synthetic, made by people down in the Factories who were sweating and dying just to keep food and water in their mouths. They burned through thousands of calories, so weak they would fall asleep while working, only to be woken up by their superiors. Sent "home" for the first time in months, they slept on the steps outside until day came again for another gruesome shift. Jeremiah felt bad that this is how people lived continuously, and everyone knew it, but they were out of sight, and therefore they were people who shouldn't be worried about. He had issues of his own. He continued his fervent walking and passed by the closed store-fronts full of clothes.

Vendors began to pop up as he closed in on the Deep, and the world seemed to populate itself. It was like a long loading bar on his holoscreen. The world decided that it would render in people to interact with or avoid. Their movements seemed robotic, and routine. Jeremiah drifted into the shadows, in case people were still looking for him here. Hopefully the explosion had distracted everyone enough, even gone on to think that he had died in that blast. Someone was after him, again, and there was nowhere to hide, he knew. First the explosion in the Precinct, then the brothel. Someone was tracking him, but how? *Maybe through the holobadge? That must be it. They must have updated the code over the air to install a tracker.* He mulled it over, and that made the most sense. No one went after him until he had picked up his badge. Whoever it was, they had waited, and watched his badge stay in the same spot, and once he was dumb enough to get it, they moved in.

"Fuck, how could I be so stupid?" he mumbled to himself and felt eyes move on him as if everyone in the simulation had heard him. Jeremiah found himself amongst the bustle and chaos. Men and woman walking by all turned their heads to him. Their eyes pierced through, like he was an enemy of them all.

Jeremiah needed his badge to access most of the world in ways he felt he needed to. Ditching it was not the best option but, it was the only option. He quickly disappeared to the shadows and made his way to a local café named Cyber Syrup. They were well known for their thick version of coffee, dosed in liquid sugars which made them unpalatable. Jeremiah walked up to the front and bought a small memory stick with fifty Petabytes of storage, way more than was needed to download the AI, data, and framework from his badge.

The computer he plugged his badge into and memory stick was old, the holokeys were starting to dim and become unresponsive, the nice vibrant blue almost gray now. The thing needed a nice reboot and to have its software and hardware updated. If it was literally exchanged for anything, even tech from the following year, it would have helped Jeremiah as he started to fume at how long it was taking him to do what he needed to do. The copy transfer was taking a dreadfully slow time, it was estimated to take about three minutes, when it should have taken less than a tenth of that time—at least that's how fast transfers worked at the Precinct when Jeremiah was still there. The transfer completed, and Jeremiah ripped the badge and memory stick from the computer, rushed out the door from which he came, and slipped into the throng of people passing by.

Down the road, near an old out-of-business building with police lines out front, he tucked himself into an alley and magnetized his badge under a large dumpster. It had been collecting water from the condensers and probably housed some poor resident from the Slums who had walked too far out of their district. He made a mental note of where he placed his badge. For now, the black boxed software of his AI and all of the permissions he had would suffice until he could get somewhere to scroll through the code he knew so well from years at the Academy, and delete the intrusion which was making his life a living hell—again. The neons looked muddy down here in the Deep on the border of the Slums, almost like a thick coat of dust was laying on top of them, turning everything from a world of color to a black and gray photograph with an odd tint to it. People, buildings, vehicles, they all seemed to be a mix between a lack of color and sepia tones. AI holograms played outside of buildings, walking back and forth, trying to coax those in the Deep—either by standard of life, or on vacation from work looking for their next score, whether it be drugs, crime, or sex—into their storefront.

It always fascinated Jeremiah how they worked. The Holo AI all ran off of the same deep mind of a neural net specific to the geographic area in which they were located. Business owners applied for a Holo, the more common name for a Holo AI, and poof, there it was, as if there was no need for any technological installations. They appeared and began their work. It seemed they had been there the entire time. In fact, they assimilated so well, it was like everyone alive never remembered a moment when they weren't around. *I hate them. Holos. AI. All of it. They're hollow.* Jeremiah laughed to himself. *Ridiculous to name them after themselves.*

"Come on in. We have clothes of all assortments, cheap to classy. Financing available."

"Hey. You need something foreign, something young, something old? We got you, just step inside," one of them dribbled from its static mouth. Its body a mesh of frames which lit up the darkness of the area. Jeremiah could see and walk through it.

"Uppers, Downers, Spirals, Twisties, Crystal-Mind, Transience, we got it, and you look like you need it." The messages played over and over on a loop for everyone to hear. Jeremiah was so used to it by now that the voices had become background noise.

"Massage inside. Can include a happy ending for the soul. We specialize in all sexes. And if you're a little less daring, we have your standard body rub. For the more experienced, we have other more daring options available." The Holo waved its hands to show all of the pills and injections behind it that it was offering.

The Precinct always loved coming down here as a group trip when partners had time off together. They blew off steam, and as long as no one ended up dead, the higher ups didn't give a shit what went on. The Precinct's only job was to stop murderers it seemed. Everything else in the world was fair game. Theft? Go for it. Get caught or found out by who you stole from? Hopefully it was just a beating. But someone always wound up dead. Jeremiah remembered those nights well. Theft was so common that it was too much to waste resources on. Theft was legal at this point, just as everything else was—legal where people didn't have the creds to do anything about it. He looked for the walls of the UC and knew beyond it laid the formidable Capitol at its center.

Jeremiah walked until he felt hours had passed and the Deep became more vibrant as he pushed closer to the UC—maybe it had been minutes—but all the time mulling over ideas and thoughts about how he had gotten here made him feel like it was enough time and distance between him, the police, and the last cybercafé. He went into another one and went to go pay for a private room in the back.

Shit. All my extra creds were on that badge. Jeremiah sighed, walked out of the café and moved down the road and across the street to a small dark alley. There were no neons near him. He sat and waited, watching everyone and everything going on as he took in his surroundings and planned his next move. He couldn't afford another visit to a cybercafé with his creds from the Furnaces.

In the ceiling, code mixed with the condensers, and chemicals were pumped through holes so tiny, they couldn't be seen with the naked eye. The reaction caused the new molecules to form and speed towards the ground. Jeremiah noticed it had begun to rain. He let the water run over his body and knew his next move.

Down the road came a burly man, not nearly as big as Mason Davis, but large—larger than Jeremiah. He was young enough, probably around five years younger, and still had a pep in his walk. By the look of him, Jeremiah guess he worked in the Mines or in the Furnaces. He was covered in a black film, and definitely ate better than most, which meant he either worked longer or stole from the people around him.

Jeremiah crossed the road and tailed him. The man moved fairly quickly, taking turns down side alleys and roads Jeremiah did not know to exist.

He stopped in a doorway to some run-down building, and passed through. Jeremiah closed the gap and entered the door behind him before it closed. The walls down the long hallway were covered in artwork, old, definitely from some place Jeremiah had never seen. There were statues, foreboding, muscular, and fantastic. One was encased in thick tamper evident glass. It was a hand reminiscent of a bird. *Interesting.* Jeremiah thought. *How does this man have artwork?* There was a small holotag he assumed once had the name of the piece or the artist. It was blank now. *Never seen anything like this. Even in the UC.*

Jeremiah walked forward, mesmerized by what he was seeing. Photographs, and sculptures made of reflective yellow. Faces of men who wore the heads of birds or monsters. Heads attached to horns. Beasts that must have walked Above before, way before life began down here. *The man.* Jeremiah forgot to follow the man. He scampered away from all the artwork and followed the twisting hallway as quietly as possible.

"It's beautiful isn't it?" A voice called from behind Jeremiah. He turned around. The man he was tailing was in the hallway looking at the same sculptures.

"Yeah, it's pretty amazing." Jeremiah's voice cracked as he got worried. *This might have been the wrong guy to rob for some creds.*

"I know you were following me. I assume you're hungry by

the look of you. I can feed you and send you on your way." His voice was deep and booming through the tight corridor.

"I'm not really hungry. I just need some creds to pay back a debt."

"And you figured you'd steal them from me." It was more of a statement rather than a question. The man laughed. "It wouldn't have worked, my friend."

"I'm just gonna go." Jeremiah tried to look over the man's shoulder at the doorway.

"That's not going to happen. You can either stay for some food or deal with us and leave empty handed—if you leave at all." Jeremiah turned around and noticed another man and a woman had entered the hallway behind him.

"I think I'll stay for dinner." *Fuck.*

15

In front of Jeremiah was the corpse of a bird, plucked of all its feathers, its feet cut off and tied behind it. It reminded him of one of the weirder sex shows he had watched in the Deep when he was undercover. It was on a bed of something green he had never seen before. The three people he had just met sat around the small circular table gazing with Jeremiah at the scene in front of them.

"Aren't birds in the GUC endangered?" Jeremiah asked.

"Yeah, they say that. They also say we're supposed to report any so they can be brought back to one of the Sanctuaries in the UC," said the man he had been tailing.

"They say a lot of things that aren't true, like everything in front of you is impossible," the woman said as she scooped up a mound of white from a bowl and placed it on her plate.

"What is all of this anyway?"

The man Jeremiah had followed answered for everyone. "Over here we have mashed potatoes with garlic, then here we have chicken sitting on some spinach. There's rosemary on top, and lastly," he got up from the table, "we have some red wine." He picked up a bottle from a corner table and returned, filling Jeremiah's glass first, then the woman's, the other man, then his own.

"I haven't even heard of most of this stuff."

"You wouldn't have. Most of it is from Above. The wine we stole." He chuckled.

"So, you got it when they first came down here? Then used a replicator for it?" Things weren't adding up for Jeremiah.

"Almost." The woman laughed.

"We can discuss this later. Let's eat and introduce ourselves."

"I'm Jeremiah." He started off first as the other three looked on and let silence fill the room.

"I'm Acacia," the woman said. Jeremiah got his first good look at her. She was fair, blue eyed, and slender. Only slightly shorter than the men around her.

"I'm Gabriel," the man he had been tailing interjected.

"Babyle," the last one said. His eyes a bright hazel which stood against his dark complexion. His head perfectly smooth.

"He doesn't talk much," Gabriel said. "So, what's your story, Jeremiah? What debt do you have to pay?" He started serving himself and passed the plate around to let everyone cut their own piece from the chicken.

"Just some gambling debt." Jeremiah was handed the plate by Acacia, who had already cut some pieces off and left them on the plate. Jeremiah was not wrong in assuming they were for him.

Gabriel chuckled like he knew Jeremiah was hiding something. "Okay, Jeremiah who has gambling debt. What's your real story? I'm not a fan of lying guests at the dinner table." He placed his silverware down, interlaced his fingers, and rested his chin on his knuckles. His eyes locked in on him, and suddenly, the joke was over. Electricity filled the air and Gabriel simply smiled.

Jeremiah sat there looking between his food and his hosts, trying to figure out what had been poisoned.

"No poison," Acacia said, cutting into Jeremiah's chicken, scooping some potatoes onto it, and sipping from his glass. "You can relax here. But I wouldn't push your luck any further than you already have..." Her words hung in the air and Jeremiah raced through the castle inside his head.

He took a breath and did the same actions Acacia had done as he tried to stall for time. He was blown away by the flavors which danced in his mouth, coating it from the tip of his tongue to the back of his throat. "What's that burning taste I'm getting at the back of my throat into my nose?"

"Garlic," Babyle said.

"It's fresh, which creates a different taste and feel. The wine will get you drunk like normal alcohol."

Jeremiah knew about getting drunk, but never with wine. Usually he would just inhale a packet or drink some clear liquid which burned all the way into his intestines, then flooded his brain immediately with a dizzying fog. The wine was nice, tender, a deep maroon, and contained flavors which he never knew existed.

Everyone sat and waited as Jeremiah shoveled the food down his throat, missing his tongue, and at times forgetting to chew. He had forgotten the question, relishing in his new found delights, things which made him forget he was in the Deep of the GUC, a place of no sun, artificial rain, and loaded with technology most of the population could not use. Jeremiah realized they were all staring at him.

"Sorry," he said, trying to regain his composure. He wiped his mouth with a cloth napkin from the table.

"Don't be. It's all new to you," Gabriel said. They all smiled at

Jeremiah, making him feel welcome for the first time since all the shit in his life exploded. Twice.

"I, uh, was a detective." He started out with simple facts, going on to mention Mason, his time in the Furnaces, and his safehouse. He left out where he had hidden his badge, but told them he was being tracked by it. "And I think if I black box it I can get into the code, find the bug, possibly reverse engineer it, and find out who's been behind everything and what they've been hiding in the Precincts."

Babyle grunted, while Acacia stared intently at Jeremiah, dissecting everything he had just said to them.

"I think it's about time we finish up dinner," Gabriel said. "I'll personally make dessert when we're done, but I think we have to show our friend something. What do you guys think?"

Babyle mulled over the idea long and hard, as if he was lost in time, combing through towers of thought and language to find the reply he deemed right. He nodded in assent rather than waste the energy on speaking.

"I believe everything he's saying, but I think Jeremiah here is playing something close to his chest for fear of being found out." Acacia allowed her thoughts to enter the mix, talking like he wasn't even there.

"Understood. Jeremiah if you'd come with us. We have some conversations and work to be done." Gabriel stood up and motioned for Jeremiah to follow as they all went towards the kitchen. Gabriel pressed a small tile on the brown wall covered in gray-green grime, like decades of dust had created a barrier against the real color. Silently the floor began to open up. *How are they doing this?* Jeremiah wondered. *There's no sound. It's impossible.* Down a staircase they went, and the floor closed above them. It was lit with the same blue neons as outside in the Deep, casting ghastly deformed shapes against the walls as they walked, though their neons were bright in comparison.

The walk was short, but time slowed for Jeremiah because of his nervousness. His eyes like pinpoints trying to take in his surroundings. A strong steel door stood in front of them. It had no handle, and did not slide open when they approached. Gabriel, Babyle, and Acacia all put their right hand against it. A biometric scanner beeped and buzzed against their hands, then took a scan of their full bodies.

"Welcome friends." A robotic voice cut through the concrete. Its voice reverberated through Jeremiah's spine. Through the door there were huge screens plastered on the walls. All of them were dark. They surrounded the room, which was lit up overhead by a pale white-yellow glow. The middle was a long desk lined with chairs which bounced up and down, suspended in mid-air by technology Jeremiah never took the time to understand. *Nothing spectacular here. Looks like the same chairs we had at the Precinct.* Jeremiah's mind flashed to small memories.

"What is this place?"

"Jeremiah, have you ever wondered what the Aboveground looked like?"

"I mean, yeah, but, from all the stories, I assumed it's just like down here, except rubble."

"Have you ever wondered what the sun looked like? The moon?" Gabriel kept the questions flowing as he crossed the large room and placed himself in one of the chairs below the screens. His body caused the chair to sink, but it rebounded and pushed back into the air never touching the floor.

"It's a big floating ball of fire. Science told us that in the Junior School System," said Jeremiah. *What else is there to say?*

"Yes, that's right. But they never showed us pictures. No one in the GUC knows what the sun or moon looks like."

Jeremiah dwelt on it but came to no big conclusion. It was a ball of floating fire, probably whipping against the sky. What else could you picture? Fire in the sky. It makes no sense. Yet, Jeremiah believed what he was taught without ever questioning it.

Gabriel pressed some buttons. The screens lit up and came to life once more.

"This is the Above. Right now."

Jeremiah could see buildings, massive, and terrifying looming over the streets below them. It was bright outside. The ground was white. Gabriel tapped holokeys which made the screens change.

"How are you flipping between cameras? Where are these anyway?"

"They're Above."

"How do I know you're not lying to me right now? This could be any 3D rendition in a computer system."

"Jeremiah, I'm sure it's hard to believe a group of strangers is showing you the world Above, but this is, in fact, what it looks like. And, occasionally you'll see a few people wandering aimlessly. They look over their shoulders often."

"How do you *know* this is the Aboveground?" His question accusatory. Gabriel spun in his chair locking eyes with Jeremiah.

"We've been there," Babyle said sternly.

Jeremiah sat there staring at them while trying to take in what they were actually saying and the repercussions of it.

"I'll let you process this for a moment," Gabriel interjected, giving Babyle a quick glance as if he was not supposed to tell Jeremiah the truth yet, but quickly let it pass and began flipping through the cameras again. Like he was attempting to find one he liked and would settle on for the moment.

"How did you get there? What's up there? Why is there life?"

"Now that's a question I'm not willing to answer yet, Jeremiah," Gabriel retorted, not angrily, but with an odd kindness.

"Why's that?"

"Well," Acacia interjected, "you're being followed by someone high up, and you're trying to black box an AI we have no knowledge of. That's dangerous. You're dangerous. Our operation is dangerous. And we've spent a lot of time limiting danger. None of us here want to get caught just yet."

Jeremiah looked around the room and saw no one had anything to offer to that explanation, not even Babyle.

"Then why are you showing me all of this?"

"Because," Babyle started but closed his mouth, as if unsure how much to reveal.

"You've been on the inside and see how things work," Gabriel finished. "You're dangerous and an asset. For us and them."

He was clear and to the point. Jeremiah now understood they were trying to do something drastic. Yet, they wouldn't divulge their secrets. He understood, and he was miffed about it. A pawn in someone else's game. Reflecting on it, he was going to use Gabriel to be a pawn in his own. They weren't so different, he guessed, but he still hated to feel this way.

"Give me your black boxed badge," Gabriel stated, holding out his hand. It was more of a demand than a request. There was no option, Jeremiah realized. He either handed it over, or he was not leaving the room.

He reached in his pocket, pulled the drive from its hiding place, and handed it over to Gabriel. Relief washed over Jeremiah, like a terrible secret he had been keeping from family that had been brought to the light, and there was no judgment in it. Jeremiah had given someone else the burden, and they were going to take care of it for him. Hopefully.

Gabriel walked to a different chair, reached underneath, and began re-arranging wires. "Poin, I need you to do a few things for me." His voice echoed from under the table.

"Yes, sir," the metallic voice called out again, sending a shiver through Jeremiah. *Great. It's back.*

"I need you to disconnect this server from the rest. Make sure there is no outbound traffic to the rest of our servers. Then, can you please scramble the addresses? Move them to different areas around the GUC every fifteen to thirty seconds, changing the timing as you see fit."

"Of course. And, sir, may I also recommend that I turn off general connections every third and fifth minute. It shouldn't affect you while you work except for a minor stutter. There may be a frame freeze, but it would help our cause."

"Thank you, Poin." Gabriel crawled out from under the table, and pulled a chair underneath him as he plugged the drive in. All of the code displayed itself on a green holoscreen in front of him.

"Best leave him to work," Babyle said as he crossed the room, and brushed for Jeremiah to leave with him and Acacia.

"Do you think he'll need any of my help? I've seen all of that code before, years ago at the Academy. I could probably help."

"I doubt he needs your help, Jeremiah," Acacia replied. "He set all of this up himself."

She was underhandedly telling Jeremiah that he was nowhere near as smart as Gabriel, and he felt it. He had reeled Jeremiah in without any trouble. *Bitch.*

They made their way to a different room and waited for what felt like hours as Gabriel worked.

"Any luck?" Jeremiah asked when Gabriel had joined them again.

"Yeah, I found it and pulled it. Tried to reverse engineer to give itself away, but it's too advanced for me and Poin together. Someone's blocking it."

"Not good," Babyle interjected.

"Not good at all, my friend."

"So, what's that mean?"

"It means, you pissed off someone with a lot of power." Acacia smiled as she looked to Gabriel and back to Jeremiah.

Jeremiah felt a cold sweat come over him. Who was at the head of all of this, and what is it they wanted and were hiding? Who were the people he stood in front of? What was their goal? His head was swimming through dirt and rock with no end in sight. *Maybe I should have stayed in the Furnaces and worked diligently. Never grabbed my badge, never used my old creds. Stayed with my new identity and lived it out as peacefully as I could.*

"You have a lot going through your head right now," Acacia stated, snapping him back to reality. "Don't worry, it will all come out in due time. Most of it anyway."

"I think I need to lie down."

"You know, sleep sounds wonderful now," Gabriel retorted. "We can talk more in the morning. I can show you to a room, and you can make yourself comfortable. We can even get some new clothes for you, if you'd like."

They proceeded back to the hallway Jeremiah had come in through. Gabriel led the way, and pressed a hidden panel on the wall, opening a door which turned and twisted up. They went down a length of hallway, then spiraled back downwards. Jeremiah felt like he had been in a maze, with more twists and turns than the Slums and the Deep itself. Artwork hung the entirety of the way interspersed with statues and sculptures encased behind thick glass or barriers of electricity and static.

One statue caught his eye, massive and white which stood on a landing of the staircase they were taking. Parts of it had broken off, but it was a man gripping a woman. His hand pressed against her thigh. It almost looked like actual skin. He had stopped to inspect all the minute details of it.

"It's made of marble. Many, many years ago. Tough material to work with, and it was all done by hand. True artistic value." Gabriel came up behind him and spoke into Jeremiah's ear.

"How did you guys get your hands on all of this stuff?"

Gabriel smiled and walked away taking more steps down, allowing Jeremiah to either follow, or marvel at the works he was surrounded by.

Jeremiah caught up with them at the final landing, standing in front of a massive door. It was a dark metallic which radiated a coolness. It opened in front of them after a quick scan of Gabriel. Inside the lights were white, the walls light brown with a chocolate trim which ran along the base, and around each doorway down the straight hallway. They entered and Jeremiah couldn't hold the question in his mind any longer. It permeated everything about his life, firing on all synapses until nothing else remained.

"What's with all of the art and statues?"

Everyone turned around not expecting that to be the question he asked them after having been presented with a cozy place to sleep for the first time in ages.

"Art is necessary for life," Babyle answered for them.

"To expand on that idea, without art we are really nothing in the universe except a species which works, fights, and dies. We would simply be animals with a deeper understanding of life, yet, we don't do anything with this understanding. Art and creativity are the answer to that emptiness and fulfillment for human life," Acacia said.

"They're both right. People who can't appreciate art are people complacent and ready to die as they work every day for the rest of their lives," Gabriel said.

"I think that last part may be a bit unfair to the populace here. Most can't move up and out of working every day. How do we know none of them are the creative types if they have to work to eat and survive?" Jeremiah asked.

"Jeremiah, that's valid to my ignorant statement. But, any one of those people could have built what I built here. All they needed was to think on it, grab an AI to help, then act. Learning is inherent with all people. Some people take longer to learn things, but it is my firm belief that anyone can learn anything if they are dedicated enough—sometimes it takes longer to understand. With an AI, learning would actually be obsolete for them, and they could have the AI develop this entire place. It's just a matter of imagination and work. That's why I believe that they have become complacent, or brainwashed to believe that life is merely working for someone else so they may exist another day. Not only that, but my statement applies to those who lived Above before their tragedy," Gabriel replied.

Jeremiah tried to pick apart the thought process there but found it reasonably sound.

Why are people just not wanting to learn, or use the technology around them to do something with their lives rather than working to keep all of this up and running? I'm guilty too. Did they have our technology Above? They must have. How would we have it now if they didn't have it then? Before the migration.

They walked inside passing through the thick metal door—the veil to a new world waiting beyond. They passed rooms riddled with furniture. Beds, couches, and chairs which looked comfier than anything Jeremiah could afford even when he was on the job.

"This one will be your room." Gabriel opened another door. Inside was a bed Jeremiah could fit on at least three times over. Another door led to a toilet and a shower basin. Acacia turned the water on and it came out hotter than anything he had felt before as he let it run over the back of his hand, burning it. She showed him how to adjust the temperature, and left him to enjoy the moment. On a small shelf one of the bottles said AFRICAN BAR SOAP. Jeremiah opened it and wafted the scent towards his face. It was better than the new smells he had discovered at dinner. He undressed.

He lay in the massive basin, letting the water soak into his skin and muscles, feeling all the years of stress finally start to break down. For the first time, Jeremiah relaxed, not from any form of medication or drug, but from a body euphoria. First his mouth unclenched, his shoulders sunk at least two inches, then his ass felt like it wasn't gripped shut.

There was a knock on the door. "You all right in there?" Acacia questioned. "You've been in there over an hour and it's been pretty quiet."

"Yeah, I'm okay. I think I just drifted somewhere else for the first time in my life." Jeremiah and Acacia both laughed.

"All right, well, when you're done, just come on out. There are some clothes on the bed for you. Take a left out of your room, and meet us in the living room."

Jeremiah swashed around, the water rippling and beating against the walls like a furious storm trying to overcome the levies and erode the sand. He depressed a button and let the water drain. He missed it as it spun away, wanting to stay in there forever allowing his brain to disappear into the nothingness vacuum it had gone to.

He walked back into his bedroom, the water to dripping off of his body with each stride. He pulled a pair of black underwear on, a white short-sleeve shirt, and then a thick pair of pants. The pants were soft, not nearly as abrasive as anything he had purchased from the stores. Lastly, he picked up a pair of multicolored socks, thick, and softer than the pants. He pulled them on, and it felt like putting on a small animals' soft fur. Jeremiah loved them. He felt warm.

"What're these pants and socks?"

"Those are what they used to call sweatpants and those socks are wool."

"From Above?"

"No, actually. We went to the Capitol and stole them from some bureaucrats," Gabriel said laughing.

"This is from down here?" Jeremiah exclaimed.

"Yes, they only save the best for themselves."

"I thought I lived good while I was on the job. Guess not."

"Well," Babyle said.

"What?"

"You lived 'well', not 'good.'"

"I'm so confused."

"Don't mind him," Acacia said. "He either has knowledge to share that you understand, or knowledge way beyond your current scope."

They all sat down, and Gabriel flicked through some discs stowed away.

"Do you want to watch anything specific?"

"You have television here? That's expensive."

"Well, we steal it. I own some old shows from Above," Gabriel smiled, "but I figured you would have connected that dot by now."

"Put on whatever your favorite is from Above," Jeremiah replied.

Gabriel popped in one disc, and the show began. It was a drama, following a genuine man turning to a life of crime based on his circumstances. Jeremiah was enthralled by it. The show was entirely different than anything played for the public in the

Deep. Most of the shows he had seen were simple reminders to be a good worker. Maybe the occasional pornography or news bulletin. Most entertainment was a paid subscription, and he could never afford that. Jeremiah had never met anyone who could, even his Captain. This was an entirely new world to him, and the more he got to know these three, the more he figured he'd be learning a lot more about the world at large.

Time flew by, and before Jeremiah knew it, everyone was ready to retire to their bedrooms. He wanted to watch more of the show to see what life and entertainment was.

"I understand that this is fictional, but, is that what life Above was like? I mean, was it possible to do everything he did, and is that what the landscape was like?"

"I'm sure it was possible, but highly dramatized," Acacia said.

"It most definitely looked like that at one point, and I'm sure that part of the Above looks similar to when these discs were recorded." Gabriel threw his knowledge into the mix while Babyle watched and let his silence be background noise. "I think more of your questions will be answered in time, Jeremiah. For now, though, I'm going to go to my room and get some sleep. You're more than welcome to stay here and do what you want, but I let Poin know you are not allowed off premises. I think sleep would be the best for you, as well."

Jeremiah was energized, but went to his room anyway. He hopped onto the bed which was elevated off of the floor and felt as if nothing was holding him up. The softness and comfort imparted onto his body was like sitting in the hot water, again. The blankets weighed down onto his chest, and he felt relaxed rather than anxious. Exhaustion quickly swept over him and he found sleep. Though he did not willingly take its hand, he dreamed.

The land was arid, hot, and dry. Browns and reds sprouted up from the ground, creating plateaus, shelves, and alcoves for shadows and light to dip into and tuck themselves away if they wished. Jeremiah surveyed his surroundings and began walking along ground unfamiliar to him. It was no longer hard against his feet, but soft so they could create impressions upon it. Whatever it was made of, little pieces of it found their way into the cracks of his skin. He dwelled on the complexity of this new texture vastly different than slabs of concrete or metal.

He walked forever onward into the land until he found what remained of a statue, the legs and a small plaque. He found it curious that nothing else remained. Time and decay had washed away what the people before him created. He passed by, continuing to where his feet wanted him to go, and as he walked the ground beneath him became harder to trek through until it began to swallow him. His legs sunk, and he struggled until he was pulled below. The ground gripping him tighter and tighter pressing against his chest until it became impossible to breathe. Darkness surrounded him.

Jeremiah woke and found himself tangled in the sheets, sweating through the clothes he was given. It pooled onto the bed. He stood, took the clothes off, threw them to the floor, and went to the bathroom to sit in the hot water again. As the water filled, Jeremiah didn't wait. He entered the basin and sat while it slowly overtook his body. His muscles relaxed.

He took in all that surrounded him now that he had the time to allow it and focused on something other than his dreams. The bathroom was beautiful. The walls were dark gray, almost black at times, but the light shimmered off of it allowing accents to show through. The sink was pure white—like the statue he had seen on the staircase—with glistening yellow handles to change the temperature of the water. The spout was the same color.

Jeremiah got out, dried himself off, and went back to lie down in the bed.

"Detective Jeremiah, may I get you anything," the metallic voice whispered to him from the doorway leading back to the hallway.

Jeremiah was taken aback. "Uh, sorry I wasn't expecting you to be everywhere, but I guess it makes sense." He paused. "I don't think I'd like anything at the moment, thank you, though."

"I can get you some music or a holopad to read. Maybe, if you feel like drawing, or sculpting, I can acquire something for you, though that may take a bit of time. It will be delivered to the street above, and then you may do with it as you wish."

Jeremiah mulled over everything, realizing the world was literally at the end of his request down here. "Do you have any material on the people who made those statues I've been looking at?"

"There are some old records I've tapped into, but they are broken. There remains much that is missing. The one of the man gripping the woman was sculpted by Gian Lorenzo Bernini. Born December 7, 1598. No record of where he was born or when he died. I've uploaded the rest to the holopad on the left side of your bed. Feel free to scroll and read, though I'm afraid I've already told you the important information. Please, Detective, let me know if you need anything else," the artificial voice cut out.

Jeremiah spent the day scouring readings of artists and sculptors. He relished in the knowledge of all the lives he never knew existed and how interesting or mundane these people were. Once or twice, he could recall Acacia knocking to enter his room, only to find him wide-eyed and deep in thought as he tried to imagine all of the places these people had come from. He did not eat and found his legs weak when he stood to walk to his bathroom again.

"Detective, are you okay?" The artificial voice returned as it had watched him throughout the day.

"I'm okay, I just need to stretch my muscles a bit."

"I've made the others aware, so expect they may check on you shortly if they don't hear from you."

"I don't think that was necessary."

"Probably not, but we take precautions here for our own. You're new to all of this information and this life. It's a lot and we do not need you to have a sensory overload or a knowledge dump. Burning out is very real, and right now, Jeremiah, none of us need that."

"I don't quite understand what you mean," Jeremiah said as he stood in the bathroom getting ready to enjoy the warmth of the water again.

"There are things you'll be needed for, but they aren't for me to disclose to you. We hope you enjoy everything, and please, if you do need anything, let me know." The artificial tone cut out again as Jeremiah was about to speak, but knew unless he needed something, he would only be treated by silence. *Stupid AI. Just leave me be.*

He made his way into the water again, thinking of all of the places that once were. Quickly forgetting his own life and what it was like to live in the Deep. The shadow of the Capitol building with the walls of the UC looming. *I want to see Above. I hate the GUC. This place is a cancer.* Words on his holopad had told him people needed to make fire to live, ships to send supplies to each other. All of this was at one time a common truth. Now he remembered that shoveling was necessary to live down here, and sleeping in makeshift huts to stave off the rain was commonplace. He didn't feel his life was much too different down below than those who had lived up Above. *Maybe all of this, it's just another repetition of human history.* Jeremiah wandered in his thoughts of the living and the dead, allowing his surroundings to fade into sepias of old lives. He tried to imagine what a ship looked like on an ocean during the 1700s, but couldn't for the life of him come to any frame of reference. *If only they had a picture on the holopad.* He dried himself off.

Jeremiah walked out to the hallway which was eerily empty. He looked around, pushing open doors he didn't feel he had the right to, and found no one behind them.

"AI, I'm hungry." His old syntax reflected on his emotions. He forgot that Poin had a name, personality, and was more than a tool to those who lived in this small complex.

"Detective Jeremiah, they've already made you food. Go into the eating area, and open the door to the oven under the countertops. Inside you will find food." *I hate not knowing where they exist,* he thought to himself as he heard Poin's voice all around him.

"What's this 'oven'?" he asked as he pulled out his food which was still warm.

"It's called a stovetop oven. The Capitol might have a few, but they're not found with any of us lowlives here in the Deep. These were common in every household Above. They're used to cook food. Vastly different than the calorie cubes you're used to eating, I suppose."

Jeremiah took his food to the screen they had watched a few days before, sat down, and asked Poin to put the show back on which he found to be enjoyable.

"The food is eggs with a sauce, spinach, and bacon. If you'd like, there is some bread Acacia baked herself. It's back above the counter. Left cabinet with the gold etchings on the bottom right corner of the dark wood."

Jeremiah didn't reply. The artificial voice was helpful, but it was grating on him that they were hiding something. He could feel it in his bones. The show played and Jeremiah ate his food, finding the eggs themselves to be bland unless he mixed them with the sauce. The bacon was the most savory part of his dish, reminding him of the gelatinous noodles he would sometimes eat. *Are the noodles made of the same thing as the cubes?* The realization hit Jeremiah. He had been paying all those creds for the same thing. *All of those food vendors are renditions of the cubes, only they charge more.* He wished he had more bacon, but didn't dare ask the AI about it. He'd rather sit in silence for the time being, knowing he was being observed, than talk to the walls. He wondered where everyone was.

Jeremiah meandered after finishing his food, trying to find something to entertain himself. There was hardware everywhere, new toys for him to learn off of. He tapped away on holoscreens, moving to keyboards made from hard plastic. He found that the keys gave a nice stiffness to his taps. The clicking was a beautiful serenade to his ears. A nice juxtaposition to the holokeys he was used to. He browsed files and pictures, trying to discover anything new in the world which had now encompassed him. *If I start digging about them, the AI will know.*

He gave up, pushing himself away from all screens, and walked back towards his room. Passing by Babyle's door, he let his curiosity get the better of him and opened it unsure of what he would find. Jeremiah was surprised when he discovered Babyle's room was stacked from floor to ceiling with ancient books. He expected Babyle to be a minimalist, but he was disorganized and messy. There was only a small path to walk between the books to the bed. The other side had a path to the restroom which Jeremiah found troublesome to squeeze through without bumping into a stack or tripping over something.

Jeremiah decided he'd check everyone's room to see how they lived. Acacia's was full of warm tones. Oranges, golds, and reds with cool accents. There were rocks and stones of bright colors which cast even more wondrous shades as the light caught the right angle. He closed her door and went to Gabriel's.

It was locked.

"I can open it for you if you'd like." The metallic tone was back. *Goddamnit.*

Jeremiah had quickly forgotten about the AI as he had explored.

"If you can open it, why's it locked?"

"Gabriel always keeps it locked, but he trusts you. I can always lock you in if necessary."

"Open it."

The door unlocked, and Jeremiah stepped through. It was drab. Dark gray all around from the bed to the floor and walls— except for one. That wall was a massive screen from floor to ceiling, reaching out to the other two it shared corners with. The room felt cold.

"Gabriel works most of the time," Poin cut in, "he finds that too much of anything really distracts from his work. He tries to keep his possessions to a minimum in his work space."

"Does he live in here? Isn't this his bedroom?"

"Primarily, yes. He doesn't frequently come out of this room except to eat and socialize when he feels the need. Even then, the complex is set up in such a way that everywhere he goes there is a place for him to work."

Jeremiah pondered what it must be like to throw oneself into their work so hard that they don't do anything else besides work. *Gabriel is either a genius, a madman, or both.* Jeremiah felt that he must get lonely at times working around the clock. *Maybe that's why Acacia and Babyle live with him, as a cure for loneliness.*

"Where did they go?" Jeremiah asked finally feeling he could have a conversation with the AI.

"I'm afraid I can't inform you of that." And suddenly he felt annoyed again. Jeremiah was tired of being trapped and not told what was going on.

"Okay. I guess I'm going back to my room," Jeremiah huffed, growing quickly bored of everything that was at a simple request and being denied of it.

Jeremiah lulled into his bedroom, trying to find something to do or study. He felt weird for feeling bored. Not long ago he was fighting to survive, now he was complacently eating and existing in some building in the ground.

The room was cold, not as inviting as it had when Jeremiah was first introduced to it. He went to the bathroom, felt the cool tiles beneath his feet, and remembered he hadn't put any socks on before he had left his room earlier. The textures of the apartment had grown familiar—he preferred to feel it beneath him rather than put an insufferable distance between him and the world.

"AI, by any chance, can the heat be adjusted in the floor of the restroom?"

"Yes."

"Can you make it warmer, like being on the same street of the Furnaces, but just passing by to feel the warmth?"

"Of course, Detective."

Immediately Jeremiah felt his feet grow warmer, but he decided against sinking his body into the basin again. He turned and looked at himself in the mirror. He could see his skin for the first time without any soot on it. His eyes were sunken in, definitely more haggard than when he was actually a detective. His cheekbones protruded from under the bags of his eyes. Jeremiah turned the faucet on cold and rubbed water into his face feeling the molecules as they slid between the wrinkles of his skin, then pooled and glided down his face back to be reclaimed somewhere and used again.

Jeremiah walked out of the bathroom. He felt cold again in his room.

"Detective, your body language and physiology say that there is something wrong."

"I don't feel welcome here, AI." *I wish this thing would leave me alone. Can't sit here without having my vitals checked through a damn camera, or a monitor keeping track of my heartrate.* Jeremiah looked around the room trying to find where Poin was getting its information, but couldn't find anything. Gabriel hid it well.

"Why is that?"

"I'm locked in a place that isn't my home. I can't do anything, and I don't feel that this place is for me."

"I assure you, you'll be able to leave, though, there are precautions we must take. I can acquire things if you'd like to decorate this room for yourself to be more homely. If you'd rather have water dripping on you and no mattress, I can make that happen." It was an underhanded comment and Jeremiah ignored it.

"Like what?"

"You've seen everyone else's room. Whatever you want, I can most likely acquire or find someone who can acquire it."

"Does that include stuff from the Above?"

"I cannot answer that at the time being, Detective. But, if you wish to obtain something no longer down here, I can pass the request along to Gabriel, unless, that is, you would like to ask him yourself when he returns."

"Can I, for now, get some neons of pink and blue? They don't need to be any signs, just straight ones and curved ones. Can I also get some black paint?"

Jeremiah wandered back and forth, between the bathroom, the kitchen, the living room, and the bedroom, bathroom, kitchen, and living room, not able to entertain himself for too long in one area.

"Detective Jeremiah, you are permitted to leave this area, and follow the corridor back to where you first came in. Your packages are outside. Though, if you do leave entirely, you will find your life to be quite short lived."

"Thanks, AI. Making me feel at home here rather than a fucking prisoner." Jeremiah strolled through the doors and followed the staircase up back through the original corridor.

Outside of the door to the street were packages of brown pulp-paper. He pulled them inside, and carried them as carefully as he could, passing by massive statues and paintings. It took him longer to get back down to his room, not only because he was struggling to not drop his neons, but the artwork captivated him again along the entire trip.

He entered his room and worked for what felt like hours, setting up the neons in a way so they would cast shadows out from behind shelves, stands, and the small table on the side of his bed. What he found was he missed being in the Deep rather than below it; the pinks and blues reflecting on gray and grime. All around him now, the pinks and blues reflected off of dark color, and cast ghastly shadows. He almost started to feel like this was his home. But there was something still missing.

Jeremiah crossed through the room, lay on the bed and tried to figure out what it was he needed to be comfortable here. The long haul was in front of him, like the corridors above, except there was no light at the end which he could see. There was no way back except a quick death, and the way in front was a thick fog. Jeremiah drifted off to sleep and only woke when he heard the AI's grating voice talking to someone outside of his room, but he wasn't sure how far away they were, nor what they were saying.

Jeremiah started to close his eyes. He heard the door to his room slide open.

"I need your help with something." Gabriel's voice cut through the stillness.

"What is it?"

"A small errand."

"Does that mean I get to leave or am I playing your butler in this place?"

"You may leave."

Finally. Back to the outside.

16

Janet looked around the basement. Everyone had split up to see if there was anything worth finding. Most of what they came across was hardware supplies, which seemed pretty useless. Though, Fox insisted that he take some nails and screws, along with zip ties he had come across. He stocked them in his pack.

Crow found a crowbar, which was slick from the damp air in the basement. It was in good shape. Jamal had peered here and there and he couldn't find anything of value for himself.

"Hey guys, why is this area a little warmer than the rest of the room?" Bernice called out.

The entirety of the group made their way across the basement and into a smaller alcove that housed all of the old boilers which had clearly stopped running. The walls were brick, light gray like the sky outside. Everyone noticed that it was warmer in this outcropping of wall, but for no reason at all. Nothing worked down here, nothing ran, and nothing was putting off any heat except for themselves. The room should not have been warm.

They began to disperse through the small room, like food dye in water, leaving traces of themselves as they moved silently. They swirled and blurred through each other's paths, trying to find the source, trying to find more meaning in their small enclosed world, free to move, yet still trapped. Janet reached a wall which was warmer than the rest of the room. She ran her hands along it, and found a small rectangular patch which cooled after she reached the next brick. It was a small area of warmth, but she had done it. She had found where the heat originated.

"Hey!" she yelled as she found the secret they didn't know they wanted to find.

Everyone ran over, swirling back through the clear, viscous ether. They waited and clung to the wall, trying to discover why it was almost hot to the touch. The warmth ran from ceiling to floor and then cooled distinctly at either side.

"Find something to bash these bricks with," Jamal said looking towards Crow, and the metal length he had poking from his bag.

Without hesitation, Crow cleared the area and began pounding against the brick as hard as he could. Nothing had chipped off after minutes of smashing it as hard as he could.

"Man, quit it with your shit and give me that bar," Jamal said as he closed the gap and took it from Crow's who had begun to gasp harder and harder for more air.

Jamal beat the bricks as hard as he could, harder than Crow had, yet nothing happened. It was as if the molecules of the crowbar weren't even hitting the brick, like a barrier was pushing back as they tried to make a dent in it. Janet stared in amazement.

* * *

"Sir, we might have a problem," Poin said.

"What? I'm busy."

"We seem to have a few people from the Above trying to get in."

"Where?" Gabriel stood up from his desk and crossed over to the massive screen in his room.

"Upstate New York. Abandoned train station. They don't exactly know what they're doing. The force barrier is keeping them out, but with any determination, they'll keep at this until they find a way in."

"At least they aren't far. I need you to get a pod ready. I'm going to meet them there."

"As you wish, Gabriel."

He smiled to himself. *Let's hope they aren't useless.*

"I've been waiting for the day someone from the Above found a way down here, Poin."

"I know, Gabriel."

"With evidence comes revelation," he said as he left the room and coursed through the channels he created beneath the streets.

* * *

Janet watched as everyone sat down in the basement, hot, sweaty, and panting from lack of breath and overexertion.

"Let's just put our heads together. Obviously, there's something here," she said.

"I've never seen anything like this," Jamal stated. "It's whack."

"Man, what if it's like, one of those electric barriers?" Fox interrupted.

"What do you mean?" Jamal asked.

"I'm saying, if it's an electric barrier or forcefield, then we find the power source, or we overload the current and blow the box, man," said Fox.

"Where the fuck did you learn this shit?" Jamal said.

"I saw something about it on the TV a long time ago, when we still had lights."

"So, how do you suggest we overload a current, when we ain't got any electricity? How does this thing have any electricity if we don't?" Jamal said.

"I haven't figured that part out yet, but I'm working on it. We do have batteries, and we have wire. Maybe we can make something to conduct some of the current and stab it against that wall and hope that it'll do something," Fox replied.

"That sounds like a lot of work for something that we don't know will even work." Jamal glared.

"Man, we don't have to do it. We can just leave this basement and pretend like there's nothing here. But I doubt any of you would agree to that. We all know something is here, and we all want to know what's beyond that wall. We're all too nosey, and none of us need to go anywhere, do we?"

"What do you mean?"

"Where do we have to be? We're going nowhere. Just wandering until the next camp." Fox was growing restless. He paced back and forth as he mumbled to himself.

"Shit. You're right. Let's try your crazy ass plan," Jamal said. Janet noticed his voice dripped with sarcasm and wondered if Fox had caught on.

Fox laughed. "Man, just remember that if things ever go south, I appreciate you. Remember that for me." Fox pulled open his backpack and began unloading everything he had. Everyone else followed suit, pooling together batteries, wire, and some metal.

Fox sat down and began stripping away the plastic from the wires, most of which were red and black.

"Which is which?" Janet inquired.

"Black is negative, red is positive. Haven't you ever jumped a car?" Crow snapped.

"No, actually. When you live in the city you generally don't have to own a fucking car, asshole."

"She's right. We just take the subway or walk everywhere."

"I lived in the city too. I never realized you didn't own a car. I didn't know you lived in the city, to be honest. I thought you were just down there when this all happened."

"Yeah, never owned one, never left the city until we got stuck in this mess with each other." Janet shot a look at everyone else sitting around, pulling apart wires to get to the copper underneath. They were her family now, filling the void which was left when the lights went out.

"That's my mistake," Crow said.

"Did you just admit being wrong for the first time ever?" Janet shot back.

"Yeah, I guess I did. I'm learning new things about everyone today."

"What if we get a few car batteries, and jump those, then we use them to overload this 'forcefield.' They're way stronger than the batteries we have, and once we jump the first one, we can jump the rest," Jamal suggested.

Everyone looked around at each other, as if that answer was so obvious and in front of them the entire time, but they were all too busy being pissed off and arguing to think logically and look at their situation objectively. They had fallen into the classic pitfall of humanity. Allowing their emotions to get in their way and cloud any reasonable judgment they might have had between them.

"Is that even possible? To jump a car battery with small ones," Bernice interjected. Everyone looked around at each other and shrugged simultaneously.

"I don't see why not. We might need to use all of the batteries we have to do it, though." Fox paused as if trying to comb through his memories. "More power I think would be better to jump a bigger battery. Just a guess, man."

"You really have a gut intuition about this working, don't you?" Janet asked.

"I do." He smiled back, then continued to work.

"Some of us need to go get batteries from up in the parking garage. We should have some wrenches around here," Crow said as he stood up and began looking around for any tools in the basement to unhook the batteries. "And the rest need to stay down here stripping wires and getting ready for us."

"I'll go with you," Janet said, as Jamal agreed to join them.

"I'll stay down here, man," said Fox. Bernice agreed to stay with Fox since she felt her talents were better suited to being away from everything, stripping wires. "Her and I got this."

"You guys know how to unhook batteries?" Crow pestered Janet and Jamal.

"Not at all," Janet responded.

"Yeah, dude, I got this. Worked on a few back in the day when I dropped outta high school," said Jamal.

"Where'd you learn?" asked Crow.

"Just some bullshit gas station that changed oil and did standard car shit in the city. Nothing special. I dipped before I could learn much else besides putting tires on, changing batteries, oil and checking fluids."

"Well that will make things easier. Janet, you're with me."

"Okay, but once I figure it out, I'm on my own and taking some tools."

Crow looked her up and down, as if he was deciding to argue but then decided it wasn't worth it.

Janet and Crow found a car that didn't seem too weathered after they split from Jamal.

"Okay, so first things first," Crow said as they opened the hood of the car. "See these, the red is positive and will always have a plus sign, while black is negative." He began pointing at the different terminals on the battery posts.

"You always take the negative off first, then you take the positive off, after, of course, you make sure the right wrench fits on the right nut." He explained as he tried a few different sizes until the correct one matched and allowed him to loosen the negative terminal then positive terminal.

"After that's done, there's a clamp here and here." He used the wrench to point. "This clamp needs to come off as well and almost always the same wrench will take this clamp off of the battery. It frees it from the engine compartment, allowing you to pull the battery. Now grab it."

She pulled at the battery, not realizing it was heavier than it looked.

"Goddamn, I didn't expect to be getting a workout while my hands were getting dirty. These things are so tiny, I figured they'd be like ten pounds at most."

"Yeah, no. They're made of lead and it's dense as hell, making it heavier than it looks."

Janet disappeared after the next car battery, grabbing a few wrenches which she had hoped would be the right size for something nearby. *We already have three batteries unhooked and ready to be brought downstairs. Maybe we would get ten or so?* Janet wasn't sure how many they were actually supposed to get, just that they wanted to be overconfident rather than underconfident. *How are batteries even measured,* she wondered. *Volts or watts? What's the difference?* Her mind meandered for knowledge. *Better to be learning as much as possible, I guess.*

She came across a car from the early 2000s. She had seen plenty of them. Small, white, looked like an egg with wheels. The tip being the front of the car, the back being the bottom of the egg. They were ugly, but not nearly as ugly as some others, she thought. She unhooked the battery. *He really is so abrasive for no reason. We've all lost something. You have to accept it and move on.*

Rob. I'm sorry for thinking that.

Everyone rounded up in the cellar under the train station, carrying batteries and wires. Fox set out to run whatever small AA batteries they had, trying to make a connection to recharge the first battery. They had no indication that it was working. No sensors, nothing.

"Man, how do we know if this is working?" Jamal stood up in the room which felt like moisture and moth balls.

"We don't until we try it," Fox responded. He was surrounded by wires, looking more like a mad scientist than a wildman.

Bernice looked over at them. "What if this is a complete waste of time?"

"At least we tried. Otherwise, we're just sitting here with our thumbs up our asses until we leave again, man"

"Then let's fucking leave!" Bernice said and Jamal nodded in agreement.

"I haven't stopped you from leaving, man. But I want to know what's on the other side of this wall. Whatever it is, someone or something doesn't want us there, and I want to know why."

"We're a group, we move together, we stay together," Janet said, noticing the tension which was mounting.

"I don't think that's how this arrangement was planned. We met and we joined together, but none of us were forced to stay if we don't want to." Fox looked up and gave everyone an ultimatum. Stay or leave. No difference would be made.

"That's just dumb, Fox, and you know it." Janet replied.

"No, what's dumb is leaving the safety of a place to be out in the open. We're working towards something besides survival for the first time since we all banded together. I'm gonna stay here, and you all can leave if you want. But, if I find a way beyond this wall, I'm taking it, man."

They all stood and looked at Fox, and for the first time saw him assert dominance. Everyone in the concrete basement knew that he was the most capable among them. If he did find a way to break the current, he could take whatever it was, and make it his own with no problems from any of them. He was the sinewy man with brains and a will to live. Everyone else was simply along for the ride.

"Man, fuck you." Jamal sat down and waited on the other side of the room.

They waited, and waited, grew tired of waiting, then waited longer, in hopes that the science project would work. Hardly anyone spoke and when they did, they only spoke in whispers to those closest to them of things which held no significance.

"Is there a way for us to test if this thing has a charge now?" Janet watched Jamal cross back over and ask Fox.

Fox looked at Jamal. Janet saw him mulling something over in this head. "Yeah, man. Grab that metal pipe, and wrap the negative end around one end while it's attached to the battery. Then, take your hands off of the pipe, and lay it on the ground. Touch the positive wire to the other end, and if it sparks, then we have energy. Make sure you hold the wire by the plastic."

Jamal eyed him and looked over at Crow.

"He's right. I don't think he's trying to kill you."

Fox didn't seem to take the slight personally.

Jamal did exactly what Fox said, and there was a small crackle. As if for the first time, there existed life that sputtered into existence. Everyone smiled and felt relief, like they had finally done something worth doing. They were eager.

"Quick, take the positive end off, and grab another pipe. Wrap it to the positive end."

Everyone started to hustle. Fox did the honors. His eyes wild, ready for what would hopefully come. He dragged the battery to the wall, and stuck the negative end on first. He took a breath and slowly lifted the positive metal pipe to the wall, and pressed it on. The wall glowed a bright blue-white, forcing everyone to shield their eyes with their hands. The light grew and grew, as the sound of raucous crackling overcame their ears. Everything went dark. The air was still, as if the clock had stopped and gone back in that moment of brilliant light. It was the light at the end of the tunnel which had faded to black–a singularity, one last dense point giving off a brilliant show before it took Fox to the other side.

Everyone lowered their hands as they heard the last massive crackle disappear into the firmament. The air filled with a burnt smell, sickening to the stomach. Fox lay on the ground. Dead. His hands black, his eyes watery, and his body stiff as they all scrambled around him shouting to wake him up. Jamal kicked the metal pipes away from them, and everyone grew silent knowing Fox had died without taking precautions for the first time. Eager, he wanted to prove himself more than he already had. Anxious, he wanted to see beyond the wall, but only found what was on the other side.

"How did this happen," Jamal muttered lowly as he leaned up against the wall looking down at Fox's now lifeless body. Tears rolled down his face.

"Fuck!" Crow yelled as he kicked a backpack and disappeared in a fury.

"It's cold," Bernice said as she rubbed her feet.

"Of course it's cold, it's winter," Janet said with defeat.

"No, I mean the wall, it's cold now," Bernice said turning around feeling the area they had pressed against. "Give me something hard to hit it with."

Everyone started grabbing for anything they could find and wailed against the brick. It started to chip away covering the floor with dust and small hunks of brick. Everyone had expected huge pieces to fall off with the force they were throwing at it, but the brick seemed to be much more reinforced. The task was arduous, and they had to stop to breathe as they barely made progress.

"I think we should bury Fox before we continue going. Do right by him," Janet said as she sat and tried to catch her breath.

The group of people who had found their new lease on life—the one Fox spoke of—made their way around his body, and they picked him up together. They carried him out of the crypt, and back up to the light where he could feel the sun and the wind again. They found some ground near the river which wasn't completely covered by snow, and started digging all together with their hands and the crowbar. The ground was hard. Though they were exhausted, they struggled for him.

Dirt piled up, and eventually they had a decent enough hole that they were able to place him in. It was shallow, but it was a grave nonetheless.

"You were a good friend, whack, but a good friend," Jamal said.

"The best survivalist we had," Crow said.

Janet and Bernice remained quiet. Janet imagined his soul standing among them, thanking them for letting him be outside in the trees he loved. He'd wander there until the end of time, listening to the birds' cry, lamenting the loss of their dearest friend. The trees hugged him as he passed while wandering to see all the mountains, feeling the desert sands between his toes, and the waves against his fingertips. The open world always for him and never for anyone else. The wildest of men. And Janet could have sworn she saw him leave them as he patted each one of them on the back, making their hair stand up.

The basement of the train station was just as they had left it, only the smell of burning flesh still lingered there with the dust on the floor. They all picked up where they left off, carrying the burden of someone they had lost. The wall chipped away slowly. As time passed, the sun went down behind the clouds and it was time to cozy up for bed as best as possible. When morning came, they would toil away again, hoping that their breakthrough would be quick so they could see what Fox had died trying to see.

Ever so slowly the wall began to diminish more. Crumbs falling to the ground, waiting for something to come along and take them away. Little by little they made progress, centimeter by centimeter, then inch by inch as the hardest parts of the wall began to break off. Eventually Crow was able to stick his hand into the wall up to his elbow.

"It's going to be another day, at least, before we bust through this," Jamal said.

"Yeah, I just want to relax and sleep again," Bernice said.

Janet kept hammering away, her muscles fatigued and screaming in pain as everyone around her began to lose their stamina and morale.

"As much as I hate to say it, I think you're right, Jamal. It's going to be another day at least, but this thing could be dozens of feet thick. We have no way of knowing," Crow said as he slowed his swings and eventually stopped.

"But we could also be just a few more inches from the end." Janet tried to rally them to pick up their tools and get back to work, but she knew it was fleeting and a fight she would not win.

"We've made a lot of progress today, which I think is a good sign, but I'm going to side with Jamal here," Crow replied as he took a seat against the wall sealing the deal.

"I wish you'd all get your shit together," Janet said. "I miss him too, but the sun is still up and we can actually find out what was stopping us."

Everyone let the words hang in the air. The group had felt different without Fox around, like they were wandering around without their hearts. No one stood back up to help Janet.

They started to drift off into their dreams, but Janet stayed awake, unable to let sleep take her from the waking world. She got up and left the basement, going back to the streets where the stars hung overhead like winks from dead friends. She gazed up at the clear sky. Freezing, she pulled her jacket tight and walked down towards the river. How far she had come and far she still had to go, yet, she never strayed far from the Hudson. It flowed south now, and she felt like her life was retreating to events she tried to escape from.

Water splashed against the thick chunks of ice which had boarded themselves up against the shore of the river. There were pieces of wood, broken and shattered against the strength of nature. Nature had created it, and nature had destroyed it again, refusing to let little roadblocks get in its way.

Janet grew cold standing in place and decided to return back to the basement to find warmth. It felt like a prison to be stuck inside such a tight room with everyone. She looked around as they all slept peacefully. She forced her eyes to close.

Her dreams were fitful.

She found herself outside of an old house. It felt familiar. It was mostly wood, had a brick fireplace, and a wood burning stove which was not from any memory she had. The air around her was acrid, almost burnt. She searched the rooms and found no one. Outside lay two unmarked graves. She ran towards them and began to dig, though everything told her not to.

Her nails filled with dirt and mud. Tears streamed down her face and mixed with the grime. She pulled a jawbone from the shallow grave and easily identified it by the teeth, the two bottom front ones bent inward. She wailed knowing Robert was beneath her. The other grave was opened by her hands. Fresh light brown hair. Her breathing stopped, knowing she was about to dig up Fox and stare him in the eyes. His head swayed back and forth as it broke through the ground.

"I've seen the void." He started to move and jostled free speaking between dirt clumps which fell from his mouth.

"I'm sorry. I'm sorry. I'm sorry."

"Just get me free, man. I want to be out there." His eyes were hollow pits, like they had been picked out and blood crusted around the holes.

She began shaking back and forth uncontrollably.

"Janet, wake up. Janet, wake the fuck up."

Her eyes burst open and she felt tears starting to well in them as she saw Crow shaking her. The others stared on.

"Why'd you wake me?"

"You were having a bad dream and started to yell in your sleep." He took his hand off of her, then sat down.

"Sorry. Just stressed with the current situation."

"We all are, but we can't dwell on the past. Remember what I told you before we met him? 'The past will kill you if you stay there too long.'"

"It's still fresh, it's not like it was months ago. It was just a day ago that he was here. You can't just forget the past, Crow. It makes us who we are. It develops us as people and we either learn and grow, or turn a blind eye and bull-rush toward oblivion."

"All I'm saying, Janet, is you can feel the pain of loss, but you can't stay there forever. It's going to eat you up. We all hurt and miss him. This loss isn't exclusive to you."

"I think I'm the only one trying to mourn him," she yelled feeling as if they all didn't care that he was gone.

"That's not the case. We all need to mourn in different ways. I don't think continuing this conversation is going to help any of us." He stood up and began to dig through his pack. Crow searched for some food to cook over a fire. From his pack he pulled a can of spam, and a can of cubed pineapple.

"Hawaiian tonight? I don't know about you, but that isn't my favorite combination," Jamal interjected, trying to lighten the mood of the room. *Maybe he's just trying to distract himself.*

"We could always make some pizza and put pineapple on it," Bernice joked, then immediately frowned.

"All right, all right, I get it you're trying to be funny using an internet meme." Jamal forced a chuckle. A silence ensued as they looked around.

"Well, I'm starving, so I'll eat both," Crow retorted.

Janet crawled over knowing she had to eat and that no one there was going to judge her for her feelings of loss. They were her only chance at survival, she knew. A faux-family forced to live together as the best means for survival.

They all ate quietly, letting their own thoughts fill the space between them, and taking over the space of the one they lost.

Janet stood up first, tears welling in her eyes, and started hammering away at the wall with more force than she had mustered before. Bang after bang after bang, the wall started to chip away in large chunks. Crow watched along with Jamal, until finally an entire brick came loose. The air became static. Cold as they felt, whatever had been trapped behind the wall leaked out into their cozy basement and they forgot their predicament and lack of warmth.

17

They had managed to pull out a big enough hole they could all squeeze through, though they had to take their packs off and pass them to the person in front of them. Crow went first, breaching into the darkness. Bernice followed, then Jamal, and Janet brought up the rear. Inside was a long narrow hallway. Cables ran along the floor right up to the brick they had taken down.

Flashlights illuminated their path, like bioluminescence the walls shown an eerie blue with the white light. They walked on, trying to take in their surroundings and make any guesses as to where they were going. Ahead, they found a staircase, old and built out of clanky metal.

"This could just be an old entrance or exit that they sealed up," Jamal said.

"That's what it's feeling like," Crow replied.

"Why would it be so hard to get in here?" Janet had turned into the optimist believing they were about to find the largest secret any of them had seen. "Besides, how would that wall still have an electric current?" she asked but no one answered.

They saw a light further on as they turned a corner.

They followed the path and took a turn left to get to the light. Around the corner there was an open area they could see further on. As they reached the end, a man appeared.

"I'm Gabriel," he said as he slowly put his hands up and introduced himself. Crow had tried to shoulder his rifle but was too shocked and fumbled with it.

"There's no need for any of that."

"Who the fuck are you?" Crow blasted back. His nervousness was taking over.

"I think the better question is, who are you, and where exactly are you heading?" Gabriel smiled at the group in front of him. "I've been watching you for a while on my cameras. The small nanites in the walls keeping track of your bio-signatures. I thought you all wanted a warm welcome."

There was no answer and silence surrounded them all.

"Answer my question." Crow pointed his rifle forward closing some of the gap between them and the strange man. "Are you responsible for whatever it was that killed Fox?"

"I'll give you that one, but if you threaten me again, Poin will make sure you can't get a shot off." There was a whirring and crunching noise as the floor moved beneath them and the ceiling pulled away to produce small metal machines with red eyes.

"Would you like me to exterminate our new guests, Gabriel?" A metal voice asked.

"Not yet, Poin. I think these people don't know where they are or what they have gotten themselves into."

Jamal was visibly shaking along with Bernice, while Janet looked numb and confused, ready for the worst and accepting it.

"Now that we're on the same page, do you all know where you are or heading?" Gabriel asked.

Crow surveyed the small corridor, finding them on the losing end unless they ran back the way they came. In front, the corridor opened to a room, wide, but the lights were blinding to him and he couldn't see much except white.

"No, we don't know where we are or going." Janet answered.

"I see. How'd you find this place?"

"Mostly by chance. We were getting out of the open to look for supplies, and noticed one area of the basement to be warmer than the rest, then we found a segment of wall which was almost hot to the touch."

"That's the thing with all I've been doing, trying to find a way to disperse all of that heat. I could localize it, but I was never able to make it disappear." Gabriel had turned his head to his left and was clearly talking to someone else. "Heatsinks, Poin. We need to figure out this problem, fast."

"Look, if you'll just let us go, we'll go back the way we came, and never come back," Jamal interjected as he stared in horror at the small machines with red eyes. He was trying to beg for their lives.

"That won't be necessary. Drop your weapons and you can come in for some food."

Everyone balked at what was just said. Whoever this man was, he was letting them in, giving them food, and hopefully not killing them in the process. Crow's mind raced, debating if it was a real gesture or a trap.

"I don't trust it," Crow whispered.

"Me either," Bernice said as she looked at Jamal.

"It looks like it's our only option," Janet replied as her eyes wandered to the red spider eyes hanging from the ceiling.

She was right. He wasn't requesting them to come eat. It was a demand the way he had spoken. They were either to die where they stood, or they were going to be guests.

Janet dropped her rifle first, then Jamal, and Bernice, while Crow was the last to lay his on the ground. He unshouldered Fox's rifle from his back and laid that on the ground too, though he was not happy about where the situation was headed. He felt guilty for leaving what remained of his friend behind. *I'm sorry, Fox.*

The room in front of them where Gabriel stood had a table which was lit up brightly from the white above. They all sat down around the length of rectangular mass. It was sturdy, definitely made from real wood, Crow reckoned as he tapped on it.

"As I said earlier, I'm Gabriel."

"I'm Acacia," said a woman carrying a tray of food and placing it in the center.

"Babyle," a man said as he carried bottles of liquor and wine to the table.

"I'm Janet."

"I'm, uh, Jamal," Jamal said. He gripped the spaces between his fingers making his knuckles crack.

"Bernice." She shifted from foot to foot.

"Crow."

"That's a weird name," said Gabriel as he looked Crow up and down.

"More of a nickname that always stuck around."

"Oh, I understand," Acacia said.

"Hmm?"

"It's easy. Someone you loved gave you that nickname and now they're no longer around, so you've taken on that name as a persona to hide from the fact you want to distance yourself from the life of your real name—the life that person was a part of."

Crow went to speak but suddenly felt very vulnerable.

"Please, serve yourselves," Gabriel said as he reached for some asparagus in the middle of the table, and pieces of salmon from the tray Acacia had brought out last.

"How did you get all of this food?" Jamal asked, as he started to load up his plate.

"We can discuss something like that later. Right now, I want to ask you all a few questions," said Gabriel. "Do you know where you are? Janet does not speak for all of you."

Everyone sat letting the silence engulf them. It was the first time they were truly warm, eating familiar food which wasn't from a can, or a recently killed animal. They all looked around at each other, or down at their plates, unsure of what to say to this new group of people.

"Somewhere north of New York City beneath an old train station. We assumed that this was just an area bricked up. The electric force field or whatever you want to call it is the only reason we're here," Janet answered.

"I said you don't speak for everyone." Gabriel's voice was sharp. "You have something that can detect electric currents at distance?"

"No. Like we said earlier, we wanted to get to shelter, and we stumbled across the part of the wall by chance because it was noticeably warmer and made the room warm." Crow cut in before Janet opened her mouth again.

Gabriel made a face as if he didn't really believe them. "Poin, what are the chances of something like that occurring?"

"Less than one percent, Gabriel. Though, it is possible. Body language along with heart rate and perspiration suggest they are telling the truth," the metal voice soothed the tension in the room.

"You have no idea what you're doing or where you're going?"

"Just another day trying to survive at the moment," Crow said, not letting Janet answer. The other two were too awestruck to speak.

"Maybe we'll have to show you some things when dinner is over."

"Good idea," Babyle interjected as he covered his mouth while chewing. His voice was more gruff than the others.

"I agree," Acacia said, "it might be beneficial for them to see. Though we'll have to get them a change of clothes." She eyed them up and down. "They're a bit too grungy looking to fit in, even in the Slums they'd stand out."

"I agree," Gabriel replied.

Everyone finished eating, and Crow was surprised and glad at the same time that no one died tragically of poison, or had their throat slit while they ate.

"Please, follow me." Gabriel stood up and exited the room through two huge wooden doors.

Crow put his hand out feeling the sturdiness of the door, much like the table they all sat at. Beyond the door, they followed Gabriel through a winding staircase. It went deeper down. Their feet clanged on the metal underneath them, until, after minutes, they had reached solid concrete ground. Everything began to get warmer as they went. Crow watched as Janet peeled off her jacket, and put it in her pack. Everyone followed her lead. Crow heard Bernice quietly groan about the pain in her feet.

The air around them felt like spring turning to summer, a nice sixty-degree day to start the morning that got progressively oppressive as the sun crept in. There was no humidity around them, but after the long cold they had been suffering through, all of the warmth was welcome, except to Bernice.

"What's wrong?" Gabriel stopped moving about and spoke to Bernice.

"I got frostbite on my feet."

"Let me see." She showed him, her toes blue-black and her feet pale.

"I'll get you something for that."

Gabriel disappeared around a corner into another room. Inside they found massive stockpiles of clothes.

"Please, find whatever fits you, then get dressed."

"Do we have to?" Jamal asked. He looked uncomfortable.

"Yes. I know a lot of the clothes look disgusting and tattered, but there is a reason for it."

"Something tells me that this isn't a debate again," Crow said as he picked up a shirt off of the ground with the sleeves missing, and a hole through and through where someone's heart would have been.

Gabriel smiled. "You know, you're very quick to pick up on that, Crow," he announced matter-of-factly with a heaping scoop of sarcasm.

"Great," Bernice said as she found old blue jeans which were too big for her.

Everyone undressed and tried to find a way to guard their privacy as much as possible.

Gabriel came back to Bernice while she was re-clothing herself. In his hands he held two vials.

"Let me see your feet." Bernice listened as he pressed them directly into the tops of them. "Your feet will get better, but only after it gets much, much worse. Give it time. I promise." Bernice looked relieved.

"You'll be comfortable shortly, but this is a necessary precaution," he said to everyone in the amphitheater like room.

After everyone had taken on their new personality, they followed Gabriel into a new room, one which was grungy and old, with a stink to it that none of them could recognize.

"We're going to need to split you guys up," Acacia said.

"No," Bernice loudly replied.

"Yes," Acacia retorted. "None of you are going to be prepared for what you're going to see. It's easier if we do this one by one, so if you have an issue, we can control it."

"I'm not going alone." Bernice looked around at everyone. "I won't fucking do it. Not again. I'll put up a fight with you all right here and now."

Gabriel stepped closer but made sure not to break through her comfort zone. "Who is it you'd like to escort you out of the three of us, and who would you like to take with you out of your friends?"

Bernice stared at the man in front of her, larger than any of them. "I want Jamal by my side, and I want the woman to escort us."

Acacia smiled. "You can still call me Acacia, and maybe it's better if we get to know each other first. What do you think?"

"We can talk and walk."

"Crow, you'll be with me," Gabriel told him.

"You. Me." Babyle looked at Janet as he spoke.

18

Gabriel paced through the rooms. He was trying to satisfy some urge, but couldn't figure out what it was. There was a need to do something, and nothing all at once. He wanted to work, needed to. But was too focused on the new group of people who were taking up more space in rooms he hadn't assigned to anyone. As his mind raced, he knew he needed to leave for a bit.

Gabriel opened Jeremiah's room only to find him sleeping, rolled up in his blankets while the pinks and blues swam over the ruffles like fish jumping from water, leaving behind black breaks. It reminded him of all the things the people in the GUC were missing out on. Sure, they had all the technology in the world, and could order anything their hearts desired—if they had the creds—but the natural world Above was out of reach to all of them. A memory passed down from generation to generation, until all that remained was a vague image with a silver fog over it.

Jeremiah stirred, and Gabriel stepped into the room, letting the colors overwhelm his features again.

"Good morning," he said, making Jeremiah recognize his presence.

"Morning," he replied begrudgingly.

"Today, you can come outside with me. There's a lot happening, and I want to apologize for locking you down as I did. It was necessary. I'm sure you know much about doing what is logically necessary, Detective, even at the times when it would cause a rift between you and someone else."

* * *

Jeremiah wasn't sure what act he was trying to get at, but he felt Gabriel was trying to make himself seem less malicious in locking him down, that he needed him here while he handled some kind of business left unannounced. *Still an asshole. Even after I did that insane job for him.*

"Where are we going?"

"I believe if I told you that, you wouldn't understand. It's best if you get ready and follow me. Acacia and Babyle are waiting."

Jeremiah felt unamused. Gabriel could have answered the question, but he was back to playing his game of limited knowledge. It was growing old and childish rapidly, very rapidly, in fact. Jeremiah got out of bed and started to dress himself in the pink and blue haze while Gabriel left, allowing Jeremiah privacy. The neons snuck in between the tucks and folds of his muscles and skin. *Who do I hate more? Gabriel or the robot? Hard choice there.* Jeremiah sighed.

Gabriel would probably take him to the UC, Jeremiah thought to himself. Maybe the actual Capitol, a place few could gain entrance to. That would be a spectacle, seeing the hulking mass of utopic buildings up close, lit by spotlights shooting light hundreds of feet high until they disappeared into the black, never reaching the top. *What else could be so important that Gabriel wouldn't tell me? Nothing, most likely.*

They were winding their way through the Deep, the water from the condensers familiar, the grime their home. Jeremiah relished being out of the compound. It was the first time he left in at least three weeks, by his rough estimate. Time had begun to blur for him.

All around them, people ran back and forth, rushing to get as much food and water they could before they forced sleep upon themselves or running to meet the next escort, losing out on precious sleep just to satisfy a primal urge. Everyone had different priorities. Some needed the next high, some needed to feel full, some need to empty themselves into someone or something else. It was chaotic, and the Capitol encouraged all of it.

"All of these people could get out of here," Gabriel said.

"How? The Armed Guard at the wall would keep them out of the UC, and the Capitol is a fortress from what I hear."

"This is true, but if everyone from the Deep went to the walls of the UC, it would fall in a day. They could arm themselves and make each local Capitol fall, until all that remained was one."

"We don't even know where that building is in the GUC—it could be thousands of miles away from here."

"We'll find it one day."

"What you're saying is a fool's dream."

"That's what I bring up."

"What?"

"Dreaming."

"It's not important."

"It is. Human nature is to be complacent—to fall in line and simply complain about the way things are. The main populace does not want to do anything uncomfortable or face fear and death. They'd rather work and continue with their work."

"What's the point then?"

"Of what?"

"Of mentioning they could escape this existence and dreaming."

"There really wasn't. To overcome human nature, there needs to be an event to bring them all together against a greater evil, rather than coming together for a greater good."

"What do you mean?" *He's going off on weird tangents,* Jeremiah thought.

"If people really wanted to make their lives better, they wouldn't, even if it meant a greater good for everyone around them. The basic person doesn't care about the greater good, despite what they say and pretend to believe. People can say they believe in the greater good, but they want someone else to take care of it for them. However, if there is a greater recognizable evil, it would unite the people. If certain death came to their door, they would fight against it. Fear would have to come to them, rather than having them go and seek fear out. Am I making sense to you?"

"I believe so." Jeremiah wasn't too sure why Gabriel was talking in philosophies. *It's unnecessary. Why bring me out if you're just bouncing ideas off of me?*

"Good."

"Why mention all of this though?"

"No reason." Gabriel turned to Jeremiah and smiled. "Just being philosophical. I'm as complacent person a person as anyone else down here."

"So, you brought me out just so you could bounce ideas off of me? That's bullshit. Should've just left me sleeping."

Gabriel walked into a small rundown storefront for nutritional cubes. The table he sat down at was worn, much more worn than what was in their underground home. Jeremiah sat across from him.

"Why are we here getting nutritional cubes if we can eat anything we want?"

"Jeremiah, I find it best not to mention our food situation in public, lest someone hear of it and come asking questions prematurely." He eyed him up and down.

Jeremiah shook his head then scratched the side of his scalp.

A man walked to the table and placed a cube of familiar gelatinous consistency in front of each of them. Gabriel put out his arm and the man scanned in the creds via Gabriel's implant. Jeremiah realized even if he had overtaken Gabriel, he would have never been able to get to his credits with the implant. He could have replicated his fingerprints, but not the implant. Few in the Deep had it. It was too costly to get the small surgery it required. Even those in the Precinct near the UC and the Capitol rarely had an implant—come to think of it, Jeremiah didn't even think his Captain had a credit implant installed.

Gabriel took a small chunk out of his cube and ate it, nodding to Jeremiah to do the same. Even if he was full, he needed to eat it.

"This is all about keeping up appearances, Jeremiah. We're all being watched on their cameras. Eating here is nothing more than appearing like we ate for the first time in a few days," he had leaned forward and whispered over the table.

"I've been missing for a week or two from their facial recognition. Might think it odd."

Wide eyed and thoughts running, Jeremiah took half of the cube and popped it in his mouth. He felt the same boring flavor melt over his tongue and coat his mouth and throat. It was a familiar atrocity bringing memories of being a kid, teenager, and an adult all at once. The same meal every day. The same monstrosity being choked down.

"I wanted to thank you for getting me the necessary materials for my project."

"I almost died for it." *Why is he bringing this up in public?*

"Tell me what happened."

Jeremiah looked Gabriel up and down as they ate the disgusting cubes.

"It was right where you said it would be. There was one guard I had to kill. Once I lifted the keycard from his body, everything from there was like sitting in my old police cruiser. I kept moving forward and there were no obstructions to stop me."

"What was it like when you first saw it?"

"The lab?"

"No."

"Oh. It was a weird sense of awe. It's too distinctly robotic yet human at the same time. They could have modeled it anyway they wanted, but they chose to make it after themselves."

"It's terrible isn't it? How human ego needs to model a new lifeform after itself."

"It's odd, and I don't understand why we do it."

"Ego. Nothing more. We believe to have claim over everything, even new life."

I don't think it's exactly living, Jeremiah thought to himself, not wanting to go down that road with Gabriel. He hated the artificial life that was taking over, and now having a body for themselves to live in, rather than Holos running the streets, it was becoming a nightmare for Jeremiah.

19

UPSTATE NEW YORK, 2019

Bernice started to run. Her bandaged feet hit hard against the ice layer on top of the snow. The cold and moisture creeped through, grabbing at her skin, and began to choke the cells. Fire burned through her feet as she ran, and eventually they went numb. *Wish I grabbed a pair of shoes before I left.*

Around her, night snuck in. It had allowed her to escape the camp hoping for her sake that no one would notice she had disappeared until it was too late and she was too far away to be caught.

Behind her, in the depth of darkness, Bernice heard whistles. *Too quick. Someone must have ratted me out.* They'd move up in the group if they did—go from being a toy to getting more rations and the respect of the Traders. *Fucking cunt,* she thought to herself. She told everyone they could do it, they could overtake them, or they could leave in the night. But no, everyone was in it for themselves, she learned. And some were too tired to fight back any longer. The whistles grew louder. *I should have kept quiet all those nights sleeping in that house with the other women.*

She ran harder, felt her newly formed blisters pop as they slapped against the ground. Pus and water oozed—froze to her dying skin. There was no wind, only Bernice's breath as she ran and ran, trying to put distance between herself and the river camp. Not far away was a small town she knew—she had been there to party during her high school dropout years.

She stopped to catch her breath, felt the pang of life in her tingling feet, and knew she needed to find some place to hide, and fast. She started to run again, each step making her feet more wet. Her fingers felt at the lump in the right pocket of her torn jeans, fiddling with the robin's egg lighter. As soon as she found a place, she'd make a fire, and rub her feet back to life. *Just hold out longer. It'll be over soon.*

Minutes turned to miles, and she stopped, her feet not wanting her to go any further.

Come on, not far now. From the trees she could see an old church, it was white against the black sky. Behind her she could not see any flashlights, but still heard the shrill of whistles against the empty wind. Her feet limped inside, woefully dragging her body along with them. In a bathroom sat a small metal garbage can. *It'll do,* she prayed.

She looked around, trying to find anything she could to burn. Only bibles and a few pamphlets about Christ. She dragged the garbage can up to the highest room of the church—which wasn't far from the ground, but it would give some oversight to the world around her—and grabbed a few bibles to send back to God.

She unwrapped her feet. They were now pale and pruned. She threw bibles into the garbage can, and held a pamphlet near her wet lighter. It sparked and sparked, not wanting to hold a flame. When it did, it sputtered, trying to go back to its peaceful death as if wishing she would stop trying to resuscitate it. The flame held long enough to light a corner, then disappeared.

The bandages lay on the ground exhuming their moisture as the heat radiated from the mouth of the metal can. Bernice sat on the floor and tried to massage life into her cold feet. Nerves reacted, shooting electric signals into her skull and back. *Fuck,* she sobbed to herself, tears welling into her eyes. *If I have frost-bite, I'm fucked.* She cried silently as she had become accustomed to doing every night.

Bernice looked out of the window which stared into the darkness. She knew there were trees which could be hiding anything, and the people searching for her could still be out there. She tried to bring her feet back to life, crying as she rubbed them. *Maybe I'd be better off dead.*

Bernice fell asleep to dream of bioluminescence. All around her a cave lit up wondrous blue against the dark black. Her feet hot against the cool ground of the wet rock beneath her. She walked, going deeper and deeper until the blues gave way to pale white, and eventual nothing. The world around her was empty filled only by the dripping of water. Every which way she turned she saw nothing. The only sense her body responded with was pain. Her feet burned and burned no matter how cool the ground was. She sat to rub them in the complete dark, and then used her feet to rub against each other. There was no feeling in her toes, and the soles felt like they were being burned in the depths of hell along the lakes of ice.

The wind howled through the trees, as she slept fitfully in a church. A place of God and healing. A place of home and family. A place empty and barren with no hope for a better tomorrow. A place which had lost its faith.

Bernice woke up to her feet rubbing against one another, still burning, still pale. The fire had gone out. She stood and stumbled, each step a mark of coals. She grabbed more bibles and pamphlets and lit them up in a blasphemous cacophony. *If God exists, he won't be too upset that I'm using his books to keep myself alive. At least, if he is, then he's a piece of shit.* Muttering and cursing to herself, breaking most of the commandments, she rubbed her feet more and more. She pushed them closer to the warmth which made her feel like the skin was going to slough from the muscle, and the muscle from bone. Even if it did, it probably would have still felt better than what she was feeling. *Why me? What the fuck did I do to deserve all of this?* she asked a fake god the same two questions she had grown accustomed to asking.

The sun came up, and the wraps were dry. In the church kitchen, Bernice found plastic bags. She re-wrapped her feet. It was pale and red where the blisters were, skin flaps hanging in all directions. Over the wraps she placed the plastic bags which made for a nice cover, hopefully good enough to keep the water and snow out. She slung a plastic bag filled with pamphlets and a few bibles over her shoulder, made sure her lighter was in her front right pocket as a creature of habit would do, and left the church, hoping someone in the small town would help her. *If anyone is still there.*

Bernice stuck to the tree line which was on the side of a massive clearing of snow. It was definitely the road which connected to a major interstate. There was a trail somewhere beneath which ran the entirety of the road, but Bernice decided against trying to find it for an easier walk. It didn't hold that much cover, and if they were still out looking for her, she'd be easy to spot.

Thank god the gasoline ran out months ago They can't use the trucks to find me. Bernice started thinking to herself how it must have been a year, give or take by her count, since the bulbs burned out. The days had turned to weeks and the weeks to months. By the time they had gone by, she stopped counting. All she was sure of was that the bulbs burned out in the winter, and winter never changed to spring.

No point. Just keep going. Don't think about time. Don't think about time. But all she could think about was the time she had spent trapped by the Traders. They fed her just enough to keep her alive, but that was it. Her body was a tool, and she was no longer a person. Time had worn it all away. *Don't think about time. Don't think about time. Just keep going. It'll all be over soon.*

The sun beamed across the snow-covered landscape. For the first time it felt warm, and maybe the snow would melt again like it had once before. With the warmth of the sun she remembered what summer felt like, but then it was gone. The clouds came back and Bernice was left with only grays and white.

She found Main Street of the small abandoned town. If Bernice were to survive, she would have to keep going, find a house away from the main road just in case they were still following her. She knew exactly where she was as she passed by the deli on the left where she had spent many mornings eating egg sandwiches for her hangover. Come to think of it, they were the worst egg sandwiches she ever had. A disgrace, overpriced for a single egg, half a slice of cheese, and one slice of bacon—if you were lucky enough to get that—but it was greasy, and it was food. The perfect way to survive from the cheap beer and well whiskey that fought her guts the morning after a long night of drinking. Bernice kept on walking down the slightly steep hill the street was situated on. When she reached the bottom, she weaved between buildings and small patches of lawn until she came to where the old sushi restaurant used to be across from the pizzeria which had changed names more times than most of the college kids had changed their hairstyle. She turned right.

The road covered in snow tucked itself neatly down a corridor between buildings, and Bernice followed it, picking up all of the tiny breadcrumb memories of her past she found along the way. There was the old steakhouse she never ate at, which had been made into a church after religion threw a lot of money at the town, or at least, that's how the story went. She wasn't surprised to hear of such a rumor. *Of course, a politician would take money to allow another church to be made and not have to pay taxes. They could always just push more bullshit onto the tourists and the students. Fine the tourists and motorcycle riders, fine the students for being drunk in public.*

She passed the old Mexican restaurant which at one point was a hot dog joint, a place which tried to make a name for itself and be something different by offering simple food and great hospitality. The owners had always tried to remember every single person's name who had walked in, giving them free sides, and memorizing the nuances of their orders. Then it was bought and changed into the fourth Mexican restaurant on the same block—just what they all needed.

The road turned from businesses to livable houses, mostly split into different rented rooms or floors of apartments which only those more privy could afford, except for the brown and yellow house on the left. That place housed around eight people per floor. Bernice remembered she had stayed with a friend who lived there a few times. They slept in a small room which only had a bed and a dresser. They might have been able to squeeze a third person in there, but it would have been uncomfortable to hang out in such a tiny room. The last time she had stayed there, it had rained so bad she couldn't see the tip of her nose in front of her face. The window had been left open as they ran back to the house, and inside they found the bed soaking wet. *Our solution was so dumb. Crank the heat up on a summer night to dry that thing as fast as we could.* She remembered sweating so bad they had gotten naked to cope with the only solution they could come up with. Looking back, she thought it probably would have been better to change the sheets, but they were both too high and drunk to think straight.

Continuing her trek, Bernice opted to go back towards the trees and stay out of the main clearing of the snow-covered road. Not far from the gas station, maybe a mile or two, she knew there was a baseball park, and a small cul-de-sac. *Hopefully it's far enough away from town that there will still be something left.* She sighed, realizing that all of the reminiscing had distracted her from her feet, but now the breadcrumbs were gone and she was brought back to her reality.

Overhead the sun fought against the clouds, trying to peek through. The clouds held their ground and left a deep haze which blanketed the sky. Hail and freezing rain started to fall, and Bernice didn't want to have to warm her entire body up like her feet. She took a right, and went up a small driveway into the first house she found.

Sneaking around back, she found a door unlocked. It looked vacant from the windows, which were still intact. *A good sign, I guess.* She crept inside, making sure to limit as much noise she was making as possible. Tiny creaks beneath her feet resounded through the kitchen as she hobbled as quickly and softly as she could across the tile or linoleum floor—she wasn't sure which or what the difference was. She peaked the corners, looked and found no one. Down a hallway she saw doors and hopefully rooms with clothes and shoes still in them, but the place had been ransacked so far. Furniture was torn up and strewn throughout. There was graffiti on the walls littered with holes made by angry kids, most likely, or abusive men. *Please, don't let there be anyone here.*

Bernice swam through the ether, trying to make as little use of her legs as possible, bracing herself against the walls closest to the doors to peak in, getting as much pressure off of her feet as possible. They were burning again.

The master bedroom was the last room. Inside was a bed, not made, though it still had bedsheets and blankets on it. Her head cocked to the left, saw a closet with a sliding glass mirror opposite the bed. She walked over, her heart excited to possibly have some shoes for her feet, even if they wound up being too big, it was better than the rags and bags she wore.

She slid open the mirror door of the closet.

"Don't fucking move," a large man said as he aimed a gun in her face. "Back the fuck up." He motioned with the barrel.

Bernice backed up slowly, felt the backs of her thighs hit the bed, and tears immediately streamed down her cheeks. She sobbed uncontrollably thinking this was the end, or the start of the same story she had become accustomed to.

"Just do it. I'm tired. Just do it." Her voice was low through sobs.

"Are you alone?"

"I've been alone."

"Hey, listen." He set the gun aside and went to put his hand on her. Instantly she pulled away from human touch. He backed off. "I'm Jamal," he said as he sat on the floor across from her. He left a clear barrier between him and her.

She looked up. "I'm Bernice. Just end this, please."

"I don't want to end anything for anyone. I just want to survive and I thought you were gonna do some whack shit, or that someone was with you."

Bernice stared at the rifle. "Do you really trust me that much that I wouldn't try to grab that gun?"

"I over trust a lot of people I shouldn't."

"What if I tried to grab that gun? Why are you being so trusting?"

"That gun ain't loaded."

"You threatened me with a gun that isn't loaded?"

"It worked, didn't it?" He tried a joke to alleviate the mood, his eyes showing her a kindness.

"Yeah, I guess it did." She chuckled as she tried to wipe the tears from her eyes. They kept coming even though she didn't want them to.

Jamal looked at her and Bernice knew just what he saw. A broken woman. "There are shoes in the closet I was in and probably some clothes you can change into. There's a bathtub I've been using by melting snow. It takes a long time to get enough water in there, but if you want, I can show you what I've been doing." He stood up offering his hand to her.

Nervously she reached out and grabbed it. His grip was light.

"That would be nice."

"I'll leave you alone to change and go through the clothes. I'm gonna go to the basement and start heating up some pots of snow to try and get it melted down a bit."

Jamal grabbed the gun and left the room, pulling the door shut behind him.

Bernice sat back down on the bed, feeling the softness of it and realized how worn her clothes actually were. Covered in ice, snow, sweat, dirt, blood, everything the human body could pretty much excrete was on her. Her hands shook as she pulled the plastic bags off her feet, trying not to destroy them in the process —an alternative to tearing them off in case she needed them again. The rags had dried blood and pus on them, which made it difficult and painful to take them off her feet. The cloth pulled at fresh scabs where old blisters had been.

The closet slid open for her and she rummaged through,

found a pair of black running shoes which were slightly too large, but comfortable compared to what she had been dealing with. She also found a pair of mismatched wool socks. She kept them, making sure not to put them on her feet just yet.

In the cold unfinished basement, the walls were gray like cement, or maybe they were made from actual cement. Bernice wasn't sure what they were made of, but it was the foundation of the house, and her and Jamal were very clearly below everything. The window peaked to let them see the snowline. In the center of the room, he had two massive pots with lids, and three smaller ones with glass tops perched on metal racks from an outdoor grill. Underneath he had a fire going, small, but able to do the job.

"I figured I can't burn through concrete, and the fire is small enough that it won't spread. I moved everything away from the center of the room when I first came here." He looked up to her as she came down the staircase.

Bernice helped keep the fire going with Jamal and moved water up the stairs to the bathtub. They covered their hands with old potholders from drawers or decorative gloves which were strewn around during whatever hurricane had torn through the house. The water they poured in barely filled the tub halfway.

"We'll get more snow going, and then you should have a decent bath. By the time we get the new water added, it'll be hot enough to enjoy." He smiled at her, but kept his distance, respecting her boundaries.

Bernice felt weird around Jamal. He was too nice, as if he wanted something. But she was oddly comforted by him. It was nice to be around someone and talk about something other than wanting to escape from the Traders. *Push it out of your head. Don't go down that road now. Just hold on a bit longer. It'll be over soon.* She followed him back to the basement, and filled the pots with more snow from outside.

The snow melted faster this time around, the pots still hot from the first round.

They filled the tub again.

"I'll let you be," Jamal said as he poured the last pot in, maybe bringing the water line to two-thirds of the way full. It was good enough. The water would cover Bernice slightly above her hips, and she could sink down into the water if she wanted to.

Bernice took her clothes off, seeing the bruises and cuts on her thighs and lower legs. Her feet still hurt—they probably always would, unless it was so bad, she'd die from it. She dipped a foot in, and pain seared through it. Open wounds touched by hot water and dead skin. She pulled her foot out, let it cool, then tried to put it in again.

Bernice repeated the process until she could tolerate the temperature of the water on her aching feet. Her skin was aflame no matter how many times she tried to get them used to the water. She wished the pain would end. She rubbed her feet again hoping they would stop aching. The water around her body turned red like her skin.

She sat in the bathtub, letting the water move around her, splashing herself on all the nooks she noticed were unclean. At the camp they were hardly allowed to shower or bathe. There was the occasional bucket of cold water they had to share between them. Her hair was matted.

Bernice took a breath, put herself under the water and scrubbed her hair with her hands to let the liquid flow freely through it. It was like being in the ocean again feeling the ripples against her body as the water swirled and splashed against her. For the first time in ages, she felt content.

She stood up to get out of the tub and dry herself off. The pus and blood and dirt had turned the water. The colors swirled together, melding to form some kind of brown or an off red, depending on the perspective. Bernice tried to see what was left behind in the water. Her feet ached badly now, but the pain was life coming back into them, she told herself. *Maybe there is hope.* She rummaged through the cabinets, looking for any medical supplies. There was a knock on the bathroom door.

"You good?"

"I'm just looking for bandages."

"I'll go get them and I'll leave them outside the door for you." There was silence for a minute as Bernice waited in the bathroom, staring at the water and her feet.

Jamal knocked again a few minutes later. "I grabbed everything I found. I'm putting gauze, an ace bandage, some band-aids, and some tape outside the door on the floor for you."

She waited a moment listening to his footsteps as he departed. *He's way too nice. He has to be hiding something.* The bandages were exactly where he said they'd be. She grabbed them all and sat on the toilet, wrapped in an old, definitely used, dark bathroom towel. *I'll have to wash this thing when I'm done.*

Bernice placed gauze all around her feet, covering the bottoms, the sides of her toes, placing one or two on the top, and taping one to her Achilles heel where the skin was raw. She bit the ace bandage in half, and made use of both strips, wrapping herself as best as she could, using more medical tape to make sure it stayed in place.

In the bedroom, she pulled on the wool socks to cover the patchwork she had made. The closet held more goodies. A pair of boxers which slipped on with ease, hugging her where her hips protruded. A gray pair of sweatpants were tossed right over, and she felt almost cozy. Just like old snow days when she couldn't make it into work, and stayed in bed all day binge watching TV while the silent snow fell and muffled the outside world. There was a long sleeve shirt, black with some old rock band's name and a design of a skull plastered on the front. She left the room in search of Jamal, but turned around, remembering she had to let the bathtub drain so he wouldn't ask too many questions. *No need for him to see this mess. I'll start a fire downstairs and we can wash this towel in some hot water too.*

Bernice brought a pot of hot water up to the bathroom. Jamal followed her only and watched as she rinsed the towel she had used in the tub. The sound of a door opening made them both pause.

Quickly, Jamal grabbed his gun, this time grabbing bullets to load into it, and plodded, barefoot, into the hallway, directly in front of the bedroom door. They waited for someone to peak their head around the corner.

20

NEW YORK CITY, EARLY 2019

Janet ran down the block to get away from the madness of the city. Rob wasn't far behind her. The local bodegas were already looted, even the one that had the fat black and white cat with markings to give it a mustache. Everyone was hungry, and thirsty, and the power had only been out for two weeks. Janet, Rob, and Taco had gone through all of their water and alcohol—mostly alcohol—and now desperately needed water or anything they could get their hands on.

"I'm so thirsty. I wish we hadn't drunk all of that wine and burned the candles expecting the lights and power to come back so soon," Janet said to her fiancé.

"Me too, sweetie, me too. But we can't change that now. We have to find something to drink, or we're going to have to take it from someone."

"We are not going to do that, Robert." Janet only used his full name when she was decisive and angry with him.

"Janet, look at me." Rob pulled them into a small alley and

looked at her. "We don't have time for standards and morals right now. If we don't find water, we are going to die of dehydration. We need to find water and food," Rob reiterated.

"Why don't we just steal some matches or something and set up a small stove to melt the snow?"

"Honey, I—" He stopped speaking for a moment. "I think that's a brilliant idea. We still have matches and lighters at the loft. Why don't we head home and gather some snow from outside? We'll try and get the clean stuff."

"Thank you, Rob," she said. The answer had been in front of them the entire time. *What happens when it gets warmer out and the snow disappears? What then?*

He smiled at her and did not reply.

"What are you thinking?"

"Nothing, I'm ready to get inside."

He's got something on his mind but doesn't want to say it. Thinks it's going to start an argument. Janet sighed, "Okay, let's go."

Janet and Rob entered their loft, locked the door behind them making sure to move their large couch in front of it for added measure. A blockade against the outside world which anyone could break through if they truly wanted to.

"I'm going to start collecting some snow off of the balcony, babe," Rob stated as he walked towards the kitchen to grab some large pots, pans, and plastic containers.

"Okay. I'm going to change into some sweats," Janet mentioned as her voice drifted off down the hallway to the bedroom.

When she returned, she saw Rob digging snow from their tiny balcony. He placed the snow into the pots and then brought them inside. Then he began to load up their containers—a mix of cheap plastic and glass which cost an exorbitant amount comparatively.

Janet sat on the couch against the door, the gray matched well with the off-white paint. She had put her hair up in a bun and tucked her feet into the excess layer of cloth her sweatpants produced at the bottom. Her arms were tucked under her armpits. She watched Rob finish filling the last of the containers and close the door.

"Can you just stop what you're doing and come sit with me?"

Rob looked over and without hesitating, put everything down, sat on the couch next to Janet and put his right arm around her shoulder. She immediately burst into tears and stuffed her face into the side of his body, wishing she could disappear into him. She hadn't showered, she was constantly thirsty, and every meal they ate was getting worse than the previous.

"I just want this all to stop. It's been two weeks, Rob—something is seriously messed up," she blurted out between snot and tears. "The police aren't even stopping anyone anymore."

"I know, sweetie. The world isn't right, but there's nothing I can do to change it. For the time being, we just have to hunker down and start rationing things. I want to head towards the docks in the next few days to see if I can find anything—maybe set up a fishing line or something."

She looked up at him. "You've never been fishing in your life." She laughed and cried at the same time.

"When I was younger, I went a few times, but you're right." He chuckled. "I know hardly anything besides putting a worm on a hook." He looked at her. "We need food, and the snow will help us get some water once we get it melted down. It's a start, but it's not going to last us long. Janet, we need to start learning to survive if we're going to get through this mess, and that starts with figuring out our basics. Water, food, and shelter. We have shelter, we'll have a bit of water, now we need to figure out food."

Janet was still crying, though silently now. She was angry and sad all at the same time, and wanted to see the world disappear into the dark, but she knew Rob was right. They needed to make headway, otherwise they would die. Plain and simple. Dead. Nothing. No joy. No love. No life.

It wasn't long until Janet fell asleep against Rob.

When Janet finally stirred she saw the sun begin to rise behind the clouds of gray and black smoke. At her movements, Rob woke up too.

"Good morning, sweetie."

"Morning."

"Did you sleep well?" he asked.

"Yes, probably for the first time since all of this, but I had dreams I wish we were still living. It was Christmas, and we were opening our gifts. The loft was warm, and the smell of coffee filled the air. Outside it was overcast, but it hadn't snowed yet. The TV played music, and we both sat in our underwear laughing as we opened our gifts. You got me the biggest stuffed penguin, and you laughed as you opened your gift of the dumbest bad taxidermy. We were happy, and now we're here, awake—just trying to survive. It's not good, Rob. None of this is good."

"Shhh, it's okay. I'm sure I would have loved that bad taxidermy, and once this is all over, I'll make sure you get the biggest penguin you've ever seen." He chuckled and hugged her trying to lighten the mood.

"Rob, please stop. You're trying too hard right now."

"I'm sorry." He stopped hugging her.

"We should get up and moving. We need to make water and get some food." Her tone changed drastically, as if a something had ticked inside her, realizing that survival was going to take everything they had now.

She stood up and went to the bedroom. She took off her sweatpants and began to layer herself. She put on a pair of leggings, followed by jeans, and lastly snow pants she had purchased years ago during the one time Rob and her had gone skiing in the Catskills. After she had fallen for the hundredth time, she decided skiing wasn't her forte. She couldn't recall why she kept the pants, though Janet was glad she did. She laced her boots and waited for Rob to finish getting his clothes together.

"Grab a backpack, Rob. We need to get supplies." *How are we even going to do this?*

She watched him grab a large backpack in silence and wondered what he was thinking. He had grown dark and broody. *He still thinks all our problems can be solved by stealing from someone else. It's not moral. Our neighbors are our neighbors and we can't take what little they have.*

"I'm going to fill up our water bottles with the last of our supply. Tonight, we can melt down some more snow," Rob stated as he walked towards the kitchen.

Janet appeared from the bedroom and pulled the couch away from the door. The feet scraped on the wood floors she fell in love with. They gouged marks, like nails against skin trying to fight back an attack. The wounds were deep, and the light brown underneath would leave scars—even if they were covered, they'd remain noticeable in the future for everyone to see.

They left together, pulled the door shut tight, locked it and each took their key with them. They knew if either of them got separated to return and wait inside. They would always meet up here, wherever they were, they would always meet up. Their souls were bound to each other, through thirst and hunger, they needed to stick together. Janet kissed Rob as they had always done, and together they walked out of the building, not hand in hand, but as partners against the world. A small kitchen knife sat on each of their hips.

Janet and Rob made their way south to the harbor, hoping they'd find some shipping containers loaded with food when they got there. Clothing, furniture, and paper littered the streets. On the way back she would have to stuff as much of that paper in her pack as she could. It would make great kindling. The apartment was getting noticeably cooler, and eventually, they'd have to make a fire inside. *However, that would work. But it still needs to get done.* She fiddled the handle of her knife and started jogging ahead of Rob.

"Honey, wait up."

"No, Rob, catch up to me. We have to get there and back before the sun goes down again. It's bad enough that we had to leave our apartment. It's only going to get worse as the day drags on."

The sounds of the city were cacophonous already, and they would only get worse. The wind whipped into the shattered windows and it just reminded Janet of how horrible their situation was. She heard Rob sigh before he picked up his pace to match hers.

Around them windows were busted. Doors had holes in them, either from being kicked in or punched, possibly even hit with blunt or sharp objects. The smell of fire lingered everywhere they went. Around them lay the shells of charred buildings. *The fire department must have gotten to them before they spread*, she thought but then decided they must have burnt themselves out. As they walked, Janet noticed an entire block was gone, burnt to a crisp and wondered to herself how many had died there. *Entire families could have been taken by those flames.*

The flames must have whipped and fanned against the buildings, and she imagined the horror children and parents must have faced when posed with the threat of dense smoke, and fire —not being able to see as the air became too hot to breathe. Feeling skin become taught as water dispersed from the body and nerve endings flared with searing pain until it became too much to bear, and then the pain stopped, but they continued living for a few moments longer. Terror would have set in until it no longer existed.

Janet shook her head, trying to push the thoughts of death from her mind, and focus on what was important: Rob. The person she loved more than anything in the world, as cliché as it was, she truly did. Rob would do anything for her, even with society crumbling and his own life on the line. She turned around and saw that Rob had fallen back a bit, the expression on his face told her he was lost in his thoughts.

"Can you hurry up, Rob," she called. She saw the moment he was shaken out of his thoughts.

He didn't speak, only quickened his pace and closed the gap between them. On the street, animals began to appear more frequently than usual. Rats were commonplace in the city, but now they seemed to be in abundance. Janet saw raccoons begin to peer out of their hiding places. She thought she saw a deer prance out of the corner of her eye, but wasn't sure if it was one or a lanky dog. What a wonder it was, to see nature begin to come back into a steel and glass city so quickly.

Janet continued on, wondering why Rob couldn't keep focus today. He had made such a big stink out of this survival business, and now he kept on losing track of himself in the world. She was beginning to get frustrated with him. Everything around them was in shambles, and the only thing they had to rely on was each other. *Maybe I'm wrong. Am I the only one I can rely on?*

The streets opened up from the claustrophobic bindings, and

in front of them, a roadblock of cop cars, fire trucks, and dumpsters blocked off the street.

"Hands up!" someone screamed.

Rob and Janet stopped in place. They were in the open with nowhere to hide, nowhere to duck away to. They were too busy running down the middle of the road trying to get where they wanted to be—rather than being smart, taking their time, and calculating the risks—to notice they were everywhere they shouldn't have been.

"Where the fuck are you two off to in such a hurry?" A man holding a rifle stepped on top of one of the police cruisers.

"To the docks, trying to find food," said Rob.

"No food there. Get your ass to the right, and you," he pointed his rifle at Janet, "turn around and walk back, I want to see the ass I'm going to have fun with later."

Janet turned to her right doing a half circle, walking back with her hands in the air. Fear filled her as she looked at Rob, who was following her with his eyes. He shot a look to the left, and mouthed to her, "run." She knew exactly what he was planning. She walked slightly faster, but didn't want to startle the man talking to the people behind the police cruiser, the ones they couldn't see.

Janet was about to reach the edge of the barricade when she took off, and Rob followed. They had a road which looked clear, and they took their chance, sprinting down it, staying on the right-hand side of the street, ready to dive into a doorway or alley at their earliest convenience.

Behind them there was a shouting of men and women. A single shot came from the barricade, but no bullets passed by them. Ammunition was too valuable for people who looked to have nothing, Janet guessed to herself. They needed those bullets for real threats. She peaked over her left shoulder and saw at least three people racing towards them.

"Do you know where you're going?" Janet asked as they ran.

"Yes."

She knew he was going in the general direction of home. She wasn't the best with directions—but she knew the city. Rob was a map, he knew the twists and turns, shortcuts, and roads with construction like it was programmed into him since birth. She never understood how he could pass by some place once, and know exactly how to get back, but he did, and he never failed her. Janet wouldn't second guess him now, not with everything at stake.

They turned to the right at the end of the block, then ran across the street, tucked themselves into an alley, hopped a fence, continued to the left, made two more rights, and one left. Rob had taken them close to their apartment, and apparently lost the gang near the fence. They ran the last few blocks, and then continued on, their apartment entrance on the left waving hello as they passed. They looped around the block just in case they were still being followed. There were dumpsters in the back which they hid behind, waiting and listening to see if anyone came. People shouted and chattered far off, but no one ever came within two blocks of their home. They went inside, considering it a good day, all things considered, and went to lay in bed. *Maybe we should have waited, just in case they were staking us out and waiting for us to make a move,* Janet thought to herself as they tried to get settled.

Janet stayed up all night collecting snow. She stuffed the white powder into metal and plastic containers. She decided the best place to build a fire would be in the oven. She set a small rack at the lowest slot, and placed a cookie sheet underneath it wrapped in tinfoil. It reminded her of ugly chrome.

On the cookie sheet she placed some newspaper and lit it, having two small pots on the rack. She kept the oven door slightly open, keeping an eye on the snow, making sure it melted and came to a boil, then replaced the pots with more pots. She funneled the water into three-liter jugs they had found and cleaned out to the best of their abilities. The apartment filled with smoke. Janet cracked the door to the balcony and took the batteries out of their smoke detectors.

Rob had collapsed onto the bed while Janet collected snow. He slept while she labored away in the kitchen. Outside the world was dark and loud. Somewhere a man was getting his head beaten in with bats and a woman ran frantically to avoid a mob that was chasing her. Somewhere a man was defending someone less fortunate, but he was the only one in the world doing so.

Everything had fallen apart, and Rob slept through it, while Janet prepared to face the world head on.

Morning came and went again, while Janet stayed up without sleeping, trying to make as much water as possible. Rob walked into the kitchen and found his pack emptied out. All that remained was his kitchen knife and multiple water bottles attached by elastic cord to the straps.

"Are you okay, babe?"

Janet looked over at him, but didn't respond. She turned away and began filling more water bottles. Rob took her silence and made his way to the living room. Janet watched as he stepped outside on to the balcony.

She wondered what he was thinking about. After a while he came back inside and scribbled on a piece of paper while Janet went about her business in the kitchen.

"Can you come in here, babe?" Rob's voice pierced the apartment.

"Okay," she replied.

"I need you to grab your pack, and get ready. We're going out within the hour. We need to watch that group of people to see how dangerous they are and how close they are to our home."

"Are you serious?" Janet was pissed.

"I'm very serious, babe. If they got a hold of us, I'd be dead, and I don't even want to think about what they'd be doing to you." He fumbled through his pack and began to stuff water into it.

"But what if they find us? Hasn't that crossed your mind?"

"That's why we're going to watch them."

"From where, Rob? We can't go down that road again. What do you expect us to do?"

He pulled the paper out that he had crudely drawn on. On it was the street they had gone down and every block they had run through. There was a layout of blocks of the city drawn as squares with smeared black where Rob's palm had gone over before the ink dried.

"I don't know where their other roadblocks are just yet, but we know this is one side. I assume they have more barricades here, here and here." He made small circles on areas where roads would be.

"Why do you think that?"

"A lot of foot traffic when the lights were on. Obviously, the city is always heavy with traffic, but this allows you to cut through areas and avoid others. Also, if they took these roads, it would mean they could get into these buildings here." He put triangles on them.

"I'm waiting for the part where you tell me why they're so important."

"Because they're the tallest buildings in that area, and they can see everything and everyone for blocks. If they had a couple of radios, they'd be able to tell anyone exactly what street people were going down. These buildings would also mean they had complete control over all of these blocks." He circled largely on the paper. "They'd be able see north, south, east, and west. It's mostly common sense if you know the city." Anger rose in her and the look in his eye told her he regretted saying that last part.

Janet knew the city, you had to in order to live in it. She knew where to go and where to be, which trains or public transit took her there the fastest even when other lines were down. She also knew where to walk and what blocks to avoid after a certain time. It was usual stuff, but nothing crazy. New York City wasn't ingrained in her brain like Rob had ingrained it in his. She knew major landmarks, but he knew every building and apartment —apparently.

Outside the wind was howling, and the clouds were dark with winter. There was no snow, but it threatened to squall at any moment. Janet and Rob were dressed from head to toe in their warmest clothes, and still, they felt the wind biting through their layers. It felt like fire on their fingers, and they were forced to go back inside and get gloves. They joked about it after their trek and kneeled on a roof a few blocks away, looking at the barricade through binoculars Rob had hidden somewhere from some vacation they gone on together in an ancient world. But the jokes didn't last long and the air around them quickly grew awkward and silent.

Men paced back and forth. Not many, maybe three, but it was hard to tell at that distance, and they all seemed to dress the same. Black jackets and green pants, shouldering rifles that looked meaner than anything used for hunting. The snow began to fall again, and light snowflakes made seeing through binoculars difficult. The snow and wind picked up. With the wind, it looked like flying at lightspeed.

"We should get moving around them, put our backs to the wind," Janet stated.

"You're right, but it's not going to be easy. We don't know where they are or what buildings they have lookouts in. This snow is fucking everything up."

"If we just make a bigger loop out, and find some tight alleys and streets until we get on the other side, that might work. If we go slow enough, I think we can do it."

"I guess we could try that, but I'd rather wait until dark."

"Can you get us there when the dark sets in like that?"

"Yeah, I can get us there. It's just going to be a lot slower than you or I want it to be."

Darkness crept in slowly, trying to push the sun from behind the clouds, but it seemed to drag along more than they could have guessed, even with the sun setting early. Leisurely it strolled around the earth, as if time did not exist at all. It seemed to have gone and completely forgotten to lay over the city like a nice blanket. Janet wondered if it had forgotten to show up entirely, and just as they were getting ready to leave to pass the time, darkness showed up like an old guest, casually late to dinner but always the life of the party.

Rob led the way through twists and turns of the sprawling maze of New York—always a city rat—more domesticated than most. *All people who lived in the city are rats,* she thought. *Unloving and unforgiving of the people around them. Everyone just looked for the block of cheese at the end of the L shapes and long corridors.*

Rob and Janet sat on a rooftop, not far from a huge lookout post. The tall towers of ancient days now used to call down to those below about intruders and ransackers. It was in the shadow of another building they sat where no one could see, not from that angle. They sat and waited staring off into that far distance of home and familiarity culminated with anxiety and loss. They could see nothing coming towards them and only everything they needed out of reach.

Lights drifted in and out, from fires and torches. Shadows of men and women weened in and out of existence as they passed through windows, some dark and some bright with fire. Apparitions of consciousness. Rob lay his head on Janet's shoulder, and they waited. Her breath long and deep, his short and shallow. She did not motion to get any closer to him, nor did she pull away.

"We watch them all night, Rob."

"Of course, babe."

"Are you actually listening to me or just agreeing?"

Rob looked up. "I always listen to you, every single thing you say. There's nothing I need to add to it. I heard you. We need to watch them, and we need to get food. I want us to survive. I want to see another day with you."

"Please stop romanticizing our existence right now."

"What do you mean?"

"You want to see 'another day' with me. You already have me in your life. We need to survive, and our love life shouldn't be the focus of this right now. What we need to focus on is food. Watching them now seems to be nothing more than a waste of time."

She knew her words stung, but they made sense. Rob was focusing too much on her, and not enough on themselves. In his own way, he was being selfish, believing more in his love than their lives and their survival.

They watched and studied, seeing the rounds these people made like clockwork. There was a routine they had built in their small community. People paced back and forth, and after what Janet's watch deemed to be three hours, someone came and rotated out. At the end of the second hour, someone had decided to sit down and light a cigarette. *They still have cigarettes,* she thought. How she would love to feel that smoke in the back of her throat, burning her tongue and sliding into her lungs, harsh and welcomed.

Around sunrise, a group of men and women came out to one side of the building, and huddled near a car. She could see a fire behind the sedan's door. They were using it to stop any wind from blowing down at the fire and fanning the flames. *Maybe they're cooking,* Janet thought to herself. People began to wander away with bowls, shoveling something into their mouths. Maybe stew, maybe soup, maybe hot water. But they were eating by any account of the word. The old ritual of bonding over food, archaic and the basis of all holidays and social gatherings.

"Let's head home," Rob said.

"What's the plan?"

"I think we need to decide if we're going to try and sneak in during the night, or if we're going to keep our distance and find a way around to the docks."

"I don't think it's a good idea to try and sneak in to this place."

"I agree, but we need to weigh our options or we're going to starve."

Rob and Janet ran home, taking a different route over the one that led them to the building they adorned like angels looking over hell. They were watching the suffering from afar, doing nothing to alleviate the pain of those who had condemned themselves in life. *Maybe through this suffering, the world was on its way to redemption,* Janet thought quietly as they went home.

Their apartment was quiet and closed off. Shut away from whatever society was left and the rambunctious laboring of a world struggling to kill itself. It was like seeing the origin of the wind. They struggled to stand up against the turmoil going on around them, and on the other side, nothing. An area completely separated from itself—a chasm of almost serenity encompassed by terror and strife.

The door opened slowly, pressing against the nothingness on the other side. It held them back, eventually gave way to their home, and allowed them once again to enter into a sanctuary for weary travelers who changed so drastically from when they left to when they had returned. Janet felt the growing rift between them. As they undressed, she felt Rob embrace her from behind. Naked and vulnerable they played each other's bodies like friends spending their first night together after both had longed for the other the entirety of their friendship. It was almost awkward. Their movements seemed jerky and rash whenever one had chosen to do something the other had not planned.

Morning came again. The sun stood behind the clouds trying to peer in onto the life below. A pervert outside a window. Fingers and toes intertwined with legs wrapped in hair and sweat. Their bodies like old cords placed in one spot, tangled and taught, unsure how to unfold the matted nest they had gotten into. Janet was the first to wake herself from that void of pleasure and anger which they had relished in after returning home.

She shouldered her pack and waters after quickly dressing, and disappeared from the apartment while Rob slept away, undulating through dreams of love and hope. Outside the world woke to hate and violence once more.

Snow blew and wisped through alleys and streets, among broken car windows and torn clothes, biting at barren skin, and stubble from not being able to shave. Janet pulled her jacket tighter, and grabbed duct tape she had carried, taping over a gash in the right leg of her black pants, attempting to seal the breach so no more wind could get in. It was minor, and futile, but the wind stayed out while the cold continued to creep in. She trucked on hoping the city would come back to life soon.

The world looked like it had been a giant ant farm of twisting mazes, and the static birds which soared and overhead watched the new television show. Smoke and scavenging at every turn. People dying, and taking advantage of every neighbor they had known. One pigeon perched itself squarely on a small fence, and zoomed in on Janet weaseling through her pack in the snow which had built up overnight. She looked at it, wondering why a New York pigeon was watching her, rather than being an asshole and trying to come at her for food. *Whatever, it's nothing, just a dumb bird in a dead city.*

Her footprints left traces in the banks, but luckily, as if maybe God was looking down for once and not turning a blind eye to suffering, it began to snow again and covered her tracks so she didn't have to.

Rob woke up from his dreams of love and hope where Janet was smiling and Rob was sitting behind her, enjoying her comfort as they watched television on the floor of their apartment. Outside it was gray and snowing, but the lights were on and it was warm, like putting on sweatpants which had just been taken out of the dryer on the first really cold day of winter. His dream was cut short by glass breaking outside, close, maybe even across the street. He rubbed love from his eyes, slipped into pants and grabbed a bat. *Where's Janet?*

He looked around the apartment, her clothes were gone along with her backpack. His head reeled as he tried to figure out what happened outside and where the fuck she went. On the counter he saw a note, scrawled quickly—almost out of necessity.

Out. Be back soon. Love you.

Where the fuck is "out"? Why didn't she tell me where she would be if I needed to meet her? He pushed the couch up against the door again, then appeared on their small balcony. Outside he could see fresh glass on the pavement across the street. Someone had decided to smash their way through a building abandoned before the bulbs burned out. Rob turned back into his apartment and sat down, anxiously waiting, and overthinking about why his fiancé wasn't there. Why someone had broken into an abandoned building—where they had gone. What if they were in their building? What if they were coming up the stairs? What if they came into the apartment? What if Janet was dead out there? What if she was captured? What if this was all a dream? Why did he have to wake up from a dream he was having to such a terrible white wasteland? He took a breath.

Metal glinted while being carried from point A to point B and back and forth and back and forth. Rob filled and emptied the containers over and again. If he was going to wait around and be anxious, he was going to at least make sure he got as much water as possible while it was still snowing. Outside it was piling up fast, quicker than he was able to fill and empty the tubs, containers and any kitchenware they still had. He thought to himself, maybe he could go to one of the neighbors who never returned and steal from them. Why hadn't they thought of that before? Some guilt ran over him and he knew why he and Janet didn't do that. They didn't want to steal from the people they knew in case they came back. It had been weeks, and none of them returned after venturing out into the world again. *Mostly Janet. She never wanted to take from anyone. But she's not here now.*

Rob pulled the door firmly behind him, feeling the metal tumbler click into place once again. He went to the closest door down the hallway and tried to open it. The handle would not twist to the right, so he attempted to turn it to the left, and it yielded the same result: no entry. He went back to his apartment, grabbed a bat and a hammer. He smashed the handle, severing it like an extremity with a sharp instrument. It broke off instantly. It had been waiting for him to take it off the entire time.

Inside there was only vacancy, complete silence and a longing to be filled with joy once more. The air felt stagnant, it almost burdened Rob to be there. He was not welcomed. He had entered against the wishes of the apartment, though it did nothing to stop him.

Pantry doors opened and closed. Some cans were found to be edible, mostly corned beef, small sausages, and canned ham. Another cabinet had a bag of unopened tortilla chips, the small bite sized ones which held salsa really well—they were Rob's favorite. Another had a few bags of microwavable rice and protein bars. It wasn't a lot, but it was calories and they needed as many as they could get.

After Rob had made multiple trips back and forth with his score, he went into the bedrooms to see if any clothes could be found or worthy of a cause. He made the trip multiple times with multiple apartments, only allowing himself to go down two floors. Some were left unlocked, and what startled him the most: one had already been looted. Not like the looting he had done where he opened cabinets and took what was needed. This apartment was absolutely devastated.

Inside, clothes were strewn everywhere, furniture was turned upside down. Plates shattered and silverware on the floor and sink. It was a shitshow, and before he decided to continue in, he left the apartment choosing to return to his own sanctuary. He closed the door behind him. Darkness was coming, and he had hoped Janet would be back shortly. *Why is she still gone?*

Their apartment felt barren though he had stuffed it with as many supplies as he could find, those which were necessary, and some which were frivolous—like a bathing suit he had found with black and white vertical stripes. It wasn't needed at all, but he felt if summer came, maybe they would come in handy, or if they decided to finally venture out of the city and go south, somewhere warm, where he and Janet could fish for their food, and make a life worth living other than the barren husk of a once great city. Then the bathing suit would be a much needed treat for the future.

Night strolled in right on time, unlike the other night when they had gone to stakeout the group of men and women. Janet had still not returned, even though Rob had spent as much time as he could distracting himself from the loneliness of his life. Being alone had proven to be more difficult than losing power, losing light, and losing sleep. Social isolation. The loss of social media, the connection with the world and people around him, and lastly, his better half. Now, he was alone with himself and his thoughts. Years of conditioning through his cellphone and company with Janet had never actually let Rob be alone with himself. How was he supposed to cope? How does anyone cope with the loneliness of their own company if they've never had the pleasure of enjoying it before?

He sat down in the dark living room trying to get his mind to quiet itself, but every time he tried to, he could only focus on how his mind wouldn't quiet. *Where is Janet? Is she alive? What's going on? Should I go outside? Should I find someone to help? Should I stay put? Should I go somewhere? We never made a plan to go anywhere if we got separated, except here. What if she can't get back? What if she needs my help and she's alive and being tortured?*

Rob found himself on the verge of hyperventilating. He stood up, then sat down, only to get up a few minutes later to pace. And when pacing didn't distract him, he began to do push-ups, squats, and then jumping jacks. He started to sweat, and he thought about it pouring out his body along with all of his anxiety. There was a series of knocks on the apartment door and he ran over to pull the couch from it. He threw open the door without looking through the eyehole hoping it was Janet. Outside was a man shouldering a shotgun aimed directly at Rob.

"You stole from us." Rob tried to raise his hands and ask what had happened or who they were, but all he heard was the sound of the shotgun going off and the feel of pain before the darkness took. His body slumped and his consciousness embraced the black nothingness of non-existence.

* * *

Janet sat waiting and watched the group of people. Above, the sun was beginning to set and she knew she would have to get back to the apartment eventually. The people Janet watched walked and strode and strutted through the snow. They made no motion to come towards her building in the shadow of the giant watchtower she had assumed was being used. With her binoculars—from a vacation she took so long ago—she couldn't see anyone overlooking her. Darkness came as it always did, pressing down, making it feel like something wasn't right. It was the unfurling of anxiety and nervousness, the strange groan of loss in her chest. The world had lost something when the darkness came, and Janet felt it, like a different light had gone out. Once it had completely set, she got off the roof and made her way home. Rob was probably worried about her by now, she knew. He was reliant on her company.

It was cold. The way back took long. By the time Janet returned, she felt it was around midnight, and her watch affirmed that feeling. When she returned, she found Rob dead in the entrance to their home. She ran to him after she crested the last steps. Tears ran down her face as she saw what little remained of his skull. It would always remain midnight on the cold day after the lights went out when she found Rob lying dead at the entrance to their apartment with his face caved in. Blood congealed under his body and in his boots and hands. It was almost stringy. He smelled terrible, and his body was already stiff. She sobbed long and hard, screamed at the ceiling, and tried to clean the blood from her hands and shirt while looking at Rob. She searched for anything about him that was familiar.

She stood up, took snow from outside, and heated it over the fire. Everything she made she poured into the bathtub she shared memories of Rob with and sat in what little water was there. Her skin turned red, but not from the blood which covered her. She closed her eyes and started to hyperventilate Janet realized she was acting out in a state of shock, trying to distract herself from her dead partner laying in the entranceway.

The water started to turn red from the blood which covered her, and Janet felt guilt as she held her knees to her chest. *Why did I leave? Who killed Rob? Why had they killed him? What the fuck happened while I was gone? I have to do something.* Tears ran down her face like thoughts and words she didn't want to utter to the world.

Janet wrapped his body up in their rug and dragged him in the living room. He was heavier than expected. Literal dead weight. She grabbed everything she needed to get through the winter and got ready to leave for the last time. Janet piled papers up next to Rob's body, and started a small fire. She waited next to him to make sure the floors caught, then made her way outside but not before thinking about staying to die and meet him in the afterlife, whether that be heaven or hell for how they had lived. She left the door open behind her as she departed so his soul had a way out of the building. If she couldn't live here with him, then no one could live here. *I'm sorry. I'm forever sorry. I shouldn't have left. Please forgive me.*

A building across the street held a decent view. She sat and watched her life slowly catch and then flare into an inferno. Fire whipped the sky with black smoke and spread out across the city like a swarm of locusts. Janet almost felt free from the apartment, but missed Rob terribly. Her actions were rash, and she almost wished she didn't burn everything down. She felt she hadn't treated him fairly in the last few days but needed to push that idea from her mind if she wanted to live. Guilt would kill her faster than this world would.

Janet walked out of the city as she followed the Hudson line a week or so later by her own estimate—time had blurred as she lost sleep, finding any drafty building she could when she felt exhaustion finally pressing down on her eyelids. Pangs of hunger didn't arrive for a couple of days. Grief was too filling. At any rate, it had been days before she decided to leave the city, because the weather had gotten worse and it almost always seemed to be night without much day to tell the passing of time in the world. It was and remained the loneliest time of her life. The snow fell, built up along the roads and slipped through the tracks along the metal lines above the streets of Harlem.

The line looped and twisted on and on. The turns and bends of the metal rails led their way north along the river which flowed both ways. That's how it had gotten its name from the Natives, though Janet couldn't remember what that name actually was. That kernel of information was lost to the years of schooling she had not been in for such a long time—*who knows what they were even taught anymore.* Last thing she remembered about school was people putting up signs, placing stickers, and talking incessantly of boycotting the State exams because of new math. Simply—as she understood it—if you knew how to do math and add, it was considered wrong because you had to find a multiple of five and start adding and subtracting. *Completely backwards.* *Just add the goddamn numbers on your fucking fingers like a real adult,* she thought, taking any tangent which presented itself to get her mind off of Rob. Janet didn't understand the idea behind it, but it was frustrating nonetheless seeing the posts about it on the Internet. *Damn,* how she missed it. *The Internet. Warmth. Light. Rob... Rob. Rob. I'm sorry I'm distracting myself from you.*

21

WESTCHESTER, NEW YORK, 2019

C roton was probably a few days out, Janet reckoned by her pace, though she wasn't entirely sure. She never walked that far. Ever. Along the way she slept near bushes, in small coverings near rock, or abandoned buildings. The weather forced her hand and she risked her life by making a fire two nights in a row with an old grill lighter her and Rob once used for candles. It radiated and filled a small room, which wasn't much of a room, more like a lookout post for someone who used to work the railroad. A shack. The old employees used to stand there, with paint peeling off the walls around them, and radio back and forth to train conductors about where they were going. Though, now there was no technology in the small shack. Everything had been taken out and all that was left were the outlines of where the radios and computers used to lay. Two tones of paint covered the walls, like a second life long forgotten, known that it was there, but many had forgotten about it or did not want to ask where it had gone. Janet placed a blanket she had packed over the broken window to keep the draft out and the heat in while she slept. *I don't even know why I'm thinking about all of these people who aren't around anymore. Rob. Fucking Rob.* She started to cry.

It was light out, and the fire had gone cold, not even smoldering now. Janet tried to warm herself up quickly, while making as little noise as possible. The air around her still smelled like smoke. *Hopefully it's only an animal outside.* She weighed her options. Outside there was crunching in the snow which had glazed over with a thin sheet of freezing rain overnight.

Someone kicked in the door as Janet was about to peer out of the blanket window she had made. Directly in her face was a rifle. Down the length of the barrel and behind a stock stood a man, scruffy, but not poor to look at.

"What do you have?"

"What do you mean?" she asked as she raised her hands up to about her shoulders, trying not to make any sudden moves.

"What supplies do you have?"

"Just some water, a pot, a pan, an old bottle, a kitchen knife, and a wooden bat. Also clothes, a sleeping bag, and a blanket to keep me warm." She was stumbling over her words as she shook from the horror in front of her. *Rob, please,* she wished to the sky.

"How'd you make the fire?"

"A lighter."

"What else are you hiding?"

She looked back at the man, perplexed by the question.

"What fucking else are you hiding besides the goddamn lighter?" Janet noticed he was growing increasingly hostile. "Get out of the shack. Now. Don't touch a fucking thing."

Janet walked out, and the sun began to blind her as it radiated off of the glossy snow topped with ice. Her legs were trembling and walking became the hardest thing she had ever done.

"Face away from me, and don't move, or I will shoot you." She heard the man rustle around her belongings, violating any privacy she had.

"What's your name?"

"Janet. What's your name?" She questioned him, not expecting an answer as he tore through her pack.

"Crow," he said returning to her, his rifle slung around his arm. "And who is this?" He handed over a photo she carried, not of her and Rob, but just of him, standing in a bathing suit during the sunset on a beach in Aruba. It was a nice vacation they had gone on, shortly after moving in together. The sand was warm and got in between both of their toes. He had walked down towards the water, turned around just a few paces away from Janet, and smiled as she had pulled out the new Polaroid they brought along with them. She had snapped the photo. A memory in time of a blessed vacation in their pure world full of love and hope.

"That's Rob," she said with tears welling up, her voice beginning to crack. She hated this man who had gone through her memories like that, but he held the only thing that could be carried right now. Death. *Fuck it,* she thought, *why not just run at him and end it once and for all? Just go back and be with Rob on that beach. Our laughter and joy. No more lonely nights and cold.*

"I'm sorry for your loss." Crow handed the photo over to Janet. He seemed to almost understand, like maybe there was humanity left in him. Janet reached out to accept the photo. She did not snatch it, but cherished the small treasure and held it with the softest grace she could muster trying not to ruin it in any way.

"If you're heading north along the tracks, you're going to get caught. And if you're heading into the city, there's nothing left." He looked at her with pity.

"I'm leaving the city. There's a few hotspots left, and they have guns and supplies. But there are way too many for me to stick around. I thought about sneaking in and stealing from them, but I'd rather not be in the city anymore," she replied, rubbing her thumb over Rob's face, never making eye contact with the man named Crow. "How do you know I'll be caught if I stay on the tracks?"

"I found you pretty easily, and I'm not doing much more than looking for an animal to shoot. Your makeshift insulation helped, but smelling that fire was easy. I planned on coming, shooting the people in here, and taking any food they had left. Yet, I only found you."

Janet knew he was telling the truth. If she had anything worth taking, he would have taken it and killed her before, or, shortly after he had taken it.

"Thanks for not killing me, I guess."

"Thank yourself for not having anything worth taking."

"I'd like to travel with you north, then we can split off if that's okay."

"Why would I bother taking you north? What do you have to offer?"

It was a parley now. She had to prove she was worth keeping around, that she had something to offer.

"I've made it this far by myself. Sure, I made a mistake that led you right to me, but I must be doing something right if I made it out of the city and up here."

"That's not much of an offer. Anyone could get out of the city if they had food, water, and warm clothes. It seems to me you have all of those things."

"I know places up north that still have food. Small towns near farms. I know where the old shooting ranges are. They should have more guns and ammo, unless any of the doomsday preppers hit them first," she blurted out. It was true there were small towns near farms, and shooting ranges, but she hadn't been to them since she was a child. *They might not even be there,* she thought, but kept it to herself hoping the bait would keep her alive.

"Guns and ammo are always a welcome sight for me, but that still leaves a very glaring problem in my eyes. Why the fuck should I trust you?" he asked. Janet eyed him up and down and noticed his right hand was on a knife which was peeking out of his waistband. He had been fiddling with it the entire time they had been talking, ready to use it on her at a moment's notice.

Her mind searched for the right words, hoping they'd be enough. *Rob, what do I do?* "I don't think you should trust me. I don't think you ever would, considering you've been fingering that knife."

Crow smiled and let out a small breath, almost a laugh. "You have astute observation skills at least, which might be handy if I can exploit them."

"That sounds a bit sexist."

He laughed. "You can't exactly go on the Internet anymore to complain about it, society's done. If I were you, I'd use your womanhood as a way of getting what you want."

Janet understood what he was saying, and while it wasn't the prettiest of sights, he had a very valid point.

"And when you're done, you could kill whoever you used to get what you wanted."

Janet realized Crow was coaching her on survival to make her an asset rather than a liability.

"What makes you think I won't kill you when we head north?"

"Girl," he said intently. "Just because you got out of a city doesn't mean you're hot shit. I'm sure you haven't taken a life yet, otherwise you'd be trying to take mine instead of bartering for me to take you along for the ride. I can show you how to survive, but you're not gonna like it. Your boy is dead. Recently too, by the looks of you. I'm only interested in the guns and ammo you mentioned. After that, we're going our separate ways."

Janet thought it over to herself. He could kill her the second he got what he wanted, and to tell the truth, she only knew of one shooting range she had gone to as a kid when her father had taken her for her hunter's safety course. *Who knows if that was even there twenty years later?* Maybe she'd never find it again, but she trusted the maps in her head. And, just maybe, she'd be able to get out in the dead of night while he was asleep.

"Then teach me how to survive."

Janet watched his face as he mulled over what she said. "Only until you're of no use to me."

She looked at him, deciding how to respond. Her voice felt weak, and her thoughts fleeting. Overhead, the sun began its transit behind the clouds. It would be dark soon.

"Can we start moving? I'm getting cold."

"As you wish, Princess." Janet heard the sarcasm oozing from his voice.

They walked, Crow telling Janet to stay in front while she dragged her feet. She was being threatened, but for the first time since she left the city, actually, the first time since this had all gone down, she felt safe. She loved and missed Rob, but he was weak, he wasn't ready to survive. If he was, he'd still be alive, and they'd be together. *God,* Janet thought, *if only I hadn't left that morning, he'd still be here, and we'd either be in the apartment, or dead right now.* Either was fine with her. *Dead together, or alive together, not this, not this insufferable life without society and power.* The grid was dead, long dead, more dead than Rob, deader than the dreams they had planned together. Just fucking dead.

Janet wondered if anyone could the get electricity going.

Maybe with power could come lights, with lights and power could come order. Janet wondered how deep these outages really went. Why hadn't she seen any Army or National Guard? *Did the Government go into hiding? That must be it. Better to hide and let society fall apart than to try and hold it together.*

Snow crunched beneath their feet, like bones of a million corpses breaking with every step they took towards the future unknown. The skeletons watched from afar, and underneath Janet and Crow as they passed, strangers too afraid to say hello as their bodies were trodden on. They wanted to stand up, put on their jackets of old skin, take their eyes from the pockets of their torn jeans, shove them back into the sockets they belonged to, and walk with the two wanderers. How they missed life now that they knew death and stared into the endlessness of it. Together they would all march—eyes dangling with nothing to hold them in, knuckles missing, and legs falling apart with every added step of pressure—to reclaim the world that had buried them beneath the snow. They all watched as the two figures drifted away, like fleeting dreams forgotten as soon as they were remembered.

They crossed a small warm brown—or cool red, depending on who you asked—bridge on the Hudson and approached a platform where some snow had accumulated, but not too much considering the overhang. The faint yellow lines close to the tracks were still there and though the sign had not been cleaned off, Janet knew she had made it to Croton-Harmon. While they had hardly spoken, time had gone by again, quicker than as of late, and night arrived to greet them with stars and the moon as a present.

"There's a building over there that we could probably hole up in," Janet said without turning to face the man behind her as she surveyed the land.

"That's nice and all, but I think it'd be better towards the river and find an old train car, or to the mechanic building. It's less conspicuous. Everyone wants the easy night's sleep. And that's why they don't make it."

Janet nodded, and hopped off the platform, walking towards the empty cars, steel arteries that used to carry blood cells to and from the beating heart which needed them to survive. She made it to the first car and realized Crow wasn't behind her anymore. Every which way she looked he couldn't be seen.

"Next lesson." A voice came from her left and under a train behind where its wheel was. "Always know who you're with and where they are. Keep track of everyone and your surroundings."

"I thought I knew exactly where I was and where you were."

"You're misunderstanding me. What I'm saying is: get the fuck out of your head and pay attention if you want to live."

Maybe he was right, she wasn't focusing on the world around her, moreover, the world around was focusing on her, and she had no idea if anyone was nearby. The tunnel vision had kicked in and she hadn't shaken the mind fog from her eyes.

Crow and Janet went around the train cars, peering to see if anyone had made camp, or for signs of life other than human. There was neither.

The doors to the massive building were still locked when they tried to open them. A good sign they both assumed. Maybe it meant that no one had gone in. They walked around, edging ever closer to the Hudson. The water was dark, kind of blue, maybe purple depending on how the sun hit it, but most definitely, it was gray. Years of pollution sat in the bottom of the river, and the salt water from the Atlantic made it unpleasant to be in. Ice and snow built up closer to shore.

Crow smashed a window with a rock, and they both grabbed an end of a wooden box, heaved it strenuously over, taking at least one breather before finishing. Then they hopped through, but only after Crow had wrapped his hand and knocked off the remaining glass so they wouldn't cut themselves. They leaped through the new opening and fell the six or seven feet to the floor, hoping their tense muscles wouldn't strain anything.

Inside it was dark, darker than they had expected considering how many windows were above them. Yet, they could still see clearly after their eyes had adjusted to the shade. There were train cars lined up, with huge pieces of metal and machinery around neither of them knew the use for or how to start.

"We need to look around, then find any diesel we can use to make fires easier."

Janet remained silent and felt co-dependent on Crow. He was constantly talking down to her like a child, but she knew without him, there was very little hope for surviving. She wondered if she would really be better off running away and never looking back. The dead of night would be her best option. But, this Crow, he seemed like he knew how to survive, and definitely track. *Maybe.* Maybe it was better if she stayed and played the game until she learned anything useful.

They split up, covering more ground of the building and to make sure there were no squatters nearby. Crow found a staircase leading down, and Janet went through some rooms which yielded nothing. They both agreed that after finishing the top floor, they'd use up some precious battery and follow the staircase down into the depths of the basement below.

There was diesel in plain containers closer to the cars. They weren't marked and were pretty inconspicuous. Janet had walked by a few, and decided to open one. Immediately the smell wafted into her eyes. Someone had definitely not followed OSHA standards, and did not mark the containers for use. Janet had guessed inspections were infrequent when the lights were still on. How long had it been since the lights flickered on Christmas?. *Rob,* she thought, beating back tears. How close and distant those days seemed. She called over to Crow. He was content with her discovery.

"We should see what else is here, now," he said to her. He seemed almost happy she was becoming useful.

Janet led the way into the basement, carrying a small coffee container of diesel in one hand which they had siphoned from the bigger containers—they had found it in a breakroom that had nothing more than a coffee maker, a plastic table, and three chairs. Janet produced a flashlight and took the lead. Crow had his rifle shouldered behind her. She looked back and saw he was ready to fire at any moment. *Probably thinks I'm going to turn on him.* She debated the possibility of it and the outcome. Neither were in her favor. The stairs were easy to navigate, and the hallway below was long, dark, and narrow, like a typical scene from a cliché horror movie. It made suspense well up inside both of them until it became palpable and overflowing.

Nothing out of the ordinary happened despite their growing anxiety. All around them were storage rooms of batteries, more diesel, spare parts, and tools for probably most, if not all of the parts down there. All-in-all, it was a lackluster find.

"We could stay down here, make a small fire to keep us warm. Shut the door. The door upstairs is already closed, and I'm sure we could hear anyone on those metal stairs if we really listened. We'd definitely see any lights coming down the hallway," Janet recommended to Crow, while trying to be as friendly and useful as possible to her captor.

"I suppose you're right. We'd be able to defend this hallway pretty well with the rifle at least. Though, any escape would never happen unless we fought through them. Anyone who came could just block the way and force our hand until we ran out of food and water, which we aren't the most stocked on." He paused. "Besides, lighting a fire down here would be terrible for us with nowhere for the smoke to go. We're going to go back upstairs and take our chances."

The odd couple trying to work together made their way back upstairs and lit a small fire which vented out window they had climbed through. They heated themselves by the fire which was mostly paper soaked in diesel, and some wood they had broken from some shipping crates. Their sore bodies absorbed the heat as they dried out their socks, hoping to prevent any athlete's foot or another annoying menace. It helped, Janet thought, to keep their feet dry. It was hard to try and find ways to make life easy when so much of it was hellbent on destroying itself.

Janet fell asleep first, not meaning to, hoping that Crow would pass out, and she'd be able to sneak away, but that never happened. When she woke, it was morning, and Crow was snapping in front of her face to wake her up.

"Exhausted there?"

"Yeah, I guess I was more tired than I realized after all the travel. I think the warm fire is what did me in."

"Well, better eat up." He handed her some warm food she wasn't too sure of. It was rectangular and pink.

"What is it?" she asked holding a piece of it in her hand.

He held up the can. "Spam," he replied, shaking it in front of her.

"I've never had it before."

"It's gonna be salty."

Janet nibbled at it. It was definitely salty and porky—wasn't the best, but it was better than anything she had eaten in a few days. *Why hadn't we found any in the city?*

"When you're done, we're going to start walking. Do you know where we're headed from here?"

Janet looked at the ground, her legs crossed, hands feeding herself. She nibbled quietly on the salty food she was given.

"Hey, Janet, I need you to answer me or I'm going to fly solo and leave you here."

She looked up at him. "We need to go north, stay close to the river, then there will be a bridge."

"What's the bridge?"

"It's just after Peekskill, it's the Bear Mountain. There's a lodge there, maybe there will be food."

"What kind of lodge?"

"An old inn, State park, and a zoo."

"It might be fair to say that it was picked clean if it was a tourist attraction."

Janet mulled over the idea that they'd arrive and find everything gone, the windows broken, and all the chairs and tables trashed. Maybe there would be people inside. Maybe they'd help her out. She was lost in her daydreams of maybes and possibilities.

"We'll go and check out the inn. And decide what to do when we get there."

Janet nodded and let out a small sigh. She had no control of her own life now. *Did I ever?*

They left the building after finishing another can of meat. Outside the wind was howling, and the snow was falling. It stung Janet's face, while Crow seemed unfazed by it. She kept her eyes to the ground as they walked.

"Stop." His voice cut through the wind. He took off his pack and shuffled around in it. "Come here," he said.

Janet walked over, wary of what was going on. The man

pulled out a scarf, stood up and crossed the gap Janet had let sit between them. He wrapped it around her neck, and head, the cloth soft against her skin. He finished wrapping it, then tucked the scarf into itself. All that remained exposed to the elements was a small gap for Janet to see through, which kept most of the snow and wind out.

"You should be able to see in front of you better now."

"Thank you." Her reply was muffled but he could still hear her. The gesture was nice, but was it something more or just to keep her on track? She found herself questioning him more and more the longer they were together. The snow started to get heavier and it was harder to see as they walked along the river, winding north.

"What's this Camp Smith?" Crow inquired after walking for the entire day through snow and ice. Their headscarves slick and wet. Both had wished they owned waterproof winter gear, but the best either of them had was a water-resistant jacket, and some old athletic spandex underneath their pants.

"I'm not familiar with it." She wasn't lying. She didn't even remember that there was a military camp this close the city. "But, the bridge to the inn is right there." She pointed to their left.

"You're telling me you've driven past this and have never noticed it?"

"I was here for a wedding. I wasn't really concerned with my surroundings. I got off the train in Peekskill, called a cab, and got in to go get shitfaced. Then I was here as a kid to go ice skating and visit the zoo. That was a lifetime ago." Janet reflected on her memories of being warm and bundled up to go fall on the ice more than her parents had wanted her to—though they still laughed each time she did. The zoo wasn't of much interest. There were birds, mostly caged alone, staring off with blank eyes.

There were old rocks behind glass of the small museum. Janet thought she saw a bear there, but couldn't be sure if that zoo memory was blending in with another memory of a different life.

"Do you want to stop at that Camp and see if there are any supplies?" Janet inquired as they stood still and let the snow collect on their shoulders.

"I'd like to go there," Crow responded. "I don't think it's a good idea if neither of us know the lay of the land just yet. I say we go to the inn, then decide if we're going to back pedal and take a closer look."

"Aren't you the one who brought me along to go to a firing range?"

"Yes, a firing range in the middle of nowhere. Not a firing range on a military camp with a tank sitting at the entrance to it. My gut tells me people have already tried going there when everything went to shit and who knows, they might still be there. The only thing left is small groups and the Traders." He was lecturing her.

"You can be a real fucking dick, you know that?"

"I may be a real fucking dick, but I've gotten this far by myself by being one. Compassion and kindness get you killed nowadays."

He had a point. Weeks ago Janet was willing to steal from anyone to keep her and Rob alive, now she was playing on rash thoughts without thinking them through. She felt like she was taking steps back. In a way, she was looking for a place to die quickly. Just to wink out of existence. Blink and never wake up. *Rob? Are you ready? Will you welcome me with open arms?*

"Let's get going. I don't want to be standing here waiting for someone to see us," Crow said as he turned to follow the road towards the looming bridge, dark gray against a gray sky. There was a beauty in the monochromatic grayscale, phasing from almost white to the darkest of grays on the side of the mountain as the trees poked through the snow, reaching for the sky, like phalanges ripping through the earth, grasping for life.

Crow went to the left side of the building as they approached, and could clearly see the ice-skating rink Janet spoke of. He walked up the steps, found a door to a dining hall, and busted the glass pane next to the handle with his fist wrapped in the scarf he had been using. It tore as he pulled his hand out, the glass catching and tearing through the fabric to cut into the meaty part of his hand next to his right pinky. He kept the scarf wrapped around his hand, minimizing any blood from dripping down onto the floor.

They entered the inn, which was brown covered in white. The glass on the windows was intact. A good sign, they agreed once again. Their bodies needed a rest, and it looked like they had found the place they needed. The sun was passing away into its nightly death.

Inside the chairs had been stacked on top of each other, and pushed into the corners. The place had obviously been turned down when the lights had gone out, and all the workers seemed to have left, perhaps they chose to go home rather than stay at work. Who could blame them anyway? It was better to watch society crumble in the comfort of your own home than at the place which paid your bills.

They both stayed close to each other as they made their way out of the dining hall, and through a set of double doors. Inside they found a bar made out of wood. It was beautiful, old, and stained from years of wear, along with alcohol, and drunk filled nights where stories had been shared, emotions spilled, and relationships lost. Janet and Crow sat at the bar with ghosts walking among them, laughing, crying, cursing, and running all about.

Crow and Janet felt the years moving through their bodies.

An ether wind dancing and touching against their hearts and soul, trying to find its place between dimensions of time past and present. They sat and played with the glasses still on the bar. Droplets of alcohol dripping down the inside.

"Wait," Crow said. "There are people here."

"How do you know that? I didn't hear anything."

"The glasses."

Janet looked, not fully understanding. *They could have just been left out.* She kept her words to herself.

Crow crossed to the doors and looked into the hallway to the right. It led to rooms. "We have to go tonight. I think it'd be better to stay here right now. We can pass under the cover of dark when the sun finishes setting. We'll go through the windows."

"You're saying we stay inside with the people who are already here?"

"If we leave now, we're open targets across the field and the bridge. They have to come down the hallway to us."

"This seems risky," Janet stated.

"Look at me. We hole up here, barricade these doors with the tables, and smash the window behind us." Crow started pacing.

Janet crossed the room, watching over her shoulder. "Okay, if we need to, we can get onto that overhang, then drop ten feet or so."

"Exactly," he said. Janet watched Crow as the muscles in his face constricted and he smirked.

Is he excited about all of this?

They started to gather the tables, laying them so the tops faced the doors, and the legs came towards them. They made a small wall. The tables were staggered so the legs were never directly on top of each other as they stacked them. When all was said and done, they had made a light wood colored wall about four feet high give or take a few inches. It was solid but a light push would knock the top row right down. The chairs in the corner solved that problem for them as they moved the heavy stacks over and placed them as braces for any kind of push someone would try. It wouldn't hold long, but it would give them just enough time to fight back while someone tried to break in.

They heard footsteps approaching.

"Hey," Crow shouted. "You better be ready to fucking die," he said as the footsteps got closer, and then stopped.

"I'm not ready to die yet, man. It sounds like you guys are just as afraid of me as I am of you." Janet watch a skinny man peek the right doorway. He eyed them up as they stood behind the bar then quickly tucked his head back behind the wall. "That's a nice .223 you have there. I had one myself. Now I carry around a 30-30." He ducked his head back and took a step away, waiting to see if a shot rang out.

Crow waited to see if the man peeked his head over again, ready to blast him, or if his footsteps would fade down the hallway like the echoing of rocks falling on pavement.

"I go by Fox," the man called out as he moved further down the hallway making sure they couldn't hear him as he did.

"How many you got with you, Fox?" Crow shouted back.

"Just me."

"They why are there so many glasses on the bar?"

"You pay attention, man. But I was always told never to mix alcohol with other alcohol. You either drink it neat or you don't drink it at all, man."

"So, you're just here drinking away as the world falls to shit?"

"Yeah, sounds about right, man. I was living in these woods long before the lights went out."

Janet didn't sense the man was lying. An odd honesty in his voice as he replied quickly.

"How'd you get in here anyway?" Crow asked.

"I don't give my secrets away to strangers ready to shoot me, man."

"Well, I don't know if you have a gun either."

"I'll come down there with my hands up, but I gotta trust you won't shoot me."

"How do you supposed we do that?"

"Give the girl the rifle, and move to opposite sides of the room. I want you by the bar, and her by the windows in the far corner."

"Why would I give her the rifle?"

"Cause she looks like she hasn't shot a gun at all, so I feel safer knowing she'll miss even if she does shoot at me, man."

Janet was insulted, but the man named Fox was definitely right. She shot a gun once as a child with her grandfather. Her arms felt like noodles as her adrenaline began to course through her body with the anticipation. If she had to shoot, would she even be able to hit him? Janet doubted her abilities. She came to the conclusion that she'd definitely miss.

"What do you wanna do?" Janet whispered to Crow.

"I wanna know why he's here and what he has."

"Then give me the gun." She stared at Crow while he glared back. He handed it over to her and made sure the safety was off.

"All right, she's moving to the windows, and I'm going to the bar."

Janet waited as Fox peered through the glass doors, clearly able to see Crow behind the wooden bar. Fox leaned further and locked eyes with her.

"Don't shoot." Fox raised his hands, and presented himself in the glass double doors, but kept moving so she couldn't sight him in. The rifle was heavy for her, and she had trouble holding it steady with her arm fully extended for so long.

"What is it you two are doing here?"

"We could ask you the same question," Janet called out.

"Well, I was here first. That makes this my domicile. I just wanted to get inside from the weather, and found this beautiful place and a nice stock to enjoy the night." Fox referenced the bar and the alcohol ranging from a couple bucks to a few hundred a bottle.

There was a silence between everyone as Fox waited behind the pillar separating the two glass entrances and the wall they had built to keep him out.

"Janet came here as a child. We're heading north and wanted to stop in to check for some supplies."

"There's food here. I could show you, but I need you to put the gun down and slide it to the middle of the room. Away from both of you."

"Why would we do that instead of killing you and taking everything?"

"You haven't killed me yet. Means you guys probably don't want conflict, man."

"Janet, kneel down and slide the rifle to the middle of the room," said Crow.

Janet gave Crow a weird look. This would not have been her move, not after everything they had just gone through about surviving.

"Do it," he said. She nodded back though she still wasn't sure this was a good idea.

Janet slid the rifle across the floor. Fox peeked his head out to make sure they both were still unarmed of any gun he had not seen. Knives he could deal with if he had to. He stepped from behind the pillar, and kept his hands in the air, then took a step back, waiting for them to break down their wall, partially, at least, so he could get in.

Crow crossed the room and pulled the corner of a table out so he could enter. Then he pushed the table back in place. He looked Fox up and down. Janet couldn't help but think that the name fit him well. He was shaggy and thin limbed, almost like he was perpetually trembling and making jerky movements, but they were smooth and coordinated, not giving him away at all if he were to be outside. Fox flowed naturally with the wind.

They all sat down, leaving the rifle between them all, and far enough out of reach.

"There are plenty of canned goods in the kitchen. I think some of the meats stayed preserved in the freezer since everything went out. Luckily for us, man, that it's been cold ever since. Though, I haven't tried to eat any of it, just sticking to the canned stuff."

"Okay, that's good to know."

"There's a camp over that bridge."

"Camp Smith, yes," Fox cut Crow off. "It's not empty, and there are people there. I don't think it's something that should be fucked with, man."

"Why's that?"

"It's a lot of fucked up individuals. The Traders are the worst of them all, man."

Janet chewed her lip. That meant there were supplies, but it also meant dealing with a lot of danger which would be difficult at best. Crow had told her about them once. Groups of people going around and stealing the last of everything, only to trade it back for anything they wanted. They had trucks when the lights first went out. But after they used up whatever they could find, they switched to going on foot. *Those people at the barricades must have been the first of them.*

"How do you know this?"

"I saw it myself, man. It's easier for me to move alone and not be seen than it is for you two to move. The sign for the Camp was on the side of the road, and I'm inquisitive. So, I went there to check it out. I heard rumors of the Traders as I moved about. I listened in at earshot of camps I passed by. It seems like there are a few groups of them. All separate. Moving about. They already have the guns, now they can do whatever they want as they fight for control of everything."

"How do we know you aren't just one of their scouts then?"

"Man, do I look like someone who's been eating well and carrying around a military grade weapon?"

He had a point. Fox was gaunt and from what Janet could see, the only thing he carried on him was a few knives which stuck up and poked into his shirt. He definitely wasn't carrying a pistol anywhere.

"I have my rifle, and I left that down the hallway before I came down here."

"That seems like a dumb idea," Janet said. "What if we planned to kill you?"

"Trust builds trust. You can't get it unless you give it."

They stayed up most of the night, exchanging words and knowledge. As the sun finished setting and started to come back up again, they all got tired, and broke open a few doors to cozy rooms with warm blankets. Crow, Janet, and Fox all took separate rooms after Fox was invited to join them for as long as he wanted to be near people. He accepted graciously on the condition that if they questioned him or what his intentions were, he would leave in the middle of the night only after he robbed them of every-thing they needed. His intention was to live and that's what it came down to. Nothing more.

They slept until dusk and sipped alcohol as Fox had before they barged in, each of them getting drunk and spilling stories they kept close to themselves. Janet talked about Rob, Fox spoke about the love he left behind with her father for his own selfish reasons, and Crow talked about a time when he was traveling to be with a woman he loved. Janet noticed that Fox and Crow left their real names out, maybe as a way of hiding the pain or the emotions they still had.

They retired their rooms again, this time drunkenly, vowing to wake with the sun and set their eyes north. This time Janet and Crow went together and put more time and energy into being awake and working out than they did to sleeping.

Janet woke up first and realized what had conspired that night. She felt uneasy, like she had betrayed Rob by sleeping with someone else. She looked at Crow who looked just as uncomfortable as she did. Both of them quickly dressed, and quietly agreed it was best to forget it had happened, and move on with their day.

Crow knocked on the door to Fox's room and found no reply.

"Downstairs lobby," Fox called as he heard shuffling in the hallway above.

The group of three followed the scenic road heading north. The further away from New York City the better. Nature was their survival plan. At least with animals to hunt and running water, they had some chance of living.

There was a strip of asphalt which cut through a city off to the west side of the Hudson. It was their best course for possible supplies and shelter ever since they left the inn. The small city was run down, like an area trying its best to make a return, but the buildings were hardly taken care of. It had potential but the people there treated it bad and treated each other worse.

There was glass shattered in the streets, paint peeling from buildings, and cars were torched. Fox, Janet, and Crow felt like it hadn't all happened after the bulbs burned, but that the decay had started years before. The area around them wasn't a recent warzone.

They marched down a street. The green sign said it was

Broadway but it was the furthest thing from the lights of the city. The road was a sheet of ice-covered snow. Sticking to the sidewalks barely visible and the buildings with doors which remained opened. None of them risked going down the middle of the wide street. All around them lay nothing but openness. It was way too risky for strangers in such a new place.

A shot rang out and clipped the ground beneath the snow with a small pang. Fox, scattered first. He broke down an alley, found an emergency ladder, and scaled it before Crow and Janet could decide where they wanted to go. Their thinking was clouded by alertness and panic. They opted for a small building with its front windows smashed in, taking the stairs up to the third floor, and barricading the door, but not before another shot rang out and hit the siding next to the doorway of the building they entered. Janet waited, with a piece of wood in hand she had found, while Crow moved towards the windows, shouldering his rifle. The second shot had come from somewhere directly across from them. *How had they missed again? Bad shot or bad location?* Janet thought.

Outside she saw nothing out of the ordinary, no movement, no people, not even the wind forced the dust of snow to make movement to trick the eye into seeing someone who was not there.

"Where the fuck is the other guy?" Crow whispered over to Janet.

"I don't know. The snow just popped up and then he was gone before I could get a bearing of what was going on."

"Motherfucker," he cursed beneath his breath.

"Did you hear that?" Janet asked.

"No, I don't hear anything. That's the problem."

"It was a small pop."

Crow furrowed his brow.

"I didn't hear anything, Janet."

Janet gazed out of the window looking for any sign of someone in or on top of a building. A man entered out onto the street, skinny, carrying a rifle slung over his shoulder.

"Fox, what the fuck are you doing?" Crow yelled from one of the windows.

"They're dead, man," he yelled back.

Janet and Crow both looked at each other, confused, trying to figure out what the fuck was going on and who this guy was. They linked eyes and tried to communicate without talking, but only had more questions arise than answers.

They left the building, checking the road each way as they did. They soon spotted Fox.

"Just one. Not gonna be any trouble. I got him in the top of the head." Fox made a distraught expression. "He might still be alive, unfortunately, but he's gonna bleed out and die, man. No one can come back from that without plenty of medical attention, and I don't think they're gonna get that here."

"Where's the body?" asked Crow.

Fox turned around and pointed at a gas station. "Right up there, top left corner closest to us."

"We should get up there and see what they had," Crow said, and Janet agreed.

Fox turned and started to slink away, closing the gap between them and old capitalism.

On the roof the man lay on his back, still very much alive, wiggling around. Fox shouldered his rifle, placed it firmly on the bridge of his nose, and pulled the trigger to end the man's suffering. He picked up the small rifle he was using.

"Hey, why'd you shoot?" Crow burst up the ladder and questioned Fox.

"He was still alive, man. I needed to mercy kill him." Fox's voice was harsh cutting through the still air. He turned to them and his eyes were like storm drains already full. The rain water washed right over the grates. "Here's a .22, Janet." He handed over the rifle.

"Thank you, Fox."

"It's a lever action, so just put your hand here and pull forward." He began showing her how to use the rifle, including how to reload it.

Crow walked around them, and began going through the man's bag. He found a bottle of water, a small medical kit, a pack of cigarettes in an orange box, a few cans of peaches and one can of green beans.

They walked on, trying to put themselves far from death, but it loomed over them, reminding them that this world was no longer kind and they had to lose their morality to survive in it.

Fox quickened his steps, putting space between him, Crow and Janet.

The world crawled on, whispering of the trio and what they had done, where they were going, and what they had been through. Trees leaned to their neighbors, while houses yelled across the street after the trio were out of earshot. Wind carried their stories far and wide, spreading the gossip over the grid. It would return carrying the same message back of people trying to survive. Doing things they never would have wanted to in their perceived normal lives before the world changed. All the stories were the same. Good people doing bad things, and bad people doing worse.

Fox trudged through, wishing he had stayed alone. If he had, he wouldn't have killed that man. Soreness took over his head, and it felt like someone was rubbing the middle part of his brain with sandpaper.

They closed in on a town—small and rustic—after camping

for days. The building on the right side of the road at one of the entrances to the town was a hulking mass of old wood. The left, brick painted over with a scene of magical creatures underneath a man climbing a mountain—a mountain all of them could see far in the distance. A self-rendition of the view which the brick building blocked if you stood on the porch of the wooden one.

"Either of you been this far up?" Crow asked as he looked between the two and the painting.

"Never," Janet stated.

"Yeah, I'm from here. My old house isn't too far away."

Crow furrowed his brow. "Why were you so far south?"

"Why are you so far north?" Fox snapped back. "Nothing here for me, and I'm sure you can say the same coming from the city, man."

He made a point. "Is it worth going to check your old house? Or did you empty it before all of this?"

"I left that house before everything happened, man. Gave my keys to some homeless dudes. I'm sure my place is a wreck at this point."

Crow and Janet had a lot more questions starting to well up. The middle of the road wasn't the best place to ask them.

"Take us to your old house," Crow demanded.

"All right, man."

They walked on and on, down side streets, avoiding the main road in and out of town. All around them rustic buildings, some brick, some having pure white siding against the white snow, and some, a mixture between the two. As the roads narrowed and began to be surrounded by trees again, Janet noticed the changes. To one side, a sign that said bird sanctuary and a small path leading to a smaller bridge over a small creek.

An entrance to a golf course was further on, and Janet found it peculiar that there was a golf course smacked down by humanity in the most random location. They were in the middle of nowhere, beside a mountain, with no real population. *Why put a golf course here? Old white money didn't want to travel from their little town of perfection to do their hobby someplace else,* she guessed.

"Here it is," Fox said, as they stood outside of a huge house not far from the golf course. Massive windows faced them, like eyes trying to take in the new world. It recognized its old owner, and almost felt like comforting them, but remembered how he had left it to people who didn't care how they treated things.

Inside, through the light-colored door, the place had been destroyed. Fox, Crow, and Janet felt it had been looted and trashed after everyone started to disappear, but they all knew that wasn't the case. Whoever Fox gave the keys to, they had been the ones to destroy the place, not anyone who came after.

The walls had been covered in black and red graffiti, the carpet stained, and the wooden floors gouged. Dishes, glass bottles, and furniture broken lay broken at every turn of the head. Fox started to feel guilty about what had happened to his house. He knew the hours and all of the time it had cost him to get the house. All of the people he had to screw over in the business world to make the money. It was upsetting, but at the same time, Fox felt he shouldn't care. Everything here was material, and therefore, it wasn't truly important. But something rubbed at the front of his skull. The idea of time and the loss of it. Fox was proud to have purchased this house at one point in his life, and now he felt the pang of guilt for how other people had treated it.

A shot rang out, as Fox's head crested the wall next to the staircase. The air around him was cut like a hot knife through paper, sizzling as the bullet whizzed by him. He fell backwards on the staircase, and Crow caught him as best he could, falling down under his weight and surprise.

"Fuck, man," Fox whispered, a hand on his chest as if he was trying to keep his heart from bursting out of his chest.

"Hey! We aren't here to cause any shit," Crow yelled to whoever was in the house.

"I was just checking on my house, man. This used to be where I lived," Fox yelled up.

"I don't know you, why the fuck should I trust y'all?" They heard a man's voice reply to them, but it only echoed down the hallway. He hadn't yelled loud enough for Janet to pinpoint where he was exactly.

"Man, if you go in one room, there's a bathroom with a blue toilet, and in the hallway is another bathroom with a blue tub and a white toilet. There's a guest bedroom if you come from the staircase halfway down on the left, inside the walls are white with a thick black trim. There should be a bed in that room. I haven't been here in ages, so that could be gone and destroyed by the squatters I let take over, man," said Fox.

"Throw your weapons up the staircase and into the kitchen, we can talk after. If you show your face past that wall again before I see any weapons, I'ma drop you."

Fox looked back at Crow and Janet. A silent agreement passed between them.

"I'm gonna throw my rifle up there after I unload it," Crow called out, "then my friend will do the same." He looked at Fox.

They both unloaded their rifles, freeing the ammunition from them and pocketing the precious material for future use. Fox walked to the last step up, and placed his rifle on the ground and pushed it hard across the carpet into the slick floor of his kitchen, refusing to toss his rifle. Crow did the same.

"Aight, you can come with your hands up, and we can talk."

"Man, do you think we're that dumb? To let you get a shot of us head on? I'm gonna come up and go to the right, into my living room. You need to lower your rifle to the floor in front of you, then my friend, Crow, will come and join me."

"Why should I trust you?"

"Why should we trust you? We just gave up our rifles. For all we know, you could have someone in a window waiting for us to make a run for it. Put your weapon down too. We gave trust. You give trust now, otherwise we're at a standstill."

There was a long pause, like listening to the empty space between being awake and falling asleep where the only thing heard was the static drone of the air and mumbling of words.

The group heard a clink as the man placed whatever he was holding loudly on the ground. Janet shuddered, knowing whoever was behind it didn't know what they were actually doing. They hadn't been raised around guns, didn't understand that slamming it to the ground wasn't the proper way to handle one. Whoever was using it was simply using it to scare and kill, not to survive and as a tool for their survival.

* * *

Fox peeked by the wall, saw a tall man standing in the hallway. Behind him, a short woman. On the floor lay a rifle, probably a .22. The girl had nothing in her hands. Fox stepped beyond his protection and kept his hands raised, nodded to Crow, and he did the same. Janet stayed still and kept quiet.

"How'd you guys get here, man?"

There was no answer. They both stood motionless, waiting for someone to make a move.

Fox knew how this was going to go. They weren't a threat. They were terrified. He sat down on the carpet and waited, putting his hands in his lap. Crow stood next to him, his hands in the air. They stuck close to a wall which separated the living room from the staircase as a last resort for protection.

"How'd you guys get here, man?" Fox repeated.

"I, uh, walked up here from Newburgh after I found my uncle dead on top of the roof of a gas station. His head blown apart."

Fox let the air remain silent as the words hung there.

"How'd the girl get here then?" Crow cut through.

"I have a name," she snapped.

"Well, princess, I don't know either of your names. They call me Crow. What's your name, and how'd you get here?"

"Bernice. And I escaped from one of those slave gangs and ducked into this house. Jamal was here already."

"Where are you headed, man?" asked Fox.

"Nowhere in particular. Bernice and I are just tryna live."

Fox looked up at Crow. He nodded in return.

"Why don't you guys join us? We're trying to find some place safer and we'll have more numbers and more guns with you two along," Crow said.

Jamal whispered to Bernice and they both nodded.

"We need food and water now, but we'll join you."

Fox stood up and startled Jamal. His hand jerked. He almost shouldered his rifle, but knew it was not loaded.

"It's all good, man. Let's make some food in the kitchen." He looked down at Janet, "Come on up, they're not gonna do anything."

"You have someone down there," Bernice yelled.

"Yes, we had to keep a card in our pocket so you guys didn't hold them all," Crow said. "Janet wouldn't have done anything unless you had first."

Jamal and Bernice felt like they had been slighted. They weren't dead, and they were both thirsty and starving. Emotions of betrayal would have to wait for a better time.

Everyone gathered in the kitchen. While they were going through their food, deciding which was best to eat together, Fox walked over and handed Jamal a jug of water. Silent, he walked back, an apparition giving back to someone who didn't deserve what had been taken him.

22

PRESENT DAY

Bernice, Jamal, and Acacia left the room while the others waited with the stacks and piles of clothing, still trying to readjust to their new prison uniforms and cellblock. It was lockdown.

The corridor was short, but twisted and turned on itself, going down a few flights of stairs, then looping back up until the only thing they had to do was climb, climb, climb a never-ending staircase. The door ahead of them was flat metal, very thin, almost like tin, yet extremely heavy, so heavy that it felt like it was only meant to be opened by giants. As Bernice and Jamal passed through and went to hold the door, they realized they had to put all of their strength into it just to squeeze through so their bodies weren't crushed under its weight. Neither knew what kind of metal it was made of to be so thin, yet durable at the same time. Through the door, one last hallway waited for them.

The walls around them were all the same color of the metal door. Bernice and Jamal realized that it was a fake wall they had just come through. They turned to look back, and the seam was perfect from the outside, yet when they had walked up to the doorway, they could see the light peeking through from the other side. Neither could understand how that had worked. A mystery within the mystery of the Underground.

"Please, follow," Acacia said. Her voice sweet. A serenade lulling them out of convoluted thoughts.

They walked on and found another door. "Do not be alarmed. It may be jarring at first. If you feel vertigo, or any form of anxiety, please, step back inside."

She opened the door for them. Dull light squeezed through the crack as the door was opened. Pink and blue, and green and yellow neon skulked inside. The street in front of them moved and was alive. People everywhere. They were normal, fully alive like those passing by in a small town. Something seemed off about all of them as Jamal and Bernice looked closer. Their clothes were tattered. Some were covered in soot, some cleaner than others. Men and women walked around either fully bundled, or in clothes so skimpy, Jamal and Bernice were surprised the men and women bothered at all with the little bit of clothing they wore.

"Where the fuck are we?" Jamal asked.

"That isn't an important question at the moment. We're making sure you can handle what this is, and realize there is life, though I'm sure neither of you have seen much of it in the time you've been out there."

"Wait. You know what happened?" Jamal asked.

"We have a pretty good understanding. We can discuss it when you are all back together. Right now, we are right outside of the UC. We aren't far from the Slums. We call this place the Deep. We would rather you have some semblance of normal life before we show you around more. This place is much different than the life you've lived."

Bernice's head was swirling and so was Jamal's. They had so many questions. Acacia led them on. A tour guide through a future city easing her tourists into new water.

Along the street there were vendors, lights, sounds, vehicles hovering off of the ground as they whizzed by. The vehicles looked similar to the cars, trucks, scooters, and bikes from days gone. Everyone was here and there all at once. The city was alive.

"I need to sit down," Jamal said.

"Not here. At the end of this string of buildings we can turn right and duck into an alley."

"Why an alley?" Bernice questioned.

"If you sit down here, everyone will think something is wrong. You'll draw attention to yourself. I won't be able to help you after that. If we go to an alley, you're just another bum from the Slums who came too far up." Acacia slowed her pace and grabbed Jamal by the wrist, dragging him on while trying to not draw more attention to them. "Keep your heads down."

Bernice felt eyes and quickened her speed, getting in front of both of them so they didn't look like one group of people. She turned right at the end of the buildings and waited. Acacia and Jamal arrived shortly after. *Why am I getting so far ahead and listening to this woman?* Bernice didn't like being too far away from Jamal, the only person she now felt comfortable around, and he was drifting somewhere else.

"There." Acacia pointed.

Bernice went along, turned into the alley, and set up on the ground which was warm to the touch. She noticed the pain in her feet again as it began to flare from her toes to her ankles.

"This feels too much like the city," Jamal said as he rounded the corner, his legs weak from what he was seeing.

"It is a city," Acacia said.

"No, it feels like *my* city. Where I'm from. But everyone there is dead now, they have to be. Where are we anyway?"

"You'll find out soon. Trust me. It's all going to be addressed, but it's not for me to tell you."

Jamal looked up, hate in his eyes. "Listen, you've kidnapped us, and now you're telling me that I can't go home, but won't tell me where we are." He pushed himself up off of the ground, anger giving him the ability to stand and focus on something. "Tell me where we are!"

Acacia looked at him. "Jamal. I'm going to say this one time and one time only. Respect me while we are out here. I will leave you for the Capitol Police, and when they start to question you, they'll find your story makes absolutely no sense. They will record everything. Then, it *will* get pinged in the database and someone from the Capitol themselves will have you transferred, and you'll be dead before the day is done. You'll both close your eyes and embrace it what comes next even if you don't want to."

Jamal was fuming, clenching and unclenching his fists. Bernice was nervous, knowing this woman was more dangerous than either of them realized. She got up, and touched his arm. "Listen to her, Jamal. She's the only one helping us right now. Even if you don't want to see it. She is keeping us alive."

"Until she doesn't need us anymore!"

"We don't need you to begin with. Gabriel insists that every one of you remains unharmed. We only need one of you, not four children running around."

Jamal balled his fist again.

"Now you need to sit down and relax. You're taking out your anger on someone who is trying to help you through this."

"You don't know a goddamn thing I've been through." He stepped closer to her. Bernice watched them, ready for a fight to break out at any moment.

"Take it all out on me then. Do it." Acacia closed the distance between them.

Jamal wound up and swung. He was on the ground before his arm was halfway to her. Acacia's knee in his back, his left arm behind him in a vice grip.

"Now. Are you going to get it and relax? I'll answer all your questions when we're back. I either let you go and you both die. Or I let you go and we go for a nice walk to cool down."

"Let's go for a walk, please," Bernice said as her heart was racing. She felt hot tears, like crying during a fever, stream down her face.

Jamal's face on the ground, he couldn't move a muscle against the woman. "Walk," he mumbled.

Acacia immediately let go. She offered her hand to Jamal as he rolled over. He grabbed it. She pulled him up, brushing off the bits of trash that were stuck to his torn pants.

His eyes were defeated, his body language suggested he'd rather stay on the ground and mope than continue to walk.

"Second thought," Acacia said. "Wait here." She walked further down the alley and put her hand up against the smooth metal wall.

"Can someone open up entrance B, the alleyway door, please?"

There was a static hum in the air, and they felt a slight buzzing beneath their feet, but it was so slight no one would notice as they walked the streets. Only while standing still did Bernice think she felt something so minute that it hardly occurred.

"This way and walk quickly." She motioned further down the alley. "If you push against that piece of metal, it will give way. Follow the stairs."

They did as they were told. Bernice followed behind Jamal,

his body sluggish. She turned to see Acacia pulling the metal shut, and then run her fingers over a small keypad. It sealed the door behind them, like nothing was ever there.

"Jamal, up ahead there is a door to the left. Go and make yourself at home."

He trundled down the staircase, his shoulders hunched as he headed toward the door she had mentioned. He stepped inside with Bernice. There was a worn couch, old red leather, with holes in it where the stuffing could pour out. Bernice watched as he sat on the couch and after a moment his body relaxed. She was about to join him when she paused.

Bernice saw tears roll down Jamal's face as he silently wept, not convulsing or choking on his breath, only the tears gave away that he was in his own head. She walked over and put a hand on his arm, but he did not move. She wondered if he even felt her touch at all.

"I'll make some food. If you want to leave this room, make a left and come down the hallway until it opens up into the foyer. There will be a table for you to sit at. Otherwise, you can stay here and relax," Acacia said as she came into the room.

They made no reply to her, only sat on the old couch, with years soaked into its sweet, musty leather.

Acacia walked to the kitchen, and went to a small false plate in the wall. "Poin, can you please let Gabriel and Babyle know we're in house B. I've secured it, and they can go out."

* * *

Poin crackled in the room with Gabriel, Babyle, Crow, and Janet. "Acacia would like me to inform you all that Jamal and Bernice are safe in house B."

"That was quick," Gabriel said.

"From what I can piece together through surveillance cameras, Jamal seemed to have a panic attack and was almost carried by Acacia to the alleyway entrance. I lose footage when they get down and out of sight. There's a small lapse between them going in the alley and going into the house."

"Can you scramble that footage or delete it?"

"Already have, Gabriel."

"How do we know they're safe for real?" Crow inquired to the man conversing with the ceiling.

"Poin, could you please get a portrait of Jamal and Bernice now, project it against the South facing wall."

Immediately the room went dark, and a light black and gray photograph appeared on the entirety of the wall behind to their right. Jamal had his head back, streams of tears on his face that he had not wiped off. Bernice sat next to him, her head on his shoulder, eyes closed. They looked peaceful. Crow and Janet could see the pores of their skin, and the hairs on their noses. The two looked worn, as if decades had culminated on their faces in the few minutes they had been gone.

"Janet, would you like to go next?" Gabriel questioned the dark room.

"Anything to get out of here." She looked to Babyle, who locked eyes with her, and started moving to a different door than the one which Acacia had taken her friends through.

Ahead of her, Babyle twisted and turned through a long corridor, the walls around her varied in colors. Some were vibrant, some were dull, some lit up well, and some at times were hard to see and judge what color the hallway was. She studied Babyle as they went through this labyrinth. He was bald, taller than Crow, easily pushing six feet, and his frame was well filled out. He wasn't particular toned from what she could see. He reminded her of an iron worker or a carpenter. Easily able to move hundreds of pounds, but ate whatever they wanted so their body always had a jiggle to it.

Babyle stopped and turned to look at Janet. *What does he want? Why are we stopped in the middle of this hallway?* she wondered.

"Ready?"

"Uh, I guess?"

"Okay." He put his hand against the left wall, and pushed. It gave way and he stepped through a door she had not noticed. She followed him, as he held the door open for her. They were in a library surrounded by books of all shapes, sizes, and colors. She turned to see Babyle had closed the door, which was simply a bookcase and not a door at all.

"Where I want to spend my time," he said to her.

"Where are we? Why is there no one else here?"

"Secret."

She started to look around, finding that the library had no windows, no doors to the outside world, just massive shelves from floor to ceiling.

"Follow."

He walked by her. Babyle grabbed a ladder and pulled it along the glistening track which went around the border of the ceiling until he found the place it needed to rest. He climbed, and pulled on a book. A mechanism churned and buzzed within the walls of books, like an old pulp mystery novel. There was a tiny click as a spot in front of Janet popped open. The air was different there, it smelled different. Almost like mildew. It was unwelcomed in the library which smelled almost of vanilla and sweet dust. *Rob would have loved to see this.*

Babyle appeared by her side, and opened the door for her again. He let her pass through the wall of knowledge and stories.

"Well, this isn't what I expected," she said as she found herself in a rundown room, with an old wooden desk and leather cushioned chair. She had seen a room like this before, on some old crime drama, or maybe it was a video game Rob had played. It was exactly like a cliché scene. An old gray metal filing cabinet, a glass window, a wooden door with blinds over the glass windowpane were used as the décor. The table had an ashtray on it, a long tubular lamp. Babyle closed the secret door behind them, and walked through the room, making Janet follow.

"Are you ready?" he asked as they stood in another room, with another door. There was no way for her to see what was on the other side.

"Should I not be?"

"Dunno," he said, looking into her eyes as he opened the door to the street.

Janet saw it all, like living in New York City again. People everywhere, walking, running, and speeding by. There was noise again, like being stuck in traffic or listening to everyone whiz by. It was different this time, Janet realized. Everything was slightly off. It was a reflection of the world she knew in a world she didn't. A copy of a copy which had become distorted.

The cars weren't on the ground. The people were gaunt—extremely gaunt—almost like old photos from the holocaust. Their cheekbones poked through tight leather skin. Their clothes hung lazily against their bones. Everyone looked like they hadn't seen daylight in years. Then Janet realized that Babyle had the same look to his skin as everyone else had. She blinked. Wondered what Rob would have said if he could see this world of pink and blue.

Her mind wandered to him, and tears started to form in her eyes. *He would've loved this place. All of it. Like that cult movie he loved.* She looked around, hoping to see holograms walking the street trying to panhandle.

"Where are we?" She looked to Babyle, her tears giving her away.

"Not yet. Soon."

"I don't understand."

"Soon," he said, smiling so his dull white teeth shown through, reflecting hues of color across them. He stepped through the door to the sidewalk, allowing Janet to do the same.

She stepped on to the street. Neons signs hung overhead, then she saw it, the first hologram trying to sell something as people walked through it. As they did, it kept talking, turning back and forth to everyone, trying to sell its wares, or get them to come inside the storefront, though she wasn't sure which, not from the distance she was at. The hum of the cars levitating off of the ground drowned out any conversation she tried to focus on.

"Is this paradise?"

Babyle chuckled. "No. Slums—almost."

If this is near the bad part of town, what's it like at the rich part?

"Can we walk by the stores?"

"Yes."

Babyle led the way, taking Janet towards the projections pacing the street. She was able to see right through them, like a dirty cloud of different colored dust. She was about to ask Babyle about them when the area started to change from a soft glow of light to full blown neon as they entered what Janet guessed was the business district. She was enamored by the signs and neon reflecting off of everything.

"Are there more places like this? Can you travel? What's it like to sell stuff down here?" She asked all of these questions and Babyle gave no reply, only let her continue to wonder and wander amongst the people and panhandling projections.

She walked and was confronted by one.

"Ma'am, would you like to look younger—feel younger?

Please, step inside, let us take care of you. Not only does our technique reduce the years on you, you'll also experience joy like no other." The projection was a wiry blue, like fuzzy dust in sunlight as it walked over to her. Janet could see through it.

Janet was wary, starting to realize that the world she was in was not at all like the one she had come from. She began to look around at the people, and less at her surroundings. Women and men were working in this area.

She saw men dressed better than she was—still tattered— walk up to women and other men, talk, and then disappear after they did something weird with their arms, like an aggressive bro handshake where they would grab each other's forearms after looking the other dead in the eye.

"What are they doing with their arms?" She looked at Babyle as she turned away from the men and women paying for sex in public.

"Credit transfer. Money."

She furrowed her brow, trying to think back to anything Rob might have said. "Is it like, Bluetooth or something that has been put in your arms with your bank attached to it?"

"Similar," Babyle grunted, as he pulled up his sleeve and showed Janet where to touch his arm to feel the implant. It was like touching a pimple on your chin during puberty which had not grown a head yet, hard but soft and mushy at the same time —able to be moved around.

"I want to see the higher living."

"Not yet. Home."

Janet and Babyle walked, found their way to another building with another hidden wall which led to more books and ladders.

"How many of these do you have hidden throughout here?"

"Fifteen," he replied without skipping a beat or allowing a pause to the conversation.

"Where did you get all of these books?" Janet asked as she walked to a wall and saw spines without names and crumbling pages that looked too brittle to even open to find the author.

"Above."

"What do you mean 'Above'?"

"Not yet."

"Has anyone ever told you that you are difficult to have a conversation with?"

"Often."

Janet felt herself rolling her eyes trying to figure out who this Babyle was and what made him tick.

Babyle walked through his library and pulled a book from the wall, which opened a door to another long metal corridor. Janet followed him, feeling like a lost dog following the first kind person it had found, hoping he would give her shelter and food.

Down the dimly lit luminescent corridor, Babyle and Janet found a small room. Inside, the furnishings were sparse. There was an old recliner, light brown fabric, like something a baby boomer would buy, Janet thought. And a small loveseat of the same color and style, just in behind a coffee table made of pure metal, dull and without luminosity. Janet didn't wait for Babyle to give a short command and sat in the loveseat, making herself comfortable. She watched him as he walked around the room, went to a small intercom and held the button.

"Ready," he said, with the least amount of fervor he could muster.

* * *

"Gabriel, Babyle and Janet have returned. Would you like photographic evidence of this, Crow?" Poin's chrome voice announced to the two waiting in the room.

"I don't think I do."

"As you wish."

"If you would please follow me, Crow."

Crow looked over at Gabriel. On each side of him lay gargantuan piles of clothing. Only now did he realize the scope of the room. Gabriel had to be over six foot, and the piles were at least three times larger than he was, probably more. The ceiling was so far off, Crow wasn't sure if he was actually seeing it or if the lights were so bright that they drowned out the white lid of the room. *Where did all of these clothes come from?*

"I assure you, whatever is giving you anxiety, Crow, is nothing to fret over. You are safe here." Poin's voice smacked into his head.

"I'm wary of you even more now," he called out to the ceiling and wondered if the AI was watching him from the void like God.

"Sorry. I've been keeping track of your biometrics, and your heart rate increased dramatically, along with your body's perspiration."

Crow shook his head, and walked towards Gabriel who had begun to make his way out of the same door Babyle and Janet had passed through. The hallway was cramped, just like the first one they had gone down after they destroyed the brick wall. The walls were smooth to the touch, and Crow's fingers recognized them as being cool, a familiar feeling which he almost longed for again after being inside for the last few days. Gabriel hadn't spoken since Poin called out to Crow. He simply led the way to wherever they were headed.

Gabriel passed through a small, hidden door which they both had to duck to get through. It led to a very tiny room, broken and worn out, like a bomb had gone off nearby. Glass littered the floor. They passed through the doorway in front of them, and Crow found himself behind a police line. There was tape he had recognized from a past life, but it was different. He could see through it. *A hologram.* The street in front of him was barren and dark. Even more glass littered the ground, and dark pools of old, cleaned up blood stained whatever the roads were made of. They looked like concrete. They were darker, a deep gray, almost black, with spots everywhere.

"Where are we?"

"Soon. Once you're back with everyone, I will answer questions."

Crow felt his head spinning as he looked around. Buildings made of dark ghastly metal hung over them. There was very little to illuminate the world. In the distance he could see hulking beams of light against towers and towers of white building: a marble showcase. Defiant and magnificent for all to see and gasp in horror of.

"What's that over there," he pointed to the light which could be seen from the furthest distance.

"That's our Capitol for this district. We're in the Deep right now."

"Are there more of them?"

"Many. And many grander than the one you see."

Crow looked around trying to take in his surroundings. He looked up and saw nothing but darkness. No stars to see, no moon to gaze at, no sun to light the way and keep track of direction. The world felt too big and his brain felt too small to grasp the grandeur of it. He felt like he had just contemplated the universe and his own morality for the first time. His chest got tight, and it became hard to breathe.

"Come with me, please." Gabriel started to walk away, taking Crow through the maze of streets until he stopped abruptly on the side of the road.

Ahead, Crow saw what Gabriel had seen. People. Cars. Bikes. But something was off. They weren't touching the ground. They were levitating as they went by, lit by hues of color. Crow blinked to make sure his eyes weren't playing tricks on him. *Nope. Definitely not touching the ground.* He took a deep breath.

Did I get taken through some kind of portal to another world or travel through time at some point? I feel like I'm going insane.

Gabriel turned and looked at Crow. He must of seen something in his expression because he said, "You should sit down. Count to ten and close your eyes."

Gabriel led him towards a small gap between buildings, a gap which wasn't exactly an alleyway, but was more than an indent of building architecture.

"There's a lot going on in my head," Crow said as he sat down. "I'm trying to figure out where we are, how all of this can even exist, what happened in New York, and if it's the same everywhere else. I've been trying to survive for so long. Then, we stumble on something so miniscule, absolute chance that we went into that basement, and suddenly I'm somewhere else with you. You're showing me a city, with people—people who are alive and living without trying to kill, rape, and torture everyone who's trying to survive." Crow started to rub his eyes with the meat of his palms until the blackness started to shine with flecks of color. The universe bursting into existence as stardust stretched out against the darkness. He was starting to breathe shallow deep breaths, and the world around him began to spin. *How the hell did I get it? What is this place? Maria, Lucy, I don't feel like I'm in control of my own life. Have I ever been?*

"I can answer most of your questions in time, as I've said. We can stay here a bit longer, but soon, we will have to walk a bit further."

"No. I'm tired of going on and on and on with no end in sight to this madness."

"You realize that's how teenagers act, right? They sit down and throw a temper tantrum when the fear of the future and the unknown are too much for their mind to grasp. That's the difference with adults and maturity. The ability to recognize fear and still walk towards that dark void and come out the other side."

"Are you my therapist now?"

"No, I'm simply saying that the feelings of anxiety, fear, and the unknown are sometimes heavy, and you're acting like an adolescent, demanding knowledge of things you have no need to know of yet. If that's going to be the case, I will treat you like one. I don't know the state of life you've been going through. Though, I can take an educated guess and probably ascertain a decent description of your life."

"Fuck off."

"Okay, if we're going to play this game, let's play the game, Crow." Gabriel reached in his back pocket and produced a small vial of deep translucent blue in his left hand.

"You're going to stay away from me with that," Crow said as he started to get up and backpedal. "I'll put up a fight." He raised his hands more out of fear than wanting to actually fight. A dog in a corner baring its teeth with no intention of making a move.

Gabriel hulked closer slowly as he closed his hand over the vial. Crow backed up faster, but Gabriel closed the distance. He swung as Gabriel got within reach. His blow glanced off of his right arm as Gabriel raised it to defend himself.

Gabriel wrapped his arm around Crow's punch, and stepped to the opposite side, planted his feet, so if Crow moved, he would trip himself.

"You'll be okay," he stated as he pressed the vial to Crow's neck. He hit a small button near the end of the smooth glass and aluminum cylinder. Crow's pupils grew wide so there was no iris left, and the sclera wanted to abscond from the invading black.

He threw Crow over his shoulder as his body went limp, and

carried him down the street into another building. The floor beneath them shifted. They disappeared further below ground.

* * *

Crow woke up and found himself in new clothes. There were sweatpants tucked into wool socks, and a crewneck sweater. He felt like a mental patient as he tried to smack the fog from his head and get an idea of his surroundings.

The room was empty, except for the bed he lay on, with a blanket under his body. There were no furnishings, no windows, only one door in and one door out. The walls were deep gray along with the ceiling, but it was translucent enough to let in whatever light source there was behind it. Crow blinked, wanting to go back to sleep, his eyes heavy and body sedated like after having a surgery. *How long have I been out?* He tried to get a bearing on his surroundings.

The world around was unbearable, a synthesis of human interactions with technology far beyond his understanding. To go from the natural world of survival, to this futuristic one of artificial intelligence, hyper drugs, and prostitution was maddening. He felt it creep into his mind—an insect which had crawled through his ear and start chewing on the membrane behind his eyes: a grinding of white noise he couldn't push out.

The door opened and Gabriel strode in, along with Janet, Jamal, and Bernice. They all looked relieved to see him. Their attire was similar to his, and none of them matched. They all agreed that sweatpants were the most comfortable to walk around in.

"It's good to see you, Crow," Janet said. Everyone joined in agreement.

"How long have I been out?" he asked still in the bed, feeling the stiff weakness in his legs.

"About three days." Gabriel informed him.

"Why so long?"

"I had to give you a good dose to keep your brain from exploding. You were definitely not prepared to see everything."

Crow took a deep breath and sighed it out through his nose.

"There's a lot to try and grasp."

"Correct."

"Have you brought anyone else here before?" he asked.

"Yes. Before the lights of your world went out."

"What happened to them? Where are we?"

"The one woman couldn't grasp it and started running around to people on the street trying to get them to understand where she had come from. The local enforcement took her away. I didn't want to risk that happening again, which is why I drugged you."

"We're underground," Janet said.

"Yeah. They say this was built right after World War one as a contingency for the testing of nukes. And they moved parts of the population here to different cities under the country. They call where we're from the 'Aboveground,'" said Jamal.

"Does anyone know about us up there?" Crow asked.

"No. The general public thinks you're all dead and that they can't go above. I would suspect most of the politicians do too with the exception of a handful. I could be wrong with that assumption," said Gabriel.

"So, why is this all here anyway? What's the point of all of this down here?"

"Power and control, of course. It's easier to control a smaller population and keep them below you."

"Was what happened up there planned?"

"I don't know. My opinion says yes, but politics above could be different than down here. I don't know if the GUC communicated with the old world above or if they're separate entities. Different governments and so on."

"How'd you learn about the world above you then?" Crow felt a buzzing in his head. Thoughts creeping in when he didn't want them to. Cold depression, and anxiety. *Maria, I just want all of this to stop.*

"Right now, that's not the question worth asking, but I will answer it for you, in time. First, I think it's better if we all take a break from this conversation and have some food. I don't want you to get overwhelmed again."

Crow wasn't happy to not have his question answered, but knew there was no point in pushing the subject. Gabriel clearly controlled his future. With any luck, Crow felt he could take back his life.

Janet crossed the room and helped Crow out of bed. His legs were weaker than he had realized. He could hardly stand on extremities made out of a tumultuous sea. His muscles twisted, shook, and crashed against each other. He wanted to lie down and get back into bed to sleep the nightmare away.

23

J eremiah traveled through the pod loop to meet up with Gabriel, Babyle, Acacia and the new group of people they had brought down. His small capsule—if it could even be called that—always reminded him of the inside of a floating scooter. It was oblong, like an egg—now that he knew what an egg was. Clear material stronger than metal gave him a 360-degree view to the empty tunnel before him. Attached to the bottom of the pod were small white lights which lit up the walls around him, and projected a small distance onto the tracks ahead. The chair he sat in was comfortable, slick-smooth, always ready to make him slide right out of it with the smallest twitch of his leg. There was room for another chair, but Gabriel said he never found a reason to install one. *Maybe that would change now that we have four more people to take care of. It still amazes me how he built all of this without anyone knowing. Gotta be a secret somewhere along the way with that man.*

The pod sped along its magnetized tracks, frictionless and building up speed in the vacuum it resided in. Soon Jeremiah would be under the next safehouse Gabriel had built as a contingency. It was closer to the Slums and the Furnaces. It had been a long time coming, and he was glad to revisit them—if only for a short moment. It would be a passing memory soon enough, tucked away into the back of his mind with other memories he forgot existed. Triggered only during times of reflection, sounds, or smells.

Outside, the walls were no longer whizzing by and the tunnel gave way from an eerie white under glow to green: a sign. The pod slowed into its final resting place, then behind Jeremiah a door slowly closed to the floor. He felt the pod lurch more abruptly than the entirety of the ride. His stomach dropped into his testicles. He was going up.

The glass translucence appeared through the floor by way of a disappearing ceiling. He stepped out onto the catwalk, hit a button on the cool railing, and the pod sank back through the floor. After finding its resting place, it would wait for the ceiling to rise up again for its next rebirth and passenger ride.

Jeremiah strode through the doors and hallways. He had memorized the labyrinth months ago and made a home down here below the Deep. A secret within a secret. His mind wandered to the Aboveground, and all the meaningless death and suffering that had been caused.

The way up was quick and he found all that he needed before he went off again.

Jeremiah waited amongst the crowds of people lit up greens and yellows. Their features exaggerated. He greatly appreciated white light now, even amber would suffice, but all the neons changed how people looked. He was reminded of skeletons. Jeremiah ran with the crowd. He kept his face down low. Any cameras still functioning couldn't get a good sight of him. *Better safe than sorry*, even with the scrambler implant in the back of his neck.

Gabriel, Acacia, and Babyle were all waiting in their small house by the time Jeremiah had arrived. Bernice, Jamal, Janet, and Crow arrived shortly after, with the latter stumbling in, looking like a mess of a bender.

Gabriel frowned. "You need to get some rest." He crossed over to Crow, grabbed him, and heaved the ragdoll onto his shoulder.

"'m good. Iswears." His speech slurred together.

Gabriel took in a deep breath, and let it out through his mouth as he stood and closed his eyes. He dug into his pocket and pulled out another cylinder. He pressed it against Crow's barren ankle and walked away from the gang. They all watched in silence.

"He fucked up," Jamal said.

"As long as he didn't fuck up his job, it will be forgotten," Jeremiah replied. *Still hate that prick. Why bring these people in on all of this? Big fucking mistake if you ask me.*

"Gabriel is very forgiving, though, in a moment he will express his frustrations. So far, it seems like everything has gone according to plan," Acacia said as she pulled up a holoscreen on the clear table in the room. The legs a bright metallic, like picturesque concept art for robots. She flipped through screens, her fingers a dazzling orchestra knowing exactly the moves to make to enlarge images, make them smaller, and overlay them into a cacophonous map which she processed as one piece of work. She was a sculptor and the holoscreen a block of marble.

Gabriel returned to the room, making his way over to the holoscreen and placed himself next to Acacia as she worked deliberately. His eyes darting back and forth trying to keep up with her work and speed.

"There," he said pointing to a spot on the maps. Acacia's

hands stopped, swiped away, made parts smaller, and enlarged to singular point.

"Too early," Babyle said as he gazed at the enlarged blue holo-screen. Everyone else looked on trying to decipher what it was.

"What's going on?" Janet asked as they all stepped over to look around.

"These are similar to blueprints of the Deep. Each of these squares is a building, and each one is connected to a line which supplies power. If it's a dimmer blue, then it's offline and we still siphoned energy from it."

"They all look the same shade," Janet said as she looked at Jamal and Bernice who nodded in agreement.

"You guys haven't adjusted yet. It's common in societies, ancient and modern, to not be able to see all the shades of a color another society is used to seeing. Your eyes will adjust eventually. Trust us. It's dimmer."

"So, what's the problem then? Weren't we trying to knock out power?"

"Yes. But this one isn't connected to the Furnaces for a power supply. It shouldn't be out," Gabriel paused. "We siphon from this one for our own power."

"Why is that bad?"

"If we continue to take power from a dead place, we might make ourselves known."

"Stop siphoning then." Jamal said like it was common sense.

"Poin takes care of that, and I'm sure he already—"

"I have, Gabriel. There are a few problems which remain."

"I'll let him go on."

"I had a lapse when the Furnaces blew and switched over to our reserve power. We all knew it would happen since we siphon so much energy from the Furnaces and places which are powered by the Furnaces. One of our reserves happens to be that building." They all looked over to the map, and saw the colored lines connected to the safe house. They understood now that all those lines were the buildings powering them. "Unfortunately, while I was switching over, I could not check to see if that one building specifically was up and running. I'm scanning through records and databases for reports already, but I am coming up with nothing. This could be a good sign. I might be getting blocked by someone or by the Hive who is hiding the reports. That would make this bad. Very bad in fact."

"I still don't fully understand," Janet said.

"If that building was supplying us with power while offline, then that means they can track where the power leads to. Poin's trying to say that there was no protection in the coding to deter tracking where that power was heading. If it's a glitch, we're fine. If someone is actively hiding things and deterring us, then this entire safehouse is compromised."

24

Janet was lying in bed trying to focus while using an old flashlight she had borrowed from Gabriel so she could read a book Babyle had given to her. It was worn and well read. The binding opened easily. There were creases which made the pages turn easily and allowed the book to bend over on itself.

The world was crazy again. *How did we get involved in this mess after getting out of our own mess? What's Gabriel's big plan?* So many thoughts ran through her head. They were all in the dark again, just as they had grown accustomed to the light. It was nice to have electricity for a moment, even if it only was for a few short weeks. Gabriel had promised they would be back online shortly, but they weren't taken any chances, not after their escapade from the morning.

Janet got up, and walked to the hallway. *Maybe it's the adrenaline keeping me awake.* The AI crackled over the speaker.

"Everyone. Please start exiting through the emergency pods. We have com—" There was a rumble and a thick crash of metal on metal above. The sound was like a train crash from an action movie, Janet thought.

Babyle appeared first, then Acacia and the group.

"Quick, Capitol police." Babyle said followed by Jamal and Bernice.

They scurried to the couch, and pushed it against the wall, slamming a hole as they did. A door slid open and everyone piled further down, grabbing a pod and buckling themselves in.

Babyle stood back at the keypad, punching away. Janet saw him briefly. She turned to see if Gabriel had arrived and then her pod was off. Ahead of her it was black on the tracks. Gabriel had said they had a line driven by magnets just in case they had lost electricity, but she never saw it until now.

Pressure pushed down on her chest as the void in front of her kept stretching on. Her eyes tried to adjust but it was too dark to see anything inside the pod or out. *Unbuckle, get out, make a right, go down the gangway, and wait. If no one arrives, find a way out, and hope you aren't found. Hope you aren't found. Hope you aren't found.* The words echoed over and over inside her head. *Rob, please. Help me on this one.*

The pod stopped and she followed the instructions in her head, waiting for everyone. Jamal arrived and Bernice with him. They stuffed themselves in together. *I don't think the pods were meant for two riders.* It didn't matter. They made it. Eyes wide, bewildered, and clearly shaken. Acacia was next. She led them through a simple maze like everything down here, Janet realized.

"What's going on?" Janet asked.

"The Capitol police broke in. They followed the trail of power right to us. Labeled terrorists for blowing up the Furnaces. It's not good."

Janet kept quiet as they walked through the labyrinth Gabriel had built away from the place they had started to call home. They ascended a staircase.

Jeremiah was waiting for them out on the street.

"We lost Poin," he said.

"And Gabriel?"

"He's going to meet us."

"Babyle?"

"Last I knew he was getting into a pod behind me," Acacia said.

Relief started to come over everyone. Around them the lights were back, and the buildings were grand. From where they were, Janet could see people walking, but they were better clothed than she had seen before. *This must be the UC.*

Acacia looked over. "Yes, we are near the Capitol here. You will all be changing soon to look the part. We need to get moving to our next home. Gabriel and Babyle will meet us there."

Everyone started walking, sticking to shadows, and limiting any movement on the busy streets. Janet walked with them.

"Wait."

"What is it? We can't hang around here forever," Jeremiah said.

"Has anyone seen James?"

They all looked dumbfounded, then realized she was referring to Crow.

"We never had eyes on him," said Jamal.

Acacia looked down, not having an answer.

"We will find him when we get someplace safe," Jeremiah said.

Maybe Babyle has him. Or Gabriel. Someone has to have James.

They all followed Jeremiah who led them through the UC. It was lit up by the lights of the Capitol building, Janet realized as she looked around. There were very few lights, yet everything was illuminated. She looked up and saw the monstrous building that Gabriel was working to take down. The men and women inside, governing all of them. *The Ivory tower hides bad intentions,* she thought. Jeremiah opened a door for them, and the light flooded in, but Janet only felt the darkness. *James.*

Please consider signing up for my mailing list while I work on book two in the Grid series. I will have an excerpt of the beginning chapters available soon.

If you loved the book, reviews on Amazon, and Goodreads help me tremendously.

I am working tirelessly to continue the story and hope to have it in your hands sooner than any of us expect.

-Nicholas Turner

Made in the USA
Middletown, DE
01 December 2020